A Pride & Prejudice Reimagining

Resolve
& Revelations

Pride, Prejudice, & New Adventures
Volume V

NEY MITCH

RESOLVE & REVELATIONS
Copyright © 2021 by Ney Mitch

ISBN: 978-1-955784-45-0

Published by Satin Romance
An Imprint of Melange Books, LLC
White Bear Lake, MN 55110
www.satinromance.com

Published in the United States of America.

Cover Design by Caroline Andrus

I dedicate this book to the publisher, editors and artists who assisted me in this series. I also thank the readers who gave this book a chance.

Good day, Reader,

Welcome to Volume V of 'Pride, Prejudice & New Adventures'. For the sake of clarity, this book is a *republishing*, and a second edition. Important Note: despite this being the fifth book in this series, this novel can be read independently of the previous books in the series.

And Reader, if you have made it this far, then you know how my sappy dedications are. Now pick up a cup of tea, or coffee if that is your pleasure, find a couch to sit on, and enjoy this next installment. Thank you, Reader, very much, for everything, and this belongs to you!

Ney Mitch

PROLOGUE

Under the shades of Canterbury, Lydia and Henry Darcy walked through the trees, hand in hand.

"How long has it been since our courtship began?" Lydia asked blissfully.

"I am not certain down to the moment," Henry Darcy joked, "but I can most definitely say with confidence that our courtship has almost reached a month complete."

"And do you find me as appealing as the first day that our courtship began?" She chuckled.

"Do you fear that I have not?" he replied lightly.

"A woman always fears that a man may lose his love for her once the woman no longer becomes a curiosity and rather turns into a constant."

"Is that what you fear?"

"That is very much so. Yet if you were to lose joy upon seeing me, then I must confess that I might do something reckless."

"Such as?"

"I think I might call you a bad word."

"Oh, that does sound decidedly horrible." Mr. Henry Darcy laughed. "Might I be so presumptuous as to be allowed to find out what those words might have been?"

"Your curiosity knows no bounds, I see."

"No, it does not—not when I know I will suffer no consequences because of it."

"You are that confident?"

"Oh yes," he replied smugly. "I am that confident. For you have shared so much."

"Have I?"

"Yes, you see, you have given me the advantage in this conversation. You have made me all too aware that you seek my good opinion."

"I wish I did not desire your good opinion, but I do."

"What does this mean that you seek my good opinion? I believe it should follow that you have grown to care for me exceedingly."

"I shall not confess to that." She chuckled.

"And why not?"

"I prefer to tease you."

"It is too late. For I now know that you are in love with me," Henry Darcy said firmly.

Lydia stopped in her tracks and folded her hands in front of her, fidgeting nervously.

"Henry?"

"Yes?"

"What if I was? In love with you?"

"Lydia..." he began, his voice getting weak. "Do you really mean it? Have I finally become able to earn your love?"

"Henry, yes. For a couple of weeks now, I have developed a passionate attachment. And so, without fear of being despised for being frank, I do seek your good opinion. I desire your heart if you would have me."

"Lydia..." He sighed, becoming swelled with emotion so moving that he grabbed Lydia, pulled her to him, and kissed her passionately. Feeling the urgency of his emotion, Lydia's sensibilities were overpowered, and her body weakened, amazed by the feeling of it. When he released her, she barely had the ability to open her eyes.

"Henry, you could knock me down with a feather at the moment," she gasped.

"You promise that you love me?" Henry exclaimed.

"I promise—as long as you promise to love me in return."

"I do...very much, I do, Lydia."

Henry kissed her once more and then took Lydia near a tree.

"Well, if I am to do this, then I had best do it properly. Forgive your stuffy companion, Lydia, but I want tradition at this moment."

Lydia stood against the tree and Henry Darcy stood a few feet away from her.

"Lydia Bennet, when we first met, it was basically resentment upon first insult."

Lydia laughed at the truth of this statement, for it was the reality of their relationship.

"Yes, we did despise each other so, did we not?"

"Yes, we did, Miss Bennet. And if someone were to tell me in that moment that I would grow to be knocked down off my high pedestal and grow to fall in love with you, I would have called them mentally impaired. And that past thinking of mine showed how limited my pride allowed my comprehension to be. For over time, it became quite clear that your spirit and your wisdom was a guiding light, forcing me to confront the sides of myself that needed improvement, and to improve them I did. You taught me another valuable lesson, which was humility—as well as the knowledge that before you, I had never known what true love was. Before, I had always looked on it with a vain inclination, and from a selfishness. I always thought on how the woman should please me, but never did I consider how I ought to please her. I would have continued to be this way, vain and proud, had it not been for you, lovely and most honest Lydia Bennet. Therefore, my beautiful companion, marry me...please, I humbly ask you to be my wife so that we can make each other happy to the end of our days."

Lydia covered her mouth as she began to weep. Finally, she said, "I really make you feel all that?"

"Yes, you do. Now will you say yes?"

"Of course, I say yes! How could I say otherwise?"

Lydia took Henry's hands in her own.

"My goodness, Henry," she sighed, "of all the mistakes that I have made, how can it have occurred that I had obtained something as astonishing and wonderful as you?"

"You, Lydia Bennet Wickham, are a wonder in yourself. And very soon, you will no longer have to suffer being called Wickham ever again. Mark my words, Lydia, I shall free you from that."

"You had better. Now!" Lydia smiled, taking his hand, and swinging it back and forth as they walked. Her spirits soon rising to playfulness again, she decided herself free to ask a question that was long on her mind. "There is something that I must know. How can you account for having ever fallen in love with me? How could you begin? I can comprehend you going on charmingly, when you had once made a beginning; but what could set you off in the first place?"

"I cannot fix on the hour," Henry admitted, "or the spot, or the look, or the words, which laid the foundation. It is too long ago. I was in the middle before I knew that I had begun."

"My beauty you had early withstood, and as for my manners— my behavior to you was at least always bordering on the uncivil, and I never spoke to you without rather wishing to give you pain than not. Now be sincere. Did you admire me for my impertinence?"

"For the liveliness of your mind, I did."

"You may as well call it impertinence at once. It was very little less. And for you to have been in love—or at the very least, in attraction—to my sister Jane, who is my opposite in every way. Well, how could you desire one sort of woman like her, then myself? She has peace, sense and serenity, but no liveliness of mind."

"My desire for her was proof that sometimes we humans find ourselves drawn to the last person who one ever should be. You were right, Lydia. Jane and I would have never been a perfect couple or even an acceptable one. I was so busy attempting to do what was right that I forgot to do what was right. It was my duty to myself to fall in love with a woman with greatness of spirit and liveliness. For she would awaken the life within me as opposed to depleting it. And you awaken me a great deal."

"And I shall never let you rest."

"I am content with that. Also, you did not accost me in the same tradition that other women have made in their attempt to seduce me."

"What do you mean?"

"I mean that many a woman who did not love me used many arts to draw me in, and I find any arts that women used to lure me into their web of social ambition to find success through marriage as a great evil. Many women did their best to entice me, and I saw their game for what it was every time. You were the first woman who did not shower me with false compliments so that you could win me. You were honest, you were true, but also willing to be kinder to me if I allowed it."

"Ah." Lydia laughed. "The fact is, that you were sick of civility, of deference, of officious attention. You were disgusted with the women who were always speaking and looking and thinking for your approbation alone. I roused and interested you because I was so unlike them. Had you not been really amiable you would have hated me for it, but in spite of the pains you took to disguise yourself, your feelings were always noble and just; and in your heart, you thoroughly despised the persons who so assiduously courted you. There—I have saved you the trouble of accounting for it, and really, all things considered, I begin to think it perfectly reasonable. To be sure, you knew no actual good of me—but nobody thinks of that when they fall in love."

"I did see actual good in you. Was not your defending of your sisters' clear enough a sign of your inner grace?"

"Well, yes, but how could I not come to their aid?"

"A lesser woman might have not. Yet you did. And then I saw you with my sister Helena—oh no, Lydia, there is much goodness in you. And once I saw it, not because you forced knowledge of your qualities on me, I could not help but admire you."

❧

When they reached Canterbury, Henry took Lydia's hand, and they ran across the grounds and into Canterbury House. When they entered, Cousin Thomas and Cousin Emilia were in the sitting room, in peace, while Cousin Thomas read the newspaper. But he lowered it and looked at Henry and Lydia's locked hands.

"Holding hands," Cousin Emilia cried, "what does this mean?"

"Yes," Cousin Thomas asked, "what does it mean?"

"It means, Father and Mother, that your son is getting married finally."

"What?" Cousin Emilia cried, standing up and almost falling down from surprise in the process. "Do you both mean it?"

"Yes, I do," Henry said. "You may cry out and cheer, Mother. I have just asked Miss Lydia here for her hand in marriage, and she has accepted."

"Oh, my god! Henry, my boy!"

Cousin Thomas stood up and sighed, overjoyed.

"Well, it is about bloody time!"

Looking at each other, Lydia and Henry smiled at his parents' reactions.

"Now it begins." Cousin Emilia sighed. "A whole new couple and a whole new path that must be walked down!"

❧ I ❧

ANOTHER LETTER THAT CAUSED A SENSATION

I t's a truth, universally acknowledged by all who knew her, that Mrs. Bennet was the most excitable mother in the history of mothers. Also, where her daughters were concerned, her nerves and energy could always be reached to new heights, her talkative nature even more voluble, and her volume at a higher decibel level than ever before.

Therefore, upon receiving a letter a month later from Lydia in America, Mrs. Bennet was all in excitement—then upon reading the letter, her exhilaration knew no bounds.

When finished, she left her sitting room in Longbourn, moved around the staircase and entered her husband's study, where she found Mr. Bennet sitting down and reading *The Castle of Otranto*.

"My dear Mr. Bennet, have you heard the news?"

"Whatever you are about to tell me, my dear," he said, still reading, "I'm certain that it has not reached my ears or eyes yet. Yet I see that you wish to tell me, and I have no objection to hearing it."

This was invitation enough.

"Why, my dear, you must know that Lydia and Mr. Henry Darcy's courtship was said to have been going quite well."

"Yes, I remember you reading their last letter to me, Mrs. Bennet. Twice."

"Well, I did not think you were paying enough attention the first time."

"I am paying attention now, however, but no doubt I shall hear what you are about to say multiple times till I know it by heart."

"Yes, you shall, for it is the most wonderful news!"

Mr. Bennet chuckled, still amazed that his wife was still speaking and had still not got to the point of why she had come. He lowered his book and gave her his full attention, as was her due.

"Well, then, what of Lydia?"

"She has just written to me, and Mr. Henry Darcy has proposed to Lydia at last!"

"Was she foolish enough to have said yes, or foolish enough to have declined him?"

"How can she be foolish either way?"

"My dear, I have learned that in regards to the act of matrimony, a person is foresworn if they do and foresworn if they do not."

"Oh, how can you speak so?"

"I can because I must. Now, if you will not mind, let us return to the point of our discussion."

"Oh, of course! You take delight in always throwing me off my path of conversation. You have no compassion on my topics of discussion."

"You are mistaken in that as well, my dear. I have the highest respect for them. For you have said the same things so many times that I have decided to commit much of it to memory, so that I can easily recall them for recitation."

"You have thrown me off my point again."

"Have I?" He laughed. "Very well then, I shall behave. Continue."

"Lydia has accepted him, and they are going to be married at last! Oh, Mr. Bennet, three daughters married. Oh, fortune has been very good to us."

"Yes, so it would seem." Mr. Bennet smiled, actually allowing himself to be happy for his youngest daughter. "The blasted fool, Henry Darcy, has not gotten my consent to have my daughter's hand in marriage. Yet I can forgive him for that oversight, seeing as how we are all separated by a very large ocean."

"Oh, he has asked. He wrote it in Lydia's letter that he wished to request your permission to marry her. Did I not mention it?"

"You did not, my dear."

"Well, it is not my fault. You kept continuing to distract me."

"Yes, yes, I did."

"Besides, I knew you were going to agree as well, so I figured I'd write back with your confirmation either way."

"You knew my mind and the decision I would make without asking me first? My dear, your skills and the art of intuition are positively akin. Have I married a psychic gypsy without knowing it for these many years?"

"Well," Mrs. Bennet smiled smugly, "while I never wish to compliment myself, I do have quite the skills to see into the future, do I not?"

"Do you now?"

"Oh yes, remember when I said that Jane's first engagement would be most excellent, for it would throw the girls into the paths of other rich men. And was I not correct, sir?"

"I would agree with you if it weren't for the small insignificant detail that Jane's proposal to Mr. Brocklehurst led to little else but me being amused that my daughter almost wed the most ridiculous man in all of England. Oh, forgive me, the second most ridiculous man in England. Mr. Collins shall always be the first."

"Well, still, Jane's engagement led to her being recognized by Mr. Bingley, who was bosom friends with Mr. Darcy, therefore Elizabeth was thrown into their path, where Mr. Darcy fell in love with her. Then it was through their marriage that Kitty met Mr. Darcy's cousin, Colonel Fitzwilliam, and now they are wed, and their honeymoon led to Lydia and Mr. Henry Darcy beginning a courtship and now what a triumph!"

"You truly wish to take all the credit for this, don't you?" Mr. Bennet said, amused.

"Well, I would never call myself the sole reason behind the fortune of so many—yet I believe that I am."

"Of course, you do, my dear. Of course, you do."

"But it is all so very vexing!" Mrs. Bennet continued.

"How so?"

"They are going to have the wedding in America! That will not do at all. Lydia is my prize child, and she must be married at Longbourn where all of her friends may see her."

"Surely you see that is not possible, my dear."

"No, I do not see that? Why should I see that? Why should that be?"

"Because much of that side of the Darcy family resides in America, and it will be much simpler for everyone here to travel there than reverse."

"Yet no one here in Hampshire shall see the happy event!"

Mr. Bennet put his book down, took off his spectacles, and smirked.

"Mrs. Bennet, tell the truth. You just wish her to be here so that you can make a large show of it and parade her illustrious new husband, the other Mr. Darcy, before everyone."

"Of course, I do!"

"Your honesty is as refreshing as always."

"And I find it very hard that the option of having it here was never opened to us. And Mr. Henry Darcy's pride on this matter is very vexing to me."

"Well perhaps so, Mrs. Bennet. Yet you might find Mr. Henry

Darcy to be no less proud than any other rich man who is used to getting his own way."

"Riches or not, I am proud of him, but I wished it were otherwise."

"Then might I suggest you think on it from another perspective."

"What other perspective could there be?"

"You will find, my love, that there is often more than one perspective in the world today. Sometimes there is often more than two. Yet this one, I believe, will satisfy you. If we travel to America to see Lydia wed, you can boast of being able to have travelled to a new land and watched your youngest daughter being wed to another man that many unfortunate ladies might have dreamed of. There, will that do?"

"It will not matter if twenty such rich men from other lands would propose to our daughters since no one will see it."

"Depend upon it, my dear. If twenty such should appear in the world, I shall order my remaining single daughters to court them all. Now, can you not find satisfaction in taking that letter and showing it to Mrs. Philips, Lady Lucas, and the Longs as well, so that all of Hampshire will know our joy—and be jealous of us again."

"Oh, that is a good scheme," Mrs. Bennet said, kissing his cheek. "And what shall you do in my absence?"

"Well," he replied sarcastically, "After I have finished sobbing as usual whenever I am left alone and without your presence, I am going to begin writing a letter to Mr. Collins."

"Why do you write to that odious man?"

"To inform him that while he still may inherit Longbourn, he can rest assured that our fortune is still equal to his."

Mrs. Bennet clapped her hands in delight.

"Oh, yes my dear, do that!"

"With alacrity and all the goodwill that comes from us God-fearing folk."

Mrs. Bennet left his study and as she did so, Mary came down the hall.

⊗⋙

Having returned from Hunsford where she had just visited Charlotte Collins and assisted her, Mary had been home at Longbourn for only five days when Lydia's letter came.

"Oh, Mary!" her mother cried out. "A letter has just come from America, and your sister Lydia is now going to be wed to Mr. Henry Darcy."

Mary, at first, did not reply.

"Do you not care to know the details?"

"I cannot," Mary objected. "And I should not. How can I condone a marriage that has occurred so soon after the death of her first husband?"

"Oh, you silly girl! Lydia should not waste away just because Mr. Wickham had to be so foolish as to allow himself to be killed in war."

"I have no love for Mr. Wickham, believe me, Mama, but still, it is all too quick, and it is not very moral now, is it?"

"Mary, please be quiet." Mrs. Bennet sighed. "And be happy for your sister. Just this once?"

Upon seeing her mother look so resigned, it touched Mary's heart. Though she no longer despised Lydia, having seen Lydia's character alter so dramatically, it still hurt her to see how Lydia was met with good fortune and she, Mary Bennet, was still undecided as to her future.

When going to Hunsford, Mary Bennet was pleased to find that Mr. Collins was not there. He was sent by Lady Catherine to the Continent to contact a clergyman in Spain for her and interview him for a post she was considering for a neighboring estate. Therefore, while at Hunsford, she was able to assist Mrs. Collins and Maria, meeting with the occupants of the village and tending to the poor. Such actions made her feel useful, but it also left her feeling empty. Charlotte Collins had the life that she had expected to have had instead, and to see her at Hunsford, so well settled, gave Mary a feeling of envy all the while, which she prayed she would finally overcome. Therefore, when leaving Hunsford before Mr. Collins returned, was both a blessing and a relief. She did not know where she was headed, and her studies began to offer less and less solace and satisfaction, for her nature began to change. She wanted to be of some use in the world and did not know where she fit in it. And yet Lydia, who for so long did not deserve a happy conclusion, was now receiving it as quickly as she had discovered herself.

"Very well, Mama," Mary acquiesced. "I am happy for Lydia and shall welcome Mr. Henry Darcy as another brother."

"Fine words, that is. Now join me as I take Lydia's letter to your Aunt Philips and give her the good news."

Mary agreed, but rolled her eyes in the process, for she knew what her mother was up to. Both women put on their cloaks and bonnets, then departed first to Aunt Philips's home, and then to Lucas Lodge.

۞

Meanwhile, in his study, Mr. Bennet took out a paper, quill, ink, and began to compose his letter, which would be a great deal different from the one that Lydia had sent to them.

Hunsford Parsonage

Dear Mr. Collins,
I trust you are well and that your journeying to the continent

was met with success and comfort. I also thank you for constantly inquiring about my health in your last missive to me. Your consistency in asking me if I am near death's door does not go unnoticed or not regarded. For I assume that it is meant to be out of general worry for my welfare and not anything otherwise.

I also thank you for your congratulations on the recent nuptials of my fourth daughter, Kitty, to Colonel Fitzwilliam. I do recall that you once wrote to me out of worry that Lady Catherine did not look upon the union with a friendly eye. This seems to be a constant impediment for us, does it not? That Lady Catherine does continuously have a disinclination toward the felicity of my daughters. Or that my family has a disinclination to ever be aligned with her intentions. At first, you informed me that Lady Catherine de Bourgh did not look upon Mr. Fitzwilliam Darcy's designs upon my Lizzy with kindness, and then it was Kitty with the Colonel—and now, I am not fully aware if this news shall be to her dislike as well, but my youngest girl, Lydia, might find herself under the boot of Lady Catherine's judgment.

You see, I must trouble you once more for your congratulations. My youngest, Lydia, who was recently widowed, has found a love to her liking once more, and will soon be the wife of Mr. Henry Darcy, of Canterbury estate in America. If your patroness finds herself possibly affronted with this news, I shall confess myself to be mortified, if so. Yet in regards to those intangible things such as family ties and blood bonds, I shall naturally find myself siding with my daughter's felicity and believe her to be in the right.

Yet again, if Lady Catherine could find it in her heart to enjoy this news, then I shall be overjoyed—and I shall admit that the lord hath smiled upon us, for we are still in her good graces. If not, please do your duty as her loyal servant and console Lady Catherine as well as you can. But, if I were you, I would stand by her many nephews: Mr. Fitzwilliam Darcy, Colonel Fitzwilliam,

*and Mr. Henry Darcy as well. For I believe that, in the end, they
have more to give.*

"Yours sincerely, &c."
  Mr. Bennet
  Longbourn, Hampshire

Upon finishing the letter, Mr. Bennet leaned back and smiled. Content in knowing that he had stoked Mr. Collins's pride while not being serious about anything he had just written in regards to the apologies, he had only one regret on the matter.

He had wished that while he found joy in the letter, he wanted nothing more than to see the look on Lady Catherine's face when she heard the news.

Therefore, while Lydia's letter caused much joy and jealousies all around, Mr. Bennet sought comfort that he also had another letter that caused a sensation—and it was all his own.

2

IN THE MIDST OF IT ALL

Placed on my seat in the sitting room at Pemberley, I had Caiden Darcy in his crib, sleeping, while William was crying hysterically a moment before.

'Elizabeth,' I said to myself, *'If I was this hard to handle when I was a baby, no wonder my mother suffered from such nerves all the time. Going through this five times must have been cumbersome— unless she passed us over to the servants, which was more than likely.'*

Hoping that he was just hungry and no more, I sat down and lowered my dress on one side, and raised William up to my chest, where he began to drink the milk. William immediately quieted down and began to drink to his heart's content, and I looked on him, smiling.

"You are just like your father, always wanting my attention."

I looked down at Caiden, who lay silently in his cradle, and smiled. Caiden always was quite quiet as a baby but smiled often, and I could not help but feel great warmth toward him. I loved them both, yet something about Caiden allowed a great bond somehow, and I felt it most keenly. This suited Mr. Darcy well, however, for

William seemed to always beam when his father was around, and Fitzwilliam could not help but favor him for it.

However, I decided it best to take advantage of the peace and quiet and began to read the letters I had received. The first one that caught my interest was the one from Lydia in America. Desiring to know how her courtship with Mr. Henry Darcy was progressing, I opened the letter and began to read.

Dear Elizabeth and Jane,

I hope you are both well, and I am hoping to meet my nephews very soon. Elizabeth, knowing our parents' desires to have a male heir for Longbourn and failing at it five times was always very comically tragic, yet now, seeing how you were able to have two for your first time giving birth, it just makes their situation comical without the tragedy.

Little William and Caiden must be a set of handsome infants.

As for myself, oh Lizzy, I shall not prolong this letter and tell you posthaste. My courtship to Mr. Henry Darcy has been a blessing and a gift, to which we now wish to seal with the most sanctimonious of sacraments. Mr. Henry Darcy has proposed to me. We are now engaged, and we wish to find how long it shall take for you all to have the ability to journey to America and witness our union. Lizzy, I know that you have two babies now, which will make your appearance here hard for you, but if there is some way for you and Mr. Darcy to come, that would be our greatest joy. And also, Jane, Henry bears you no ill-will and will be content to see you as well. I would like my family to see me make this correct move—for finally I have done something where I believe that you should all be proud of me. I shall understand if you cannot come, yet if you can, please do.

Sincerely,
Lydia

Upon placing the letter down, I breathed out heavily, filled with many sensations.

Lydia and Mr. Henry Darcy were actually going to be wed! This was all so incredible!

I looked down and saw that William's eyes were closing and I gracefully put him down in his cradle and rocked him to sleep. When seeing that they were both in slumber, I lifted up both cradles, left the room, and carried them to the nursery. There I found Lucy cleaning the room.

"Lucy, I need you to look after William and Caiden while I visit Jane in her classroom."

"Of course, Mistress. But if you have some message to send her, I can always go in your place."

"Oh, thank you dear, but this is something that I must do on my own."

I left Lucy in the nursery, for she always proved to be a most reliable nanny, and then went off to speak to Jane.

❦

When I arrived at the classroom, Jane was walking among the desks, looking over the students as they were writing their words.

"Now remember," she said, "if you are having any difficulties, come to me at the last. Sound the word out first, then write it to the best of your ability, and then I shall come around and correct you. The first two-syllable word is Apple. Now begin again."

Ten students looked down at their papers, lifted their quills, and began to write the word. Jane looked over their shoulders and approved of their efforts before she looked up and saw me standing in the doorway.

"Continue children," Jane said, and then she approached me, smiling. "Come to check on me, then?"

"I know that you do not need it. I came to show you this."

20

I offered her the letter, and she perused it. When she was done, she looked on me with an expression that I could not read.

"Well?" I began, "What do you feel?"

"It is strange, but I feel many things." Jane then turned to the children and told them, "To continue next attempting to write the word 'Begin' and show me when I return." Jane nodded to me and went into the hallway, out of earshot of the children, and I began to speak.

"Jane?"

"I am happy for her, but is it not too soon, Lizzy?" Jane said. "Wickham has only been dead for five months now, if even that."

"Whatever love that she felt for Wickham died soon after they were wed, and he showed her a very frightening aspect of man."

"Well, yes, that much I am certain of for sure, however it still feels like too swift of a blow. How does she know that her feelings for Henry Darcy is love or is instead a desperate attachment to the first man who allowed her to feel complete? You have seen it, Lizzy, how too often people are more in love with the idea of being in love, rather than love itself. That was a mistake I almost made once. And to think, Lizzy, what if I had not learned then that it was not a deep affection but one out of convenience? I could very easily have destroyed the man and my life if I decided to attach myself to him, making tension rise where there was none? It is a dangerous thing, Elizabeth, mistaking vain inclinations for true affection. For they can be easily confused."

"I know Jane, and if the case was any other, that would be right, yet there is one thing that I feel alters it. I am proud of Lydia now, but it is not her."

"Then what is it?"

"It's Mr. Henry Darcy."

"What do you mean?"

"Jane, you would know better than anyone. Henry Darcy has much of the Darcy pride and can not only make a bad first impression, but he was relentlessly unpleasant at first, making liking him almost impossible. Lydia would not have taken to him unless he had done something to truly show he had changed. Whatever his faults, falseness and flattery does not suit him."

"While you are right that I did not think of Mr. Henry Darcy in that way, Elizabeth, I still was thinking of him."

"What do you mean?" I was confused at first, but then a suspicion quickly gathered within me, and I worried over it. "Jane, are you hinting at a possibility that you might have begun to feel for Mr. Henry Darcy?"

"Oh, no!" Jane cried. "I'm sorry if I gave that impression. It is not that at all."

"You promise?"

"Indeed, I swear."

I sighed, feeling an immediate relief.

"Though I admit," Jane continued and again I felt my nerves rise within me, "that my pride is a little wounded, though not my heart."

"Your pride?"

"Well, I am happy that Mr. Henry Darcy has found happiness, and I was very happy to know that Lydia's decisions allowed an offered olive branch between our families. Yet I admit to the fact that so soon after rejecting him, he is courting my little sister— well, it does sort of affect one's sense of pride. And when I felt this, it amazed me, for I had no idea that pride was a trait that I possessed."

"We all do, it seems. It is almost as if it is a trait that none of us can escape."

"And it leaves no one else behind and intact, clearly," Jane sighed, "for I did not get by unscathed and here I am—a little confused and disturbed by it, even though I felt nothing for Mr. Henry Darcy. Am I evil, Lizzy?"

"No, you are not." I laughed. "You are just not used to feeling so human, I presume."

"If this is that, then it feels horrible."

"Well, take heart and enjoy the fact that such painful sensations do not occur to you on a daily basis. Now you know what your little sisters have gone through all these years. Yet before I allow you to return to your students, you mentioned something more about Henry Darcy."

"Oh, I almost forgot," Jane said, "And I hope that I am very much in error over this, Lizzy. Yet do you think there is a chance that Mr. Darcy does this, his proposal to Lydia, out of revenge against me for refusing him?"

"Oh," I gasped, unaware of how to respond. "I had not thought of that."

"Yes, and I am frightened to bring up such a point, and I want to believe that his heart is pure and that it has turned over its desires for another willingly and without vice attached to it. However, for too long my generous candor led to me being blind about people—I simply do not wish to be wrong again, and ever since the betrayal of Mr. Brocklehurst, I am more apt to desire to paint an objective portrait of everything that I see."

"I see your reasoning," I admitted, "yet if that be so, which I hope it is not, then there is nothing we can do, is there?"

"No, there is not. And hopefully, I am in the wrong on this score. With any luck, he did not woo Lydia with the furtive intention of trying to wound me. If so, then our hopes of their union bonding us all together in a stronger tie will not occur, but rather my actions, my refusal of him, would only lead to Lydia being hurt once more."

"You are afraid that she will become a victim again?"

"Yes. And this time, her husband does not serve in a militia.

This time, there will be no war to save her from remaining shackled to a villain forever. Though God forgive me for speaking so coldly about a human life lost, even if that was the life of Mr. Wickham."

"I hate to speak for him," I said spitefully, "But hopefully the almighty will not care one way or the other about him!"

"Lizzy, that was unkind."

"It was meant to be. Yet looking back on this predicament of ours, I cannot believe that Henry Darcy would do the same thing as Wickham, or that he is evil. He may be an insufferably rude man at times, but he is a Darcy, and pride is something they seem to have been raised to have too much of. Henry Darcy and Wickham were different sorts of men. Therefore, I have to hope that this is something else. However, all I can propose is to ask Fitzwilliam to take us to America at least a month before the wedding, and we shall observe them closely. If they prove to be perfect for one another and their love is a strong one, then we shall be glad for them. Yet if it be false, then we must speak to Lydia and Mr. Darcy will speak to Henry. We will do our best to convince them to break off their engagement."

"Oh, I had not thought of that." Jane smiled. "That makes we feel less apprehensive." Jane stood up, looking lighter. "I feel much more at peace now and that is of great comfort."

"You are? Oh, Jane, then I am glad we had this discussion."

"Yes. Let me know as soon as you are able of when we are leaving so that we may tell my students' parents of how long I am to be away again."

"We will do so with haste."

"Thank you, Lizzy."

Jane left me alone as I watched her retreating form move down the hallway, her expression more relaxed and clearly free of any emotional occupation.

"Jane was worried that his intention was to use Lydia to wound her?" Darcy asked me as we lay in bed.

He had come back to Pemberley after having traveled to a neighboring estate. His attempt to go house-hunting for Mr. Bingley seemed to be very ongoing. Upon his return, he joined me in our bedroom, but before I had any chance to speak to him, he had grabbed me and kissed me.

Sensing his mindset and mood, I kissed him in return and began to undress while he removed his jacket and vest. Then, when we were both nude, he carried me to bed, and we made love before we had to prepare for dinner. Now, as we lay in bed, with his lips kissing one of my breasts while his hand stroked down my body over and over, I began to tell him of all that Jane, and I had spoken of.

"Yes," I said in reply, having a hard time speaking while he caressed me so. "She is worried of her past actions having even more repercussions than the tension that was between both families. And if it were true, then now she feels she would be the direct cause of Lydia's life being ruined forever."

"If that were so, then it would not be her fault, but Henry Darcy's villainy would be the cause of it. Not her."

"Yes, but knowing Jane, she still will look at him as a beast, who she provoked into action. Yet Fitzwilliam, what are your thoughts? Do you think Henry is of the sort to go to so great a length to seek revenge?"

"I do not believe so. Not because I actually like him. You know me, Elizabeth, and I still cannot bring myself to like him so—for him and I are too close alike for comfort. Yet he believed that all he did was for the sake of what was right. It was not, yet he believed it. Which means that resorting to such malicious revenge might be below him, for he would be going against his own pride in his morality."

"I hope so."

"Yet either way, we can know nothing until we see them together. And yes, if we find them lacking as a couple in many ways, then we must say something to them."

"I shall promise to do so if you promise the very same thing."

"I can do that very easily, for as you know, I have no problem with hurting his feelings."

"And while I am proud of how far Lydia has come, I shall never be afraid to tell her the truth in the end. For if the truth will save her from making the wrong move, then I would rather have her suffer temporary pain as opposed to a permanent one."

"Yes, being cruel to be kind. It is a hard path to walk, but I am happy that you are so brave."

I raised up my head and kissed him passionately.

"Yet there is the matter of our children. Fitzwilliam, I do not wish to leave them, but I also know that a ship is no place for them."

"Yes, I had thought of that, and I thought of a most satisfactory alternative. Or two alternatives, actually."

"I am all ears." I smiled as he rolled me over and began to run his hands along my bottom. I giggled at first, but then my eyes closed as he continued massaging my skin. Then he leaned down, kissing down my back and along my bottom with such gentle firmness that I turned into the pillow and moaned.

"Well," he said, in between kisses, "I thought that either we could take our children to Matlock and have my aunt Fitzwilliam look after them or—"

"Your aunt and uncle would not wish to go with us to America?"

"If they do, then my second alternative is in order."

"Which is?"

"I know that your uncle's business will not allow him time to leave England at this time, correct?"

"Yes."

"Which means that your Aunt and Uncle Gardiner cannot attend Lydia's wedding."

"Oh!" I realized, "you think we should take our babies to be looked after by them?"

"Would your Aunt Gardiner be open to looking after two infants on top of her children?"

"I know that she would love it. She is fond of babies and besides, they will cost them little to look after."

"Then that shall be our first plan."

"I shall write to them tomorrow," I offered.

"Thank you, my dear. Now, the only matter of concern we have is simply to go to America and discover whether Lydia and Henry's love is real, or one of terrible intentions."

"Yes, and—" Suddenly a different thought passed through my mind, and I began to burst out laughing.

"What is so amusing?" Fitzwilliam asked me.

"It is a very random thing. I was just thinking of Caroline Bingley."

"Caroline Bingley? And why, pray tell, would you be thinking of that scheming and devious woman while we are in bed together?"

"True, this is not the proper setting for such a thought, but it could not be helped. You see, I have just realized that Caroline Bingley has been thwarted again."

"What do you mean, thwarted again?"

"She has missed another chance at achieving a Darcy connection."

"Oh..." Then Darcy took a moment to reflect, and he tapped his head as it occurred to him what I had meant. "Oh, yes, that is correct."

"Yes, that night when she invited herself to our dinner party, she learned of Mr. Henry Darcy's existence and you and I both know her, my dear. She has a brain that is constantly at work and not for the better."

"No, it is not. Yet surely, she could not have developed any true designs against him, for she had never met him before."

"My dear, let me tell you a little secret about the Caroline Bingleys of this world. They do not have to meet a man before they begin to lay claims on him. For you see, to them, it is a truth, universally acknowledged, that a single man in possession of a good fortune, must be in want of a Caroline Bingley. However, little known the feelings or views of such a man may be on his first entering the woman's mind. This truth is so well fixed in the minds of her that he is considered as the rightful property of her sensibilities. She doesn't have to have met him, my dear. And—to add to this all, he has the last name of Darcy! This synthesis of the perfect dream would have crossed her mind in a marked way and showing her dangerous obsession. Therefore, it is a puzzlement to me, in the midst of it all, what is Caroline Bingley thinking?"

3

THE TERRIBLE CASE OF CAROLINE BINGLEY

"That is absolutely outrageous!" Caroline Bingley cried as she sat with her brother and his wife in their townhouse, eating lunch. Mr. Bingley and Miriam had just received a letter from Kitty from America. Kitty had written to them of the news of Lydia's good fortune and expected them to be getting an invitation in the mail at any day.

"What is, Caroline?" Miriam asked, pretending to be coy, but was secretly enjoying Caroline's outburst. "Is this not the best of news?"

"The best of news?" Caroline reiterated, angry, "It is nonsense is what that is."

"And how so?" Charles Bingley asked, surprised at her outburst, for though he did his best to anticipate Caroline's complaints, this one was wholly unexpected. "Lydia had traveled to Pennsylvania with Mr. and Mrs. Fitzwilliam, and she was thrown into the path of Mr. Henry Darcy, making it all so convenient."

"But she was married to that no-good Mr. Wickham! Who was nothing more than the son of the late Mr. Darcy's steward."

"Oh, he fell on the battlefield."

"I know, Charles, you have told me so already, but how can it be that she had married so lowly before and then had the tenacity and cheek to dare set her sights on higher ground and such a distinguished liaison? That side of the family may be Americans, but still the name of Darcy must always be of importance in society."

"Be careful not to discredit anyone for being an American, Caroline," Charles warned. "For I will brook no such prejudice in my house."

"Oh, Charles!"

Miriam cleared her throat and Caroline looked at her most pointedly. Remembering that the townhouse was under Miriam's rule now, Caroline decided to be diplomatic and check her tongue, for she knew when her survival depended on it.

"Oh, of course," she said, in complete falseness, "I sometimes say the most foolish things and I should not be heeded. Yet still, this Lydia business is all so strange. How can she, who married the man who was a blight on the memory of Pemberley, and she was also a shame upon the family herself, should now connect herself to the family in a most pretentious way? Charles, you, and I both know the embarrassment she was on her family and the Darcys as well. She shamelessly eloped and was only saved because the libertine Wickham was paid off."

"Caroline," Charles warned.

"Mr. Henry Darcy cannot know her history—and if he did, he would turn her out."

"Whether he knows her history or not is not our affair, however," Miriam said simply, "And her shame, however reckless, is not of the sort that ought to make her damned for all time and shunned from all good society."

"Loose women such as her are what we are encouraged to reject," Caroline replied, resentful, "Am I now to forget such a practice?"

"It is permissible to reprimand and ask for penance to be served, but for eternal damnation because of a passion of the heart is extreme to say the least."

"Whether extreme or not," Caroline added, "it is Mr. Henry Darcy's right to know of her past."

"If it is his right," Charles said with more edge to his voice, "then it will not be our business to do so, for it is *not our business to do so*." Mr. Bingley's tone, which was usually so light and upbeat, was now stern and the marked difference could not help but have an impression on Caroline, who was not used to seeing her brother look so hard and firm. It unnerved her, therefore, she did not press the matter. Then she decided to change the angle of the discussion they had.

"Yet, Charles," she began, "I do so wish that you had taken me with you when you all first visited Philadelphia, for I would have loved to have met the American Darcys. And as for you, Miriam, it would have given me the chance to have met your family, for I have not had the pleasure and I am sure that they must be lovely."

"Thank you, Caroline." Miriam smiled, not at all believing a word that she had said, and she was right not to. Caroline was simply using another tactic to ease her way into their company, but it was too late at that point. For she had made so many bad impressions upon her sister-in-law that Miriam did not believe that Caroline had any good sides to her.

"Well," Charles said, cutting his meat, "You will meet them now, for this is an invitation that I am apt to attend, therefore, to America we shall go."

Caroline continued eating her food, but her mind was at work all the while. It were true in some ways that her chances at meeting this Mr. Henry Darcy had ended—as of yet. Suppose that he was to find out the truth of his fiancée's past, what then? He would be devastated to learn that the woman who had drawn him in with her arts and allurements could be so sullied. He would reject her possibly, and then he would want to cover his error by attaching himself to a true lady, one with a spotless history, and who also had a dowry on her side while Lydia Bennet Wickham had none.

Caroline Bingley had never seen or communicated with Henry Darcy in the course of her life. Yet her mind was an ambitious one that was also fueled by a strange fancy. She had lost out on marrying her first choice of Mr. Darcy, and therefore, when hearing that a second one existed, her mind quickly put that one in the place of the first one—and though separated by an ocean, she viewed this Mr. Darcy as a fortunate conquest. She had foolishly made him into an obtainable dream that one day she hoped she would be able to claim for her own.

And thus, with a new scheme in her heart, she stubbornly clung to it and even more proved the terrible case of Caroline Bingley to be true: a woman who tried too hard to make her own life by not seeing that she was imposing upon others.

🜚 4 🜚

THE FOOLISHNESS OF MR. COLLINS

At Hunsford Parsonage, Mr. Collins was sitting in his study, his sermon for Sunday's service half-written on his desk, and he was just finished reading the letter Mr. Bennet had sent him. When he was done, he stood up, utterly confused of what to make of it.

"Dear lord," he said aloud, for he often talked out loud to himself whenever he had a serious internal dispute that he needed to ponder much on. "Mr. Bennet has lost all sense of all that is proper and good!"

He paced back and forth a little longer, muttering to himself, but he realized that he very much wanted confirmation of his stance. Therefore, he thought it best to consult Charlotte.

Ah, his dear Charlotte! The woman who seemed to be of one heart and one mind with him, as if they were designed and made for each other.

Taking up the letter, he left his study, and then went to the parlor that was Mrs. Collins's personal parlor room. When he entered, she was sitting down, sewing, and looking like the perfect picture of a

33

wife to her husband, who mistook her desire for solitude as a sign of feminine delicacy.

"My dear Mrs. Collins, I have just received the most extraordinary news that has set my mind upside down."

"What could have occurred to have done that, my dear? And should you not be walking to Rosings Park soon so to have Lady Catherine look over your sermon?"

"Oh, my dear, do not worry of that. Though I admire your desire to always have me be punctual, for I cannot begin to express the many times Lady Catherine has stressed upon me the importance of punctuality, and as she so condescendingly says, being on time is something that always ought to be regarded as a virtue. And one of the most important of virtues in the whole cannon of virtues."

"My dear, what was it that you desired to tell me?" Mrs. Collins asked patiently.

"Oh, of course. Well, I have just received a letter from my cousin Mr. Bennet from Longbourn—which I hope he is keeping well and properly groomed, for as you know, it is my inheritance after all."

"Yes, dear, and it is very proper of you that you do not think of it often."

"Yes, it is very proper that I do not. Thank you for the compliment, my dear."

Mrs. Collins rolled her eyes, realizing that her husband may not take the hint of ceasing to always express his inheriting Longbourn because of the entail. It was most indelicate to speak of it, and yet he continued to do so—and perhaps always would.

"Mr. Collins, you may continue," she urged once more.

"Oh, of course. Well, he has written to tell me that his youngest daughter, the fallen one whose husband died in battle, is now to be wed to Mr. Henry Darcy of Canterbury Estate in Pennsylvania."

"Oh, truly?" Mrs. Collins smiled. "I was given information from

Maria that Lydia had formed an attachment to Mr. Henry Darcy, yet I had no idea that the courtship had become so profitable."

"And yet, my dear, I am most put out!"

"Why so, my dear?"

"Because we know her sordid past. And when I wrote to Mr. Bennet after her...vile act, I advised him, as a man of the cloth, to reject her entirely and have her whole family do what is right in the eyes of morality and shun her from their acquaintance and thoughts. And I felt myself correct to have done so."

Mrs. Collins closed her eyes, amazed at how much her husband never thought before he spoke.

"For her actions showed her character to be naturally bad."

"Yet, my dear," Charlotte argued, "it could successfully be argued that evil is not born, but learned over time, and you know my sentiments on the matter. Lydia learned and was allowed to be what she was due to a faulty degree of indulgence. Her parents never disciplined her, and she was left to fall to the wayside of believing herself to be right in all things. Maybe time and marriage to a man such as Mr. Wickham has taught her to enhance her character. For after all, wisdom is not something one is born with as well but learned."

"My dear," Mr. Collins said, then he smiled condescendingly, "While I value your opinion naturally, I must own, as a clergyman who has been selected by our noble patroness Lady Catherine, that I have a great deal more insight on the matter in regard to the study of the human condition. Therefore, please be guided by my beliefs this time. Please my dear, and while I do pity Lydia's circumstance, I still wonder how I shall propose this all to Lady Catherine."

"You are going to actually tell this all to Lady Catherine?"

"Yes, for as you see, even Mr. Bennet, who's heart is too soft in regard to his children, knows that what he does is walking the line of error and feels remorse for doing anything that would upset Lady Catherine."

"My love," Charlotte began, growing desperate, "While you had previously advised me to be led by your counsel before, now I must urge you to take heed of my words. I have known Mr. Bennet all my life and have learned to detect when he is being heartfelt, or when he is sarcastic and making a joke. When he wrote the letter to you, he was speaking in jest, and it was all meant in lightness. This situation is between family, and it is best that we do not interfere in it this instant. Also, Lady Catherine does not speak of the American Darcys often, especially now that both of our countries are estranged to each other and are still threatening war. She might care very little for that side of the family."

"Your thoughtfulness does you credit, my dear. Yet what is a clergyman but a servant to the mission of bringing families closer, increasing their bonds and blessings? Therefore, I am most decided that once I finish my sermon, I shall go to Rosings Park directly. Thank you, my dear, this was a good discussion."

He kissed her on the cheek and left. Upon her husband's leaving, Mrs. Collins shook her head, knowing full well that her husband had only come to hear himself speak rather than seek her advice. It was the way most of their conversations went when he had entered it, already with his mind made up on the matter.

Thus, he entered his study and began to finish his sermon, which he believed to be a work of genius—but would eventually be re-written by Lady Catherine, as it always was.

And therefore, the foolishness of Mr. Collins was always as it seemed to be—an ever-fixed thing.

5

THE WRATH OF LADY CATHERINE
DE BOURGH

Once he finished his sermon, Mr. Collins put on his coat, hat, took up his cane, pocketed the letter and then was off to Rosings Park.

He walked across the lane, over the grounds, and the great estate loomed ahead of him.

As was every time that he had looked upon the seat of his patroness, Mr. Collins gazed upon the grandeur of Rosings Park. Secretly, he rejoiced in his success at being the chosen reverend to the church of that great estate. Feeling his position too keenly and allowing the sin of extreme self-consequence to swell his pride, Mr. Collins allowed his feelings of importance to rule his actions and decisions too often.

He arrived at Rosings, was shown in by the butler, and led into the main parlor of the great house. When he entered, he beheld Lady Catherine sitting on her customary seat with her daughter, Anne de Bourgh, sitting on the adjacent couch, holding a tissue in her hands for whenever she needed to blow her nose.

Approaching Lady Catherine, he bowed as low as would be

considered permissible—or perhaps he bowed a little too far—and then he gave her a look of pure reverence.

"My honorable Lady Catherine de Bourgh, how do you do this day?"

"Very well, thank you," Lady Catherine said, "But why are you late Mr. Collins, for I have expressly stressed the importance of being punctual, and you would do well to remember it."

"I will your ladyship," he said, bobbing his head up and down, "and I apologize most humbly. It was just that I had received a letter that I believe you—"

"You have not said hello to Anne yet, Mr. Collins."

"Of course, where are my manners?" Mr. Collins then turned to Anne and bowed. "How do you do today, Miss de Bourgh?"

"I am well, thank you, Mr. Collins," Anne replied.

"And if I may be so bold, you look remarkably well, and you're not being able to be presented at court has deprived the British Court of its brightest ornament."

"Yes, yes, yes!" Lady Catherine cried. "My daughter Anne puts all the other ladies of court to shame, yet it is her birth and rank that give her all the graces that set her above the rest. And you are right to see it, Mr. Collins."

Happy that he had said something that was met with such enthusiasm, Mr. Collins smiled.

"Now, Mr. Collins," Lady Catherine continued, "let us see this sermon of yours?"

"Of course, your ladyship," he said, taking out the paper which had the sermon written on it, and handing it to her.

"No," Lady Catherine said, reading the sermon, "The first sentence is good, but the second one should be re-written. The third sentence can be cut out altogether, and the last paragraph should not be this. I shall re-write that part of the sermon for you."

"Thank you, your ladyship," Mr. Collins said, sipping his tea and eating a cake. "I am most honored by your attentions."

"Very well, sit there while I re-write this part."

While she had paper, quill, and ink brought, Mr. Collins then thought it would be wise to tell Lady Catherine of the letter he received from Mr. Bennet.

"Lady Catherine?" he began.

"Do not interrupt me before I begin to write, Mr. Collins. It is extremely vexing, for you interrupt my train of thought."

"Oh, forgive me, your ladyship, please forgive me, for I am very sorry—yes, very sorry. Very sorry. Yet I was just wishing to know if you are aware that Mr. Henry Darcy, a distant relative of yours, in America is now getting married to Mrs. Fitzwilliam Darcy's sister, Lydia Bennet Wickham."

Lady Catherine stopped her quill midair.

"What? What do you speak of?"

"I have received a letter today from my cousin, Mr. Bennet of Longbourn."

"Oh, the estate that has been entailed away to you."

"Yes."

"Well, I do hope that the estate is being well maintained so that it is a worthy inheritance."

"I hope so. That is my desire, Lady Catherine. And while I do not wish to be the means of injuring any of my cousins by inheriting their land, it cannot be helped, you know. And I must also admit that it is a lovely estate, and when I do come into it, I have great hopes of getting it all appraised to make certain that I am aware of the benefits of the living. I believe I can run the estate very well. Yet again, I do feel pity for inheriting the estate over their wills."

"Yes, I am certain that you do," Anne de Bourgh said suddenly, "However, since three of the five Bennet girls have married well enough to be settled comfortably, then fortune has found them— even more than it has found you, my dear Mr. Collins, so you need not pity them, for they have met most happy endings, especially

Kitty. Her marriage to the Colonel is a perfect match, do you not think?"

"Oh," Mr. Collins faltered, "Yes, I suppose it is."

"You are very kind, sir," Anne replied, and then she ceased to speak. All she had wanted was to point out that Mr. Collins's not being chosen by the Bennet girls as a husband did not hinder their happiness. Also, she was aware that Mr. Collins once tried to woo Kitty, therefore she found it all the more amusing to secretly press the idea of it upon him to deal a blow to his pride.

"Mr. Collins," Lady Catherine demanded, "you were speaking a moment ago about my other relation."

"Oh yes, Mr. Henry Darcy."

Mr. Collins told Lady Catherine the news that Mr. Bennet had written of and when he was done with his narration, it was as could be expected; Lady Catherine had much to say on the matter.

"Confound it all!" she gasped. "Why did no one in the family think to deliver this news to me? And it all makes me quite put out."

"But mother," Anne urged, "we barely even speak to the American Darcys, if at all. How can we demand to know of their dealings when we have not even developed a strong bond?"

"It does not matter, Anne. All that matters is paying respect where that respect is due. And to have another family member of mine marry into this Bennet family—for goodness sakes, what about them is so desirable that they can urge my nephews to want to link themselves to them so? It makes me wonder if they used arts and allurements to their advantage in a way that borders on witchcraft. No, I am not candid. And you know my sentiments, Mr. Collins. I did not look on Fitzwilliam's marriage to Miss Elizabeth Bennet with a kind eye."

"No, you did not, your ladyship, and it was understandable."

"Yes, it was, however now I have no choice but to bend to the whims and foolish fancies of others. I thought that would be the end, and then the poor Colonel falls under the schemes of that equally nefarious Kitty Bennet, and now Lydia Bennet—the most notorious of all, has caught herself a Darcy. We shall have a girl like that even more tied to the family. Is it to be endured? It should not be, and I have a mind to do something about it. No one listened to me before. Well, they will do so now. Or at the very least, I should have been notified on this all and I am quite put out that I was not considered. I find it very hard, and I shall not stand for it!"

Lady Catherine continued on her rant for a little longer before she sent Mr. Collins on his way, where he crossed the grounds of Rosings, feeling self-important by telling Lady Catherine the news that would cause a rift in the family.

However, while Lady Catherine spent the rest of the evening in frustration, she would not be allowed to last in such a state for long. For the next day, she had received an invitation to the wedding in Philadelphia of her distant nephew, Mr. Henry Darcy. Although, she could not release her anger so easily and it had to be transferred elsewhere. Therefore, she no longer was angry about the marriage but was only bitter for not being consulted first—and for the woman still being Lydia Bennet.

Therefore, the wrath of lady Catherine de Bourgh, though still not fully at an end, was so much deflated that there was no chance of her rushing in to break up a bond, but only sitting in her parlor, muttering about the injustice of her advice not being sought by a side of the family that barely even knew of her—except two.

6

THE ONE TO FEAR

When all was settled, it was amazing at the speed that all was assembled. Mrs. Reynolds—with the assistance of Jefferson—had everything arranged. Our bags and luggage were packed, the carriages were made ready, and the second carriage was set up for Lucy and another maid, who would look after William and Caiden in the carriage. In the first carriage, Georgiana, Jane, Darcy, and I were placed, and our first destination was London, where we would remain at Mr. Darcy's townhouse for a couple days, safely placing our sons in the care of my Aunt Gardiner. While in London, we would also meet up with Mr. Bingley, my parents, who also would come to the townhouse, and the Fitzwilliams, who also would be staying at their house in London so that we all could board the same ship together to America.

"I confess myself glad that we were able to get a ship from London," I said, "rather than having to journey from Portsmouth again."

"Yes, it would be more convenient all around," Jane agreed.

"And yet," Fitzwilliam said, "so early into the journey and I already have to warn you of something."

"What?" we all said in unison.

"Mr. Bingley and Miriam will not be traveling with us to America alone. Mr. Bingley's sister and husband, Mr. and Mrs. Hurst, have decided to come."

"Oh, well," I admitted, "I confess that they are not my favorite people, yet their presence will not be a terrible addition, really."

"Oh," Fitzwilliam sighed, "I was not finished. Naturally, if the married sister is coming, so must the unmarried one as well. Miss Caroline Bingley shall also be in the party."

"What?" We all gasped again.

☙❧

Aye, Reader, we did not take to that news well at all. For her appearance, though, we did our best to endure it, was very trying, and I still had my suspicions about Caroline Bingley. She always had this look in her eye, as if she was up to something. I hoped that I was being paranoid, yet when it came to painting her portrait, I had never been in error when my mind drew a sketch of her inner self.

☙❧

Our journey to London went well without incident. After a day of staying there, I rode with Jane and Darcy to Gracechurch Street, where we would hand over Caiden and William to our aunt and uncle. At the moment, their children were at the park with their nanny.

"Oh," Aunt Gardiner said to me when she and Uncle Gardiner took them in their arms. "Thank goodness they look barely alike."

"Oh, so you see it as well?" Darcy asked them. "I confess that I cannot tell what they look like, really. To me all babies look alike."

"Do not fear, Mr. Darcy," Aunt Gardiner said. "You do not

43

speak from blindness, just lacking in experience. After giving birth to four children, one can see much in a child's face that one did not before becoming a mother. For example, Caiden shall grow to probably be the more handsome one."

"You can see that already as well?" I laughed.

"Oh yes, it is very much likely. And he is the one who looks more like you, Mr. Darcy. William's features are less defined, but he smiles often and that is a good sign that he shall grow to believe it right to do so. Smiling works wonders for a man's demeanor and appearance."

"So," Uncle Gardiner said, "remember, please, to give Lydia our sincere congratulations and we have a present for her, which is in that box over there."

Jane went to the box that was on the desk and picked it up.

"We hope that she likes it."

"I'm sure she shall," Jane replied.

We stayed at Gracechurch for a little while longer, to ensure that Caiden and William would be well before we left for Grosvenor Square.

The next day saw the arrivals of so many old friends of ours. Our parents and Mary arrived at my husband's home and when entering, their reactions were as expected. My mother was filled with effusions of joy at being in such an illustrious home and my father was enjoying her reaction.

When they were settled and we all sat down in the parlor to tea, the doorbell rang again and this time it was Lord and Lady Fitzwilliam, with their son Acton, and their other son Henry Fitzwilliam!

We all met them with civility and warmth, yet I could not help looking on Henry with curiosity the whole time, and nor could Jane and Darcy. The last time that we had seen him was when he arrived at Pemberley solely for the purpose of calling out his brother, Colonel Fitzwilliam. He challenged the Colonel to a duel over

Kitty, and then fought him on the grounds. Looking on him now was most astonishing, yet it was made clear that he was going to join his family in going to America and seeing Lydia's wedding.

This, however, seemed to give off the wrong message. For he was going to the wedding of a random relative of his, who he barely knew. And yet he did not attend his own younger brother's. However, I could only suppose that it would have been easier to attend a wedding for a cousin he cared little about than for Colonel Fitzwilliam, who he fancied had betrayed him and stole the woman he thought he loved. Either way, my heart went out to Richard, for it would have hurt his feelings.

Henry Fitzwilliam, however, was determined to make a good impression, and it was evident that he wanted to eradicate our previous memory of him. We allowed him to turn over a new leaf, but there are some memories that cannot fully be erased; Henry Fitzwilliam's challenging his brother to a duel over heartache was one of those memories.

That night, Mr. Bingley and Miriam came to dinner as well, yet Miss Bingley and Mr. and Mrs. Hurst did not. They had received an invitation to dine elsewhere at a friend's house that evening. This suited all very well because it was quite a full table already.

During the dinner, I worried that our mother, who meant well very much...and I did love her...would say something to bring shame to herself and place her on the wrong end of some very impertinent remarks. Yet my worries had been in vain. I can only suppose that being in the presence of an Earl, his wife, and their two heirs was enough to make her grow quite shy again—and this only made my father amused even more.

When he was close to me, he whispered in my ear: "Perhaps I should do my best to always have an Earl near me. If they can have this much of an effect on your mother, they are worth every pound it would take to purchase them."

"Father, not even the Prince Regent has that many pounds."

"No, perhaps not."

The rest of the evening went well, however, as the women and men separated after the meal, I excused myself from my mother's, sisters', and Miriam's company, and went into the hallway to get a moment's peace.

This was the longest I had been away from my two sons and the loss was getting to me. For my mind continually fell upon them and I worried that something might happen to them while we were away.

While I paced the halls, hoping to get my mind away from such matters, I heard hushed voices from around the corner and I recognized both. One belonged to Darcy, while the other belonged to his cousin, Henry Fitzwilliam.

"And you promise this?" Darcy asked.

"Yes, I swear," Henry replied. "Darcy, do you not ever understand that you cannot always hold people down by one mistake?"

"I can when that mistake was you battling your brother over a woman that he naturally won. Richard never meant to hurt you in any way, Henry."

"I have come to terms with that, yet it still feels otherwise."

"He did not even know that you liked Kitty when he developed feelings for her. And when he did learn of it, he actually tried to release her from his affections."

"What?" Henry replied.

"Yes, Henry, he did his best to consider your feelings. So much so, that he almost denied himself the woman that he truly loved. He began to attempt that, for you, and he would have told you if you had given him the chance, but you did not. And how did you repay your little brother? You dueled him in public. Now you know my habit, Henry. All too often, my good opinion, once lost, is lost forever. Yet you are my family and I love you. Give me a reason to give you my good opinion again. Henry, be happy for Richard, and when you see him, apologize for not being there at his wedding."

At first, Henry Fitzwilliam did not respond, but then he spoke up.

"You always will side with Richard, Darcy," Henry sighed.

"Richard was always there for me when we were children. Henry, all you did was ignore me."

"What? I did?"

"Yes," Darcy sighed, "Richard did not. So, stop blaming me for my preferences."

Henry Fitzwilliam did not speak for a time.

"While I will not deny that my pride is still hurt—or at least my vanity is," Henry confessed, "I do regret my past actions and I wish to start anew."

"Then start anew. That is the good thing about family, Henry. We will give you the chance."

The next day came quite quickly, and we were all assembled, yet my thoughts still wondered about Henry Fitzwilliam. I was neither certain nor confident that his mind was mostly in the right place. His anger was lessened over time, tis true, but was it so because he had learned to overcome his passions, or because of distance? He had not seen Richard or Kitty for quite some time, and their absence could have played a great part in him believing he was up to the task of seeing them.

The mind is a strange thing that way.

We can pretend all that we like that we have gotten over something when we have put distance between ourselves and that thing. But when it comes back into our sight and company, the wound can reopen; the pain can re-emerge. And all that wrath that we kept within us can be unleashed.

I remembered the look in Henry Fitzwilliam's eye when he challenged the Colonel.

First his eyes.

Then his muscles.

And his voice.

All of it was like watching a man lose control to his basest animal instincts and become a predator—a savage. And the last thing I wanted to see was that demon rise up again on the very eve of a happy time for all.

Therefore, I feared his company, even more than I feared Caroline Bingley's.

However, on the day of our departure, while all was being loaded into the carriages and we only had to wait till the servants placed our luggage in them securely, we were greeted by a most incredible commotion.

As we stood in the parlor, hoping to leave soon, the doorbell rang. The butler tended to it, and we heard her voice before we even saw her person.

Her footsteps boomed along the floor. We all stood up and Lady Catherine entered, followed by Anne de Bourgh.

"Good, I arrived before you all departed," she said, by way of greeting us.

"Aunt Catherine," Acton Fitzwilliam said, bowing.

"Catherine," Lord Fitzwilliam said, "We had no idea you would be attending."

"I decided to do so at the last minute," Lady Catherine said impatiently. "And I have already organized it with the ship, and Anne and I will be accompanying you on the voyage to America."

With my previous fears of being apprehensive about the company of Henry Fitzwilliam, I had been in error.

Lady Catherine had arrived, and she was the one to fear... truly.

7

CONFESSIONS ON THE SEA

As the voyage was underway and ocean was all around us, there was much worry about how we would all get along. Yet there was never any tension or angst in between anyone, for the ship was large enough to allow us time to be close and time far apart.

One time, I was sitting on the ship, reading a book, and I looked up to see Jane speaking with Henry Fitzwilliam. At first, I went back to reading, but then I looked up again and watched them. Jane and he were speaking in quiet and comfortable tones, and I could tell that Henry was doing his best to integrate himself into our family one at a time. That was a smart tactic. For it was always easy to make peace with one person than think to do it in a whole group.

As I watched them, I was taken unawares when someone sat beside me, and it turned out to be my mother.

"What do you think?" Mother said, looking at Jane and Henry. "He looks like he is on the way to being besotted by her."

"Mama," I sighed, "They are just talking casually."

"No, there can easily be more there, for he is rich, and she is handsome."

"It takes more than that to secure affection between two people. Besides, their tastes, tempers and traits are so much not like one another."

"Similarity does not determine intimacy! You and Mr. Darcy are very different."

"Our souls are the same, however."

"And who's to say that theirs is not? No, Lizzy. Jane may be the age of a spinster in the making, but with her perfect face, form and features, she is sure to have a perfect ending."

"And what is so wrong with her life at the moment? She is happy."

"She is single."

"And in the eyes of the bearer, that can be enough. It is the eyes of the world that make being single a blight upon the human condition. Besides, why do you worry over Jane? You feared that when father died, we would be destitute and without a penny to our names. Yet now that Kitty, Lydia, and I have wed and can look after the family if something were to befall father, why do you still have to worry or care about Jane's destiny?"

"Because...because it makes no sense."

"Oh."

"Yes, Elizabeth, it makes no sense. Jane is the most beautiful woman in the county of Hampshire. She has all the graces that are deemed worthy..."

"And according to you, she would be the one to save the family," I finished, "and now that the reverse has come to pass, you are utterly confused, and ashamed."

"Ashamed?" my mother said, turning to me.

"Oh, Mother," I groaned. "Will you never see yourself for what you are? You believed Jane would marry well and save the family. You spoke of it often and declared it a fact. And now that fact has been proven untrue, for it did not come to pass. Since the reverse is before you, you feel at a loss and do not wish to see that maybe you have been wrong. While I know that you care deeply for Jane, surely you must see that it is not your affection for her that is hurt, but your pride. You prided yourself on something that was not right in the end. And so, you prejudice yourself against what is before you, not willing to see with your own eyes that Jane is happy single. Look at her, mother. She is not incomplete or sullen, sad, or dejected. You should come to Pemberley one day and observe her as she is teaching her students. She finds completion through it. She finds that Jane Bennet is more than what she has been often perceived to be."

"Lizzy, how can you speak so when you find all of your happiness in your married state?" my mother objected. "You who would pursue Mr. Darcy to the ends of the earth."

"He was my destiny," I said. "That much was certain, but every person's destiny is different. If Jane marries, let it be because it was meant to be, not because it *had to be*. I am saying, simply, that a woman who is single is no less important or fulfilled than one who is wed. I am saying, Mother, please...let Jane be Jane. And then see what happens afterwards."

My mother sighed. "I am too old to change my way of thinking," she replied, to my surprise, "and I know you are too resolute to change yours."

"I am."

"'Tis difficult. Lizzy, right now I do not know what to think. And if I do not worry over her and Mary, what more do I have to do? What can I fill my time with? Your father ignores me...always has."

"I know," I said, feeling sorry for her, "yet why do you not ever try to reach him by speaking of things that concern him? Mother, you never read books he reads, or ask him what is on his mind. You speak without wishing to hear his feelings. He does the same with you and, if you do not mind me saying, see what happens if you do try to connect with him instead of you both being on your own paths and never meeting to walk down the same one."

"It is too late for that."

"It is never too late for anything. Besides, you have raised five daughters. Do you not think it is time that you spent time on yourself as a reward?"

"But what if your father does not care to try at this point?"

"Then I am sorry, Mother. Yet all that I can say is that if he does not see your efforts for what they are, then ask him to."

"What do you mean by that?"

"Ask him to see how you are wishing to get better along with him, and then ask him if he is willing to try, for you are. Father is a cynical man, but even he could not turn away from such warm sincerity."

"Well, I suppose I have nothing to lose."

"No, you do not. For even if it does not work, he still is your husband. For better or for worse."

My mother, a little unnerved by these new findings, nodded to me, then stood up and walked away.

My time and adventures on sea voyages had led to me learning much about the people I traveled with, but in all my history of confessions on the sea, what I learned about my mother that day had to have been the most moving.

8

FAMILY WE HAD ALL OUR LIVES

Sailing along the Delaware River, soon Philadelphia came into view and while Henry, Lord and Lady Fitzwilliam had seen it before, it was the first time for Acton, Mary, my mother, and father.

"Oh, it is so large!" Mary cried. "It looks nice from a distance, and hopefully it shall keep looking so upon closer inspection."

"It all depends upon which street you walk down," Lady Fitzwilliam said. "As it is with any city you go to. I admit to preferring New York, but I do recall liking Philadelphia well enough."

"It is the people who I enjoyed," Henry Fitzwilliam said. "I was a child at the time, yet they seemed so full of life. Hopefully nothing has changed since then."

"Nothing much," Darcy said. "Just a war on the rise."

Our ship made berth, the boarding plank was set, and we all disembarked, walking down to Penn's Landing, and waiting for luggage to be brought down from the ship's stock room.

"How long do you think it will be 'til we find them?" Lord Fitzwilliam pondered.

"Well," Darcy said, "if I know Cousin Thomas, and I do at this point, he has learned full well when the ship was meant to arrive and what spot it was to make berth in, which means we should not be waiting long—"

"Fitzwilliam!" Came the cries of the familiar voice of Cousin Emilia. "My dear Fitzwilliam and Elizabeth!"

We all turned, and Cousin Thomas was there with Cousin Emilia, along with Kitty and Colonel Fitzwilliam.

Our joy at seeing each other was quite moving. Upon seeing Cousin Thomas and Emilia's joviality, we all met with much enthusiasm and warmth on all sides.

"I was worried that something might have occurred on your ship," Cousin Emilia cried. "Sea voyages are always so frightening to me."

"Oh, but here we all are," I said, "alive and happy to see you."

"You must let us embrace you," Cousin Thomas said, and he and Emilia hugged Darcy, Bingley, Miriam Bingley, I—and even Jane.

"We missed you quite a good deal," Mr. Bingley said. "Indeed, it is as if we are looking back on kindly shores."

"My dear Mr. Bingley," Cousin Thomas said, "And his lovely wife, Mrs. Bingley, you are most welcome as well."

"Thank you very much, Mr. Darcy," Miriam said, "And I am honored to be a guest in your home."

"Oh, you must call us Thomas and Emilia, for with such a family gathering, there are too many Darcys to go around, and as such, we shall all get each other confused."

We all laughed at the truth of that statement. Cousin Thomas then turned to Lord and Lady Fitzwilliam.

"And you are two faces I haven't seen for so long," Cousin Thomas declared, "yet they look no different."

"I am against aging," Lady Fitzwilliam smiled.

"And I am against dying," Lord Fitzwilliam said. "Now

introductions are in order. You have already met my oldest, Henry Fitzwilliam, but this is my younger son, Acton."

Kind words were exchanged before Cousin Thomas turned to Lady Catherine and my parents.

"And if I am not mistaken, this is Lady Catherine de Bourgh."

"Of course, it is, and you had better not think you are mistaken, Thomas!" Lady Catherine demanded.

"Dear lord," Thomas said, "it is quite clear that you have not changed a bit, Catherine, and that you feel the importance of your position too keenly."

"Thomas," she hissed, "be quiet."

Cousin Thomas raised an eyebrow, and he looked shrewd. Almost keen about something.

"Oh, you did not tell them?" Thomas smirked, and then he turned to us. "Catherine and I actually grew up together enough, for I was raised in England for a time. This is to my benefit, because as the older one, I would pick on her often and it has led to me never being afraid of her!"

"You are still an insolent fool."

"Oh, thank you, Catherine. I shall take it as the best of compliments, for I believe our longtime acquaintance has made me the only person completely unafraid of you."

"One of two people," Emilia said. "Lady Catherine, if you recall, I never had a fear of you either."

"And why should you?" Lady Catherine exclaimed, "When do I do anything for the purpose of inspiring fear?"

"All too often," Lord Fitzwilliam chuckled, "and we love you for it, Catherine—well, mostly."

My sisters and I hid our laughter over this interaction.

"Yes, Catherine, do not be vexed over our loving bites at you," Thomas said. "It is the habit of seeing childhood friends of the family again."

"Well, just because I have crossed an ocean does not strip me of my title and you will respect me, Thomas."

"Oh, give it a rest, Catherine," Emilia chuckled, "and learn to laugh some more."

I wanted to hug Cousin Emilia!

"And," Emilia continued, "I am assuming that the lady behind you is our cousin, Miss Anne de Bourgh."

"Yes, it is." Anne smiled. "Good day, Cousin Emilia and Cousin Thomas, it is nice to meet you all finally."

"The pleasure is all ours," Thomas said, then turned to Catherine. "You have a genteel sort of daughter here, Catherine, and you ought to be proud."

"Thank you, yes I know."

"And you are making sure to listen to her often? I know you, Catherine, and being a dominator is sometimes a habit of yours."

Now I wanted to hug Cousin Thomas! Dear lord, both him, and Emilia were the sort of parents that came from legend.

"Thomas, have you lost your mind completely, and your manners?"

"I simply like teasing you, Catherine. For I am quite good at it, you see."

"Well, you have no right to judge me, for you did not even consult me when your son decided to finally wed. Why did you not write to me immediately so that I could determine the eligibility of the match?"

"Eligibility?" my mother cried. All throughout the sea voyage, Lady Catherine and my mother had given each other a wide berth, recalling their last encounter with each other. Yet now, for Lady Catherine to question another of her daughters would be too much for my mother's pride to let it slip by. "Are you implying that you need to interrogate my daughter to see if she is suitable for this Mr. Henry Darcy, because I can assure you that she is, no matter whatever you have to say about it."

"She is suitable," Cousin Emilia said, smirking, "and Catherine, when you see them together, you will be in no doubt of it. Also, you truly expected us to seek your counsel for our son, who hasn't even met you, regarding his choice of wife? Catherine, how could we have done so?"

"I still should have been consulted, for as you know, I am often praised for my excellent judge of character. And you shall recognize it this instant, or must I make voyage back over the ocean, for I am not in the habit of being thus addressed."

"Who is stopping you?" my mother whispered under her breath. "Goodbye and good riddance."

"You are free to do so, Catherine," Emilia smiled. "Or you can let your childhood friends welcome you into their home—and learn to smile and laugh with everyone again and stop being such a drag."

"Upon my honor, I have never been treated so in the course of my life."

"Then you clearly forget how I would pull your hair when we were children." Thomas laughed, then he turned to my parents. "Now who are these jovial-looking people, for I have a hankering to know them as well?"

"Very well," Darcy added, "this is my father and mother, in-laws, Mr. and Mrs. Bennet, and their third oldest daughter, Miss Mary Bennet."

They all bowed and curtsied to one another, and then Mr. Bingley introduced them to Caroline and the Hursts.

"Lydia, Georgiana, and Mr. Henry Darcy wished to be here," Kitty said, eyeing Henry Fitzwilliam with apprehension. "But if they did, we would not have all the room that we needed in the carriages."

"Yes," Cousin Emilia said, "we had to borrow two carriages from our neighbors just so that we could accommodate you all."

"Oh, thank you so much for going through all this trouble for our comfort," Caroline Bingley said, smiling sweetly. I did not know if Cousin Thomas would be able to tell, yet Caroline could not have said it with any more falseness.

"Oh, it is no trouble at all." Cousin Thomas grinned. "Now let us get you all to our carriages, for we cannot wait to show you our home. It's been so long since we accommodated so many in Canterbury that we are all quite giddy over it."

As we progressed, I did my best to get my mother and Cousin Emilia to begin talking, for they were so alike. Yet Caroline Bingley moved with much speed and began to monopolize Emilia, asking her all about Canterbury and how many children she had. Mrs. Hurst also accompanied her, yet Mrs. Hurst managed to make it appear as if she was simply trying to get to know her host. Whereas, with Caroline, there was something else afoot. She seemed desperate to make a good impression, and I could not shake my suspicions that she was trying to make Cousin Emilia warm to her.

However, my attention was directed to Kitty and Colonel Fitzwilliam, who approached his parents and siblings. Acton and Lady Fitzwilliam were very talkative—almost too talkative, and it was clear that they were doing their best to hide that Henry Fitzwilliam did not know what to say to either of them. Looking at Henry Fitzwilliam, I could tell that he did not look bitter, but chagrin and a touch embarrassed. Kitty turned to him, smiled gently, and nodded her head to him, and he returned it with a warm gaze before Kitty looked away and continued to address Lady Fitzwilliam.

Henry, however, looked down at his hands as they walked on. Richard did not even get a chance to speak to him because Acton continued to tell him of everything that had gone on in England, while also wishing to know all that had occurred in Philadelphia. I knew Acton very little, but from what I did know, he seemed to be aware of how to be the perfect younger brother. He seemed to be of the useful sort where he understood his role in his family and how to use that role to his and everyone else's benefit.

"So, Mrs. Bennet," Cousin Emilia began, finally getting a chance to speak to my mother since Caroline and Louisa were in another carriage, "Our two children are to be wed. I hope it excites you."

In that carriage, I was alongside my mother, Mary, Kitty, Colonel Fitzwilliam, Cousin Thomas, and Cousin Emilia—for it was a grand sized carriage if I ever saw one.

"Oh, Mrs. Darcy, nothing makes me more joyous. And I am sure that my Lydia and your son shall get along splendidly. She is a lively sort of girl, but with the greatest heart, I promise."

"Oh yes, her heart is a large one. She not only has turned my taciturn son into a more amiable one, but she has quite won over my other daughter, Helena, who suffers from a mental impediment. Oh, you should see them together. She knows how to speak to Helena and is always patient with her."

"My Lydia? Truly?"

"Oh, so she has developed such compassion without even you knowing?"

"Oh, I confess to being non-the-wiser over it. Yet again, I am not surprised. I do long to see her, and I am certain your son has many amiable qualities of his own. Yet if taciturn is something that he once was, then it is all too amazing how some men will choose to transform themselves. It is a virtue in their own right."

"Yes, quite right, Mrs. Bennet."

"And forgive me for overhearing, but I was told that you had nine children?"

"Yes, I do."

"It does make my number of five appear less daunting." My mother looked at Mary, Kitty, and me. "I suppose that I should not have complained so often now."

"Well," Kitty said, "We were a handful."

"Oh, you were not so hard at all. I was just too nervous."

Kitty flinched at this, for she had never heard our mother

reprimand herself before. She turned to me, and I winked at her, indicating that I would tell her later.

"And," Mary added, "you had no heirs, which added to the stress of your situation."

"Heirs?" Cousin Emilia asked. "Male heirs, you are referring to?"

"Yes, our estate was entailed away to the male line, so my daughters would not inherit it upon my husband's death."

"Upon my honor, that must have been dreadful."

"Yes, I spent so long worried over us being turned out as soon as he passed away. It gave way too much room for agony and little room for comfort and the distribution of proper affection."

"Yes," Cousin Thomas added, "it must have been a great strain on your bond with your husband. And to have it passed down along the male line, who was it to go to in your stead?"

"Our cousin, Mr. William Collins," Mary answered. "There was much discussion over it. Yet you did not have to worry yourselves, Mr. and Mrs. Darcy, for you had two male heirs."

"Even if we did not, my children would not suffer under such a foolish rule," Thomas said. "The estate ceased to be entailed away to the male line."

"Really?" I asked.

"Aye. I went to court over it long ago. Luckily, the court system back then was so preoccupied with the war that was going on, and the loss of men to the army, that they understood the only way families could keep their homes was if they allowed them to be passed down from husband to wife, or father to daughter—in case all the sons were dead from war."

"Oh, that was wise."

"Many men belonging to great estates did that back then or were smart enough to have never entailed their estates down the male line to begin with. Therefore, if I had only daughters, my wife would have inherited Canterbury if I passed away first and then it would have gone to my daughters. I wrote it in my will as such."

"That was a great thing you did," Mary sighed.

"A person cannot control where they have been often," Thomas said, "Yet I believe we ought to control where we are going, for that is the only way to move forward."

"A very noble realization," Jane said.

"Yes," I agreed, "And if you do not mind my openness, Cousin Thomas, yet I am amazed at how you and Emilia are not afraid to speak to Lady Catherine so."

Thomas and Emilia laughed at that.

"Yes," my mother agreed, "How do you accomplish it so well?"

"We have found that, unfortunately, there are only two things that will overwhelm Lady Catherine. One, you must be older than her, and two, you have to be beyond her reach of influence. And she has to know that you are beyond it, and you must have known her longer than God has. Because only then will you know her secrets."

"You know her secrets?"

"All of them, for I was there to have witnessed much. And she knows that she must allow me to speak as I ought, or I might just let something slip one day, and she will be found out."

"Isn't that blackmail?" Mary asked.

"Yes, it is, but when it comes to Lady Catherine, it is also just."

"All too true." Emilia smiled.

"You use information to your benefit?" I asked. "Thomas and Emilia, I took you for many good traits, yet cleverness in regards to social tactics was not one of them. I have underestimated you."

"Many do. It is one of the many benefits one gathers from always appearing jovial. People mistake being good with being an idiot—when in truth, it can be very much the opposite."

I turned to my mother and smiled at her.

"I knew you would like them."

"Yes, I believe that I do."

As we rode on, Cousin Emilia also made polite and warm conversation with Jane, to draw her out and show her that there were no hard feelings about what transpired between her and Henry Darcy. Jane took it as an opportunity to tell them of her teaching at Pemberley, which they all admired and also were happy in seeing that Jane had not passed over their son simply to fall in love with another. No. Jane had refused Henry Darcy so that she could choose herself above all things.

There are few constant sources of pleasure in the world. But a family who will always be ready to accept you is one of them. Never would we forget the American Darcys, as they would never forget us, for they clearly felt as if they were the family we had all our lives—that we had only just met recently.

✿ 9 ✿

NEW FRIENDS AND OLD FANCIES

E ventually, our four carriages arrived at Canterbury. Though not as large as Pemberley, our mother still felt that there was a connection to both estates in some way—and that was that the Darcys belonged to it.

Upon our arrival, I felt the familiarity of coming home to a known sight, but also feeling the luck of that return. Due to our last parting with the occupants of Canterbury, I feared that we would never be allowed to return, and over and over that had proven to be a needless fear. Now it was my turn to return to it, and I hoped to be met with the same comfort that we had gained on our first visit. But nothing can ever be the same, can it?

For just as we pulled up, the door opened, and many people rushed out who I did not recognize and very few who I did. In the middle of the throng were Lydia, Henry Darcy, and Georgiana!

"My family is here!" Lydia cried, "come out and meet my fiancé!"

Beside her I saw Henry Darcy smiling warmly, his hand in hers, and if I were to go upon first impressions, I would declare that he was fully in love with her. He barely even looked like the Henry

Darcy I remembered. Yes, his imposing height and features were the same. In essentials, he was as he ever was, but his mood and demeanor were lifted. He had energy! Vitality. Brightness. He looked...content and alive!

Was it so possible? That tall, proud, and stern Mr. Henry Darcy, who by all accounts was a man who labored under the weight of propriety and rigidity, not only gave way to releasing himself from such restraint, but that he truly did choose Lydia? He, who had once favored Jane due to her serene nature, elegant manners, and refinement, were to then turn around and choose the sister who was spirited. And yet he looked happy, and—his sister, Deborah Darcy, had been correct! Henry Darcy had just not known what was right for him. He needed something with spirit to awaken his own rather than something that was demure. Dear lord, if my first impression was true, then he was a Darcy—through and through.

And yet, first impressions could be inaccurate, so I was going to subdue my hopes and do my best to judge the situation impartially.

We descended from the carriages and hellos were said all around.

"It seems ages since I have been to Longbourn," Lydia said, "And yet here you are, just the same, and now it feels as if Longbourn has come to America, does it not?"

"Oh, Lydia!" our mother cried. "It is good to see you! And would this be the handsome man who I get to eventually call my son-in-law?"

"Yes," Lydia said, "Mother, Father, and Mary, I believe you are the only ones to have not met him. This is Mr. Henry Darcy. And Henry, this is the rest of my family, my mother, father and my older sister, Mary."

"Mrs. and Mr. Bennet, and Miss Mary," Henry Darcy said, nervous and a little stiff. "I am pleased to make your acquaintance and are in hopes that you shall like me for a son-in-law."

"I have had my share of amusing sons-in-law," Mr. Bennet said.

"I hope you shall equally prove so. Though whether I shall be an amusing father-in-law is another matter entirely."

"Do you mock me for the sake of sarcasm or to put me at ease? I am not trying to be rude, believe me, I am just not very skilled at detecting jokes."

"Oh, then we might not get along so well."

"Father," Lydia said, "be easy upon him, and not just for the sake of making him feel comfortable, but also as a personal favor to me."

"Very well, my dear."

"You are not alone, Mr. Henry Darcy." Caroline Bingley smiled. "Wit is often hard to discern from insult with a smiling face to it, and you are the purer at heart for desiring seriousness in your address."

Caroline, I thought, *you insolent piece of rot!*

She was not even a step into the house, and she was already pandering to Mr. Henry Darcy's pride and smoothly insulting my father in the process. Knowing my father, however, he would take that as an opportunity to observe Miss Bingley's behavior and find it as a source of amusement. But I was not amused. And also, was she so ambitious that she didn't see that she spoke to Henry Darcy without having been introduced to him first?

"Oh," Mr. Bingley said, "forgive me, Henry, for my late introduction to my family, but this is my sister Caroline Bingley and Louisa Hurst along with her husband, Mr. Hurst."

"Welcome to Canterbury," Henry Darcy said, bowing slightly toward them. Louisa and Caroline curtsied gracefully while Mr. Hurst bowed but did not speak at all. This was all for the better because Mr. Hurst had no gift of conversation. From what I could tell, he only had a gift for sleeping.

Henry Darcy turned his attention back to my parents, and he smiled at my mother.

"I can see where your lovely daughters get their magnificent beauty from, Mrs. Bennet."

"Oh, thank you, Mr. Darcy."

"Call me Henry, for there are too many Darcys to go around."

We all laughed at that, for it was the second time that we had heard it.

"Ah, so this is my other nephew!" Lady Catherine de Bourgh exclaimed, stepping forward. This time, however, Anne did not follow her, but stood by Georgiana. Henry Darcy turned to her, and Lydia moved closer to him instinctively. The instinct, however, proved to be a mutual one, for Henry turned his body toward her as well.

"Aunt Catherine?" Henry Darcy began, "is that you?"

"Ah, now you remember your aunt."

"In truth, I never really forgot."

"Really? Yet you never had written to me before of your intentions to marry."

"I did not think it would be a concern of yours."

"My boy, when it comes to my family, all concerns me."

"You have not seen me since I was a child. I did not think that my choice to marry would be of any import in your eyes."

"Oh, but your choice of wife always is."

"And let's speak more of that when we go inside," Cousin Thomas said, "For before family matters ever should get discussed, introductions must be finished. Before you are some old acquaintances, but a few here are new. Guests, before you are the rest of my children."

I looked down the line and there was Henry, then Joseph, with his wife. I also saw Victoria with her husband, but the rest were unknown to me. Yet now I became aware of whom they were.

Cousin Thomas introduced the set we already knew and then he proceeded to the rest.

"This is our other daughter Samantha with her husband Mr.

Eastbourne and their two sons Joseph and Alexander, then Molly with her husband Mr. John Jay, then Ester with her husband, Mr. Arthur Martin, and Felicity with her husband, Mr. James Deacon and their daughters Ariana and Gretta. And my children, this is the long party of many friends and family. First there is Mr. and Mrs. Bennet of Longbourn with their daughters Elizabeth, who is married to our Mr. Fitzwilliam Darcy here, and their other daughters, Jane and Mary. As you can see, this is your aunt, Lady Catherine de Bourgh and her daughter, Anne. Then there is Lord and Lady Fitzwilliam, the Earl and Lady of Matlock, with their sons Henry and Acton. Lastly, these are the Bingleys, with Mr. Charles Bingley and his wife, Mrs. Miriam Bingley, then his sisters, Caroline and Louisa Hurst, along with Mr. Hurst."

It was a long procession of names and, quite frankly, I did not understand how Cousin Thomas could have remembered all of them, but he did.

There were many bows, curtsies, and 'how do you dos' offered, but it was all so overwhelming.

We all went inside as our luggage was brought to our guest rooms while we all sat down to tea.

"Well," Cousin Emilia said, "aren't we large in number?"

Everyone laughed.

"But we are missing two still," my Mr. Darcy said. "How are your other daughters, Helena and Deborah?"

"Oh, well, Helena is doing much better, but she still is a little apprehensive for such large gatherings of people. And poor Deborah could not get time from her convent to come and meet you all," Emilia sighed. "But if you like, I would love to take you to see her again as soon as you are all rested enough to do so."

"That would be splendid," Jane said.

"Oh, so you have met Deborah then?" Molly asked us. "You liked her, didn't you?"

"Yes, we did."

"I am not surprised, for out of all my sisters, she is the most like me."

"Oh, please Molly!" Ester cried, "You do yourself too much credit. If there was any sister who Deborah resembled, it was me."

"No," Samantha cried, "it was I. For I am the most spirited, and that is a vice I cling to proudly." Samantha turned to us. "A side effect of us sisters being together again in so long. We begin to relive old arguments."

"At least you wait till you are reunited after so long to argue," Kitty said. "We Bennet girls didn't need distance to bring up old rivalries."

"Indeed," Lydia added, "all we needed was to wake up in the morning and we could find something to complain of."

"Then you would have fit right in at Canterbury." Molly laughed, and added, "We bickered so often that it made our parents and Henry quite distracted all the time."

"Distracted was a polite word for what you put us through," Henry Darcy groaned. "I swear, to be an older brother to *so* many sisters is like being in a henhouse with much clucking going on."

"Oh, I do not know," Joseph said. "I rather enjoyed the clucking."

"Oh, Joseph!" Ester cried, "and you wonder why we like him best, Henry."

"No Ester, I never wondered. Besides, Helena and Deborah favor me, and Joseph gets the rest of you, so it all evened out, didn't it?"

"Not as much as you would think," Felicity said, "but now Henry has Miss Lydia here, and I believe, Miss Lydia, that your affection for Henry is enough for that of five women."

"Five women?" Lydia laughed. "I am too much for only five. Rather, I would say my love is enough to make up for fifteen women at the very least."

"And to think," Caroline said, turning to Charles Bingley, "that you complained over having Louisa and I as sisters, claiming that to be too much. Now, seeing that you had only two sisters to contend with, do you not find yourself lucky?"

"Not so, Caroline," Charles countered, "for in such matters, quality still counts over quantity. And you, in your worst moments, can have the wrath of four women combined."

"Oh, Charles! How ungenerous and impolitic of you to paint my portrait in such a negative light. Indeed, Mr. Henry Darcy, he would rather teach you to not believe a word I say in defense of myself. Is that not ungenerous of him?"

Henry Darcy looked confused at having been addressed so directly in such a crowded room, but he nodded and played along.

"Yes, I suppose it is, Miss Bingley. However, at the moment, we brothers are doing our best to paint negative lights on all our sisters for the fun of it. So, he is not alone, nor are you."

"Yes, Miss Bingley," I said icily, but still smiling. "There is always a time to enjoy the felicity of having a laugh with and at one's siblings, for it shows the deepest of bonds."

"Oh!" Felicity cried, "someone has used my name in a sentence again. I do so love it when that happens."

We chuckled as the tea was brought in by the servants.

⚜

The conversation that day proved to be most wonderful. For in a family such as that side of the Darcys was bound to be an experience that reminded me a great deal of some of the inhabitants of Hampshire. The Darcys had many stories, and my mother had many stories of her own from her experiences in raising us. Having just given birth to twin boys, I was able to speak of them for a while, while Fitzwilliam every now and again added a little anecdote here and there, or a confession of how he was afraid of the day they would learn how to crawl. For that would be the day they would begin to learn how to work some mischief.

Yet, while the afternoon proved to be a triumph as far as family meetings go, there was one thing I noticed, and I believed that Lydia marked it as well.

One moment, while Jane was getting some more tea for herself at the table, she found herself standing next to Henry Darcy while he was getting some more cake. They spoke in careful and quiet tones, and I wondered what they could be discussing. After a couple of minutes, Jane went back to her seat and immersed herself in our conversation while Henry sat back down next to Lydia.

ᘒᘓᘔ

That night, before we were to go to our rooms to get changed for dinner, I went to Jane's room. I knocked on the door. She opened it first before she moved aside and expected me to enter.

"Were you expecting someone else?" I asked.

"Yes, I was expecting our mother," Jane admitted. "I am so worried that now we are here, she might learn of Henry Darcy's first proposal to me. Oh, Lizzy, I pray she does not find out, for that shall make everything more complicated."

"Oh, I see, but actually Jane, I have come to ask you about that very point."

"Have you? And why so?"

"Well forgive me for noticing, and I did not mean to, but I saw that you and Henry Darcy spoke in confidence to each other earlier, and I just wished to make sure that he did not say anything offensive to you."

"Oh," Jane replied, sitting down, and I followed suit, "I am not mad, for it is plain that you were worried over me."

"Well, did he say anything impertinent?"

"No." Jane smiled. "It was quite the contrary. He apologized to me."

"Oh, did he?"

"Yes, and not just for his disastrous actions after I rejected him, but also because he worried about how his swift and decisive actions must make me feel. For him to propose to my younger sister so soon after being rejected by me, he was worried that it would hurt my vanity as well as make me feel that he was wishing to seek vengeance upon me. He wanted to very much assure me that it was not the case. My rejection wounded him, and he was resentful at first. But it did not make him wrathful or wishing retribution of any kind. He simply had a lot to attempt to overcome and, much to his surprise, Lydia had helped him as well and showed him how wrong he was about many things. Of all of us to reform Henry Darcy, who would have thought it would be Lydia?"

"I did not see that coming as well."

"No, nor did I. And yet, I suppose, when you do look upon it, I was not the woman for the mission, therefore it had to have been another."

"You mentioned earlier that he did not want your vanity to be hurt by it," I acknowledged. "Yet it was. You confessed as much to me."

"It was, and it still is, in a way. Yet that instinct has long been subduing now and I am able to give way to nothing but happiness on all ends. I am just so amazed that it has all ended in this happy way! And now that I look on it, maybe they are truly perfect for one another. For they were two broken souls, and somehow they needed each other to patch the holes in themselves closed."

"So, you believe them to be truly in love then?"

"Elizabeth, I can see what you are feeling and thinking. And while I do not think it wise for me to make a full conclusion based off of only seeing them for one day, but Lizzy, did you not see them together? He adores her, and she is bound to him. They did not like to move far away from each other, and they looked on each other so fondly. He never looked at me that way before—Mr. Brocklehurst did, but..."

"Oh Jane, you still feel pain over that, do you not?"

"Senseless as it is, I always might. And sometimes I did think on what it would have been like if it had all turned out in my favor on that score—and then I remember all the good that happened since it did not."

"Such as?"

"If I had married Mr. Brocklehurst, then how would I ever have been able to become a charity instructor, teaching children of the less fortunate? And if I had married him, then I would not have traveled with you to America, then had rejected Mr. Henry Darcy and forced him into a state where he had to wake up and see that Lydia was his perfect match."

"Then it follows that the choices of Jane Bennet ruled the fate of our lives."

"I do not presume to have that much power." She smirked. "But my actions did have consequences that were for the good of all."

I stood up and prepared to leave.

"Oh, but there is one problem," she said to my back.

"What?" I asked, turning to her.

"Miss Bingley has designs on Henry Darcy."

I blinked, amazed that she had noticed that.

"I had no idea you realized that," I said.

"Teaching children has opened me up to learning how to read people's silences in a way that I did not before. Before, I had given people the benefit of the doubt so often, always hoping for the good. Yet now, I do hope for the best, but I am not afraid to see the worst in people. Or to acknowledge it."

"Caroline Bingley is a fool."

"Caroline Bingley is obsessed with the name of Darcy, and that obsession will be the unwinding of her, I fear."

"It just might. And I fear that she shall never learn."

"She has been in the habit of probably never being told her faults. So, she will always be prejudiced against the idea that she has them."

"'Tis very possible."

"And yet, what I cannot understand is how much she could have misread a situation. Why would she set her sights on Henry Darcy, who is engaged to my sister, rather than turning her attentions to Henry Fitzwilliam, who is single and the son of an Earl? It makes no sense! Not that I would encourage Henry Fitzwilliam to court her at all, or fall prey to her schemes, yet still. Why would she therefore make the wrong choice?"

"Because she is a blind fool."

"Yes, she is."

I was startled, for that had to have been the fifth insult Jane had ever uttered in her life.

"Jane, that was fantastic."

"She has given me no choice but to see her as she is," Jane replied, "therefore, whatever judgment I make on her, she has forced my hand in the matter."

"Yes, I suppose she has. Still, we must be wary of her."

"Yes, we must."

Happy that I had a strong ally in Jane, as always, I left her room, pondering our situation in Canterbury and how we had come back upon new friends and old fancies—some fancies of which were benign, others were possibly harmful.

❧ 10 ❧

A HARD CONVERSATION TO START
AND END

Carefully and quietly, Mr. Darcy walked down the hallway. He had inquired after Henry Darcy with the servants, and when he found out that Henry was alone in the billiards room, he made his way there, hoping to look inconspicuous.

When he entered, he was lucky that his information was accurate, for Henry Darcy was playing at billiards by himself.

"Mr. Darcy," Henry said, bowing.

"Mr. Darcy," Darcy replied, nodding his head. "I was told that I would find you here."

"Oh," Henry faltered, "you came looking for me then."

"Yes, I have."

Henry placed down his billiard stick, folded his arms, and prepared himself.

"Well, I suppose I was anticipating this."

"Were you?"

"Yes, I was. I recall your last words to me very often before you left Canterbury."

"I said what I had to."

"Yes, you would see it in such a light."

"You do not?"

"I see it as well, but it still is very hard to speak of such things. It does hurt one's pride. But I can see that you are afraid."

"Yes, I am. I understand the need to regain emotional security after experiencing a loss or a humiliation. Therefore, it makes me wonder about the validity of your changing courses to Lydia."

"You are afraid that my designs on her are ill-founded and out of spite."

"I fear that you are a man who has been heartbroken, and you will do anything to show the world that you still have your self-respect—and that your shame is erased. We humans have a natural inclination to attempt to eradicate any embarrassing moments of our lives by having the world see us in glory. Henry, I am not trying to insult you, so do not take offense. I am simply doing all in my power to protect Lydia."

"As you have done so before," Henry Darcy replied. "Lydia told me of her past with Mr. Wickham. She always did know what you did for her, but she was in denial of it for so long. I did not know if you knew that."

"Thank you," Darcy replied, "for I did not."

"Well, now you do. Fitzwilliam, we are too much alike to ever get along. I see that about us, but as I said, we are similar. Would you propose to the sister of a woman who rejected you, just for the sake of getting revenge on that woman? Would you resign yourself to such a fate just to have a moment of spite achieved?"

Mr. Darcy pondered the question at first, yet it took only seconds for him to determine his own will.

"No, I would never do that."

"Precisely. Angry at Jane Bennet I was. Spiteful, resentful, and even going so far as to wish that she were to feel the pain that she made me endure. I do not deny this. Yet that is the natural reaction of any heartbreak, so I do not feel especially sinister for confessing this. Yet upon seeing Lydia when she arrived here, I had no designs on her as a prize to win and achieve revenge through. In fact, I hated the very sight of her."

"Did you?"

"Jane may have not been there, but her little sister was, and I was very much content with expressing all my anger on Lydia."

"You were planning to punish her for what her sister had done to you?"

"Yes, I admit that."

"Henry, please say something about yourself that could possibly redeem you in my eyes? Or I do not know if I shall censure myself."

"I am trying to tell you the truth about myself. And how Lydia was able to get through to me in the end."

"How did she?"

"She stood up to me." Henry sighed. "And she was not afraid to point out all of my flaws and somehow spoke in such a manner that I had no choice but to listen. And the turn of her countenance I shall never forget, when she spoke the very same words that you spoke when you reprimanded me all those months ago. She and you both said that I was the last man in the world who any woman should ever be prevailed upon to marry."

"She said that to you as well?" Darcy asked, surprised.

"Yes, those were your words. You know not, you can scarcely conceive how they have tortured me—though it was some time, I confess, before I was reasonable enough to allow their justice."

"I was certainly very far from expecting them to make so strong an impression. I had not the smallest idea of their being ever felt in such a way."

"I can easily believe it. You thought me then devoid of every proper feeling, I am sure you did. Yet like you, what did Lydia say to me that I did not deserve? The recollection of what I then said, of my conduct, my manners, my expressions during the whole of it, is now, and has been many days, inexpressibly painful to me. Her reproof, so well applied, I shall never forget."

Fitzwilliam Darcy sat down, looking at his curiosity of a cousin and wondered at him. Could they really be so alike? Was it possible that Lydia Bennet suited Henry Darcy in the way that Elizabeth suited him? Could life really be so much of an entangled thing?

"So, you promise me," he continued, "that you love Lydia? That you are certain she loves you and that this is not a rash step just to rebuild each other's confidence?"

"I admit that she does help me feel stronger, but only in the way that love naturally does make one feel so. I love her, Fitzwilliam, and Jane Bennet is an angel. For if she had not rejected me, then I would never have gotten the chance to marry where I ought. It turned out that creation truly can come from someone choosing to say 'no'."

"Yes, it always is possible. I had to say no to things myself." Mr. Darcy stood up and straightened his jacket. "Henry, if you speak true, then I am happy for you and Lydia. I do not believe though that we shall ever be close."

"No, for we are too similar."

"Yet still, I wish you all to be happy, and if Lydia did deserve someone, then it would be you."

"Be careful Fitzwilliam, you are coming dangerously close to complimenting me."

"Yes, well..."

Mr. Darcy nodded and then left the room.

☙❧

Both Mr. Darcys were left to dwell in two different states.

Henry Darcy went back to playing billiards yet wondered all the while at how his hasty marriage would be perceived by all. Would he constantly have to defend himself from naysayers who doubted his true affections, or would they begin to observe his manners and see that he had truly changed? Whatever be the case, he was happy that his nature was not of the flimsy sort where because others doubted the sincerity of his feelings, he would begin to doubt it as well. Oh, no! Whether it was out of stubbornness or strength, his heart would not be shaken, for he knew that he did care deeply.

However, he knew he would have to speak to Lydia to make sure that she had not told her parents of his history with Jane. He had been getting on so well with them, especially the mother who was quick to adore him, that he did not want to lose their affection because of suspicion.

With Mr. Fitzwilliam Darcy, however, he walked the halls, still worried that Henry did not admit all to him. But he was still content in knowing that at least he was given the truth. For in such moments, Henry Darcy was incapable of lying, and even if so, he was not very proficient at it.

Therefore, his mind was at rest for the present as he walked to find Elizabeth, content in knowing, out of a sense of family loyalty, that he had undergone a hard conversation to start and to end—and that he had ended it to the best of his ability.

✲ II ✲

A CONVERSATION THAT IS HARD TO
BEGIN, BUT EASY TO END

Cousin Thomas was in his study with his account book, going over the figures that his estate made roughly that month when the door opened, and he was graced with the presence of Lady Catherine de Bourgh.

"Oh, hello, Catherine," he said pleasantly. He stood up to receive her properly. "Still not in the habit of knocking, I see?"

"You look as if you knew that I would come," Lady Catherine huffed.

"It is because I did. Please sit down and tell me the mountain that you made out of a molehill now."

"Someday, you might actually say something funny, Thomas."

"And some day you might actually give advice that is needed."

"My advice is always needed," Lady Catherine said, sitting down opposite him.

"And why do I get the funny feeling that you shall display your words of wisdom right before me?"

"Because I will, for I am of the mind to point out your inadequacies."

"No, Catherine, you are in the mood to be a pain. As usual."

"Oh, you take delight in vexing me!"

"Interesting, how now you sound like Mrs. Bennet."

"Oh, do not insult me that far. I could never resemble that odious woman."

"On the contrary, your souls are clearly very similar."

"Now your insults are going too far."

"It was not so much an insult as it was an observation. In truth, I quite enjoy Mrs. Bennet's company."

"Are you insane?"

"No, I simply like a woman who talks a lot."

"Of course, you do, which is why you married Emilia."

"I should rectify my speech. I enjoy women who talk about things worth talking about. Unlike in your case, where a woman speaks and does not wish to hear any response. You still speak in speeches, don't you, Catherine?"

"And that is another thing you must cease to do, you impertinent cur. You must stop insulting me all the while."

"I only do so to remind you of something that escapes you often."

"And what is that?"

"That you are human. I do it to remind you that you are human, like the rest of us, and that you can be wrong as well."

Lady Catherine sneered at Thomas, but he only continued to speak onward, not afraid at her soon-to-occur rebuttal.

"Tell me something, Catherine. When did it happen?"

"When did what happen, Thomas?"

"When was the day that you woke up and told yourself that you were right to always dictate others? When did you forget your humanity?"

"I have much humanity."

"No, you mistake your desire to control as such, but it is not. It is only your pride."

"And what of you, you blind fool! You knew why I came, so do not pretend to be coy about it. How could you have been so foolish to encourage this engagement of your son to Lydia Bennet? You do not know her past, do you?"

"I am aware of it all."

Lady Catherine faltered, not foreseeing that her strongest argument would deflate so swiftly.

"And you still allowed your son to propose to her?"

"I do not see what is so very dreadful on Lydia's part. She is young, and her mistake was one made from such youth, and did not do harm to anyone but herself in the end. She has served her penance and ought to be absolved from her ties to that worthless late husband of hers. Besides, that all happened in England. This is a whole other country where she can move away from such perpetual reminders of something she has the right to forget."

"Yet such an action still should haunt her character."

"She ran away with a man because she loved him and made a mistake...what evil was in her intentions?"

"The evil of not following the rules and regulations of good society. She should be called out to spoil!"

"No, she shall not be under my roof, and she is Henry's choice, which I am happy he has taken. Now, the question then becomes, why do you care? Why does Lady Catherine de Bourgh, of Rosings Park, who has not cared about her American cousins for so long, suddenly strike an interest in their doings—especially at this turn of the year and a war between two countries upon us? What is Lady Catherine's secret reasoning? Shall I tell you what I really think, Lady Catherine, of what is really on your mind and moved you to action?"

"Your words shall mean nothing to me, for they will all be false, so pray tell, what lunacy have you concocted?"

"The lunacy of one who knows you too well. Admit it, you are not mad that my son is getting married to Lydia but are angry that Henry did not choose your daughter, Anne."

"You see," Thomas continued, "you forgot about us here on the other side of the ocean, but then the Bennets begin to learn of us, they begin to attach themselves to us, and your anger gets awakened. Lord Fitzwilliam told me about your wishes for Anne to marry Fitzwilliam Darcy, and he ultimately rejected her so that he could marry Elizabeth. That must have been a great blow to your pride. You felt hurt, didn't you, Catherine?"

Lady Catherine did not reply, but only looked out of the window, staunch and defiant.

"And then Kitty goes and marries Colonel Fitzwilliam, which was another possible choice you thought of for Anne as well, did you not? For naturally, after it did not transpire between Anne and Fitzwilliam, Richard would have been the next good candidate. Therefore, you were thwarted by another Bennet girl. They were interrupting your machinations at every turn. Yes, I do know your mind all too well. Then when you heard news of my son marrying Lydia Bennet Wickham, that was the final straw. And so, you crossed an ocean to see a family you have not seen in decades, all so you could defeat one Bennet girl. Then, if Henry and I were compliant to you, you would then have him attached to Anne, just so that your victory would be complete. Am I wrong, Catherine?"

"You are not nearly as smart as you think, Thomas. Not even half so smart."

"I am, and you know it. For I merely pretend not to have a clever bone in my body—I have learned that maintaining a pretense in that manner is always necessary."

Lady Catherine sat down, resigned—and angry that she was.

"You will not listen to my advice, no matter how right I am."

"No, I will not heed your warning, for there is nothing to warn me against. My son is a grown man, and this is his choice to make. Yet, you will do something for me."

"Why would I do that?"

"Because you do not want me to let slip to anyone in our company all that you have just said."

"You would use our conversation as collateral? Are you that low, Thomas?"

"Yes, I am, and to give you further incentive, I also shall not tell anyone your secret."

"You are evil!"

"I am when peace needs to be maintained."

"That is your excuse?"

"Yes, very much."

Lady Catherine picked up a quill from the desk and threw it at Thomas. Thomas, however, did not flinch when it struck his chest, for he had been on the receiving end of Lady Catherine's wrath before.

"Very well! What do you want?"

"I want you to accept everyone here, Catherine," Thomas said. "I want you to be kind to my children, the Bennets, and all else. I want you to be happy, Catherine, and not ruin this happy event by having to hurt others. Can you promise me so?"

Despite her pride and stubbornness, Catherine was secretly moved by his demand.

"And that is all that you want?"

"For the moment, yes, but one side request."

"And what is that?"

"I want you to begin to have tea-times with Mrs. Bennet and Emilia, and let the young women go off and enjoy each other's company. Including Anne. Let her go off and join them, where she shall be allowed to mingle amongst company."

"What pathetic reason do you have for that?"

"Anne is a young woman now, and she follows after you like the pet you have raised her to be. She clearly is eclipsed by your shadow, Catherine. Why do you not let her be and see how she will turn out if you allow her to grow on her own?"

"She is sickly and needs me."

"She needs her voice. She needs to be allowed to grow up."

"And who do you think yourself so superior to me that you can lecture my skills as a mother? I raised my own child, thank you."

"And I have raised nine of them, seven of which were girls. And the daughter we have who has mental damage has more confidence than Anne does. It's too strong a prejudice that we men are said to not care for our daughters. Too strong a prejudice! Therefore, that is my request. Take it or leave it. While Anne is here, see what happens if she is allowed to bloom on her own. Agreed?"

Lady Catherine stood up and balled her fists.

"Very well, but only because I would like to have time to myself as well, and not because I submit to you in any way, shape or form."

"Very well then. Today the ladies shall go to visit my daughter, Deborah. Tell Anne to accompany them, and if she likes it, then encourage her to mingle with my daughters, who I promise will treat her with affection and respect. We do not forget family here."

"Fine, yet if she does not like it, I shall not ever listen to you again."

"I know you shall not, Catherine. Yet thank you for listening to me now."

Lady Catherine walked to the door, then remembered something and turned back to him.

"Thomas?"

"Yes?"

"There was a time where you were an ambitious man who gave respect and credit to decorum and propriety. When did you forget yourself?"

"When I learned something very important."

"And what is that?"

"I became a father."

Lady Catherine's mouth clenched shut at the reply, not knowing how to respond to it.

"And because," he continued, "I learned an important thing. Sometimes our children will love us. Sometimes they shall hate us. Yet one thing we should always give them is their right to be heard. For if we only teach them to listen but never give them their honor to be heard, how will they ever learn how to stand up to the world? And I learned if they cannot stand without me, then I never taught them how to properly stand at all. Anne is not my child, tis true. She is yours, but while under my roof, I will care for her. And people such as you will call me foolish, Catherine, but a long time ago, I stopped fearing the world. Can you say the same?"

"We shall see who is right in the end, Thomas."

"There is no end, Catherine." He smiled, and added, "There is never an end."

Lady Catherine huffed, thinking him a fool, and then left. Thomas smiled to himself, knowing that nothing had changed with Lady Catherine. For she had always been a woman who always had a tendency to specialize in a conversation that is hard to begin, but always easy to end.

12

A CONVERSATION THAT WAS LONG OVERDUE

Mrs. Bennet just left the sitting room where she had a tete e tete with Cousin Emilia and Lady Catherine de Bourgh. This meeting had been wholly unexpected for her, and partly unwanted, for she did not wish to be even in the same room with Lady Catherine. However, being specially invited by Emilia Darcy, who was the mother of her daughter's fiancé, made her obliged to attend, in hopes of gathering even more connection to the family.

To her surprise, Lady Catherine was perfectly cordial for the entire tete e tete, and even went so far as to ask about what was it like to have raised five daughters. The three ladies spent the whole afternoon actually exchanging stories about their children and the mischief they got up to when they were little. With Emilia being the only one to have sons, her stories were the most varied, yet all three ladies were able to add their own experiences to the discussion quite successfully.

This triumph of an afternoon led to Mrs. Bennet feeling particularly light and breezy, giving her a confidence that she had not felt for some time. This newfound spirit kindled a sense of purpose in her and she decided to put a plan she had into action at the nearest opportunity.

When free to find her husband, she went looking for him in the only place she knew him to be—the library of Canterbury.

When she entered, she looked through the shelves and was not surprised to find him seated at a desk with his feet resting on a footstool and reading a thick novel.

"Mr. Bennet!" she began.

"Oh, does someone want me for something?" he asked, not looking up from his book. "I was hoping that in such times as these, the wife would have to do all the work and we husbands were allowed to be completely inactive."

"No, you are not wanted for anything directly—well, unless my company does count. I simply needed to speak with you."

"Will it be more fascinating than my book? Because I am at a very good chapter, so if you would not mind coming back in a half an hour, then I would be much obliged."

Mrs. Bennet took the book from his hands, threw it on the desk out of his reach, moved his feet from the footstool, sat on the footstool and looked up at him.

"My goodness," he said, perplexed. "You must have really desired my attention."

"Yes," Mrs. Bennet confessed, "I did want it. And now you shall give it to me."

"Very well, what could be so pressing?"

"I wished to speak to you about our situation."

"My dear, I cannot increase your allowance for you are already—"

"I am not speaking of our economical one, but our emotional one. Mr. Bennet, let us be honest, we do not make one another happy."

Mr. Bennet's face froze out of astonishment. Whatever turn he had thought the conversation would take, it had not been this one.

"We almost never agree on anything," Mrs. Bennet continued, "and there is not much of a mutual respect for one another that now I see is required in every marriage. I know that my taking so long to confront this might have it be too late for rectification, but I shall be confident and believe that it is better late than never. My dear Mr. Bennet... I wish for us to find peace with each other. Or do you not see what I speak of?"

"Yes," he whispered, "Yes I do."

"And this is not just a whim of the moment, but one that I have been contemplating for quite some time. We have three daughters wed. Our mission and duty is complete unto them. Yet how about if we attempt to improve ourselves? Let me share your library—we can speak about books. And you, take a concern in matters that concern me. Let us speak with the workers on our estate together or consider taking trips to the continent with one another. For too long, we have been so separate, and I will confess that part of that fault is my own. What say you?"

"I say...goodness, Mrs. Bennet, I know not what to say," he began. "It is so unexpected. Yet I fear, that at a time in our lives now, we are so much who we are, so defined and set in our ways, that it is too late to find our way out of the mazes we have made for ourselves."

"You are determined not to try, then?" Mrs. Bennet asked, unable to hide her pain.

"I did—Mrs. Bennet, are you about to cry?"

"What would you have me do?" she exclaimed, "Have you no idea how hard this was for me? And here I would sacrifice, fight my own nature, and to hear you say that you will not even try to battle yours... well, you have broken my heart, is all. It was badly done, Mr. Bennet. Badly done."

When done, Mrs. Bennet stood up and began to walk out of the library. Just before she reached the door, Mr. Bennet stood up.

"Mrs. Bennet! Please forgive me."

Mrs. Bennet turned around but could not bring herself to look at him.

"You have to understand," he began, "that after so long of us not fitting properly, I have grown used to it. Therefore, I was not prepared for your sudden change of thought. Yet I am allowing myself to be prepared for it now. Mrs. Bennet, are you sincere in your promise for our relationship to improve?"

"Yes," she sighed, "I was. I cannot deny that I will sometimes fail you, and that you will fail me. Yet I am willing to give us our chance. If you will have me."

Mr. Bennet, utterly amazed at this new request of his usually silly wife, walked up to Mrs. Bennet, wrapped his arms around her, and they kissed.

When they released each other, he smiled down at her.

"When is the last time that we did that?"

"Too long." She laughed.

"Yes, it..." he then kissed her again. "I suppose I am willing to give us another try."

"Mr. Bennet, my dear Mr. Bennet, that is wonderful to hear."

They stood in the library, wrapped in each other's arms, and Mrs. Bennet chuckled silently, astonished that they had successfully undergone a conversation that was long overdue.

13

A CONVERSATION THAT I DID NOT
FEAR TO HAVE

Our carriages arrived at Sister Mary Ignatius's convent, and Deborah met us all with eagerness. Our company included all her sisters (though not Helena), Mrs. Bingley, Miss Bingley, Mrs. Hurst, Georgiana, and us Bennet daughters. Therefore, we were a company of fifteen women that Sister Mary Ignatius came to greet, and our number was not lost on her.

"You are like a miniature army!" Deborah Darcy laughed. "It is most amusing."

"You have got to be the worst nun ever, Deborah!" Samantha replied.

"And why is that?"

"You are too happy."

"Oh, shut it, Sam. And learn to say something good for a change."

"Deborah," I said, "it is good to see you again."

"It is nice to see you as well," she said, smirking knowingly.

"And what is that look for?"

"For being right, it is. You see, I told you all that we might be sisters in the end and lo and behold, I was correct, wasn't I?"

"Yes," Jane said, "you were correct in the end. It was only the details that turned out to be quite different."

"I am a nun, not a mastermind. I only have a hand in the large plan of all, and not the details of things. Therefore, I can still claim to know much."

We introduced her to those of us she was not yet acquainted with, and Mary did her best to show her all she had learned from reading *Fordyce's Sermons*.

"It is always very well to do so, Miss Mary," Deborah Darcy said, "and I admire a lady who shall always seek to improve her mind through extensive reading. Yet remember that those great men who write, their words are no more or less great than your own. You have learned morality yet remember to live by your own philosophies as well."

"See, what did I tell you?" Samantha laughed, "Deborah, you are a terrible nun."

"Oh, do not pick on her so," Ester interrupted. "You would think you were sisters who rivalled all the time."

"You forget that we did," Samantha said, and then she turned to us. "When we had just recently come of age, we both liked the same man."

"Oh, not that story again," Ester groaned.

"It's their first time in hearing it," Deborah said, "so it can't hurt."

"Yes," Samantha agreed, "and we went to war over him. Literally, we pulled pranks on each other and everything."

"Well," Jane laughed, "how did it end?"

"Well, we did not kill each other, so that was a good outcome, however we did ruin some clothing because we would pour ink or tomatoes on each other."

"It also did not end because we decided to make peace with one another," Deborah replied. "It ended because the man we liked fell in love with another woman."

"Oh," Kitty began, "well if you think about it, that was the best thing that could have happened. Say he chose one of you, then the other would have gone through torment and have been left to feel inadequate."

"Precisely, therefore our sisterhood was saved because the man made the correct choice."

"And I went on to marry my husband," Samantha said.

"And I was left to fall in love myself, and then ultimately choose the church afterwards."

"Then you were in love before?" Mrs. Hurst asked.

"Of course, I was. Many women who become nuns were in love once. At least once to be honest."

"Truly?"

"Yes, it is a little-known fact, for many seem to think women who become nuns do not like men, however many of us love them terribly."

"Then why did you become nuns?"

"Because we liked our faith more. Or because we had that one great love, and it did not work out to our satisfaction, and we would rather turn to a life in a convent rather than turn to a life of something else."

"How amazing. Yet with you, Mrs. Eastbourne, if I am not mistaken, your husband and you almost have the same name. For one is Samuel and you are Samantha."

"Oh, you noticed! Yes, we both sometimes even go by Sam to each other."

"That sounds like a match made in perfect harmony," Miss Bingley said. "And it is pleasing to see two people who fit together so well. For too many a time a woman has used her arts and allurements to draw in a respectable gentleman and proved not to be deserving of him."

Could I slap her?

It was very clear that she was implying Lydia, at that moment, regarding Henry Darcy. Not only was she indirectly insulting my sister, yet she was also clearly showing her designs on a man who was engaged to another, and she had barely known that man. It was altogether ridiculous.

However, before I could open my mouth, Kitty had smiled and decided to speak up.

"This does occur undoubtedly, yet those women are no more dangerous and guilty than men who do the same thing as well. And yet I believe that they are even less guilty than the women who use criticism of other women to make themselves appear superior. I have learned to be wary of that sort, for that is an art as well, and is a cruel kind. That is what I find to be the worst way to draw someone in."

Miss Bingley began to open her mouth to speak again, but Deborah Darcy beat her to that score.

"So, which one of you has made the acquaintance of the President of our United States yet?"

We all turned to her, startled.

"No, were we supposed to?"

"No, of course not. I just had a great desire to change the subject and startle you all, and that was the first thing that crossed my mind to say."

❦

As we walked along the grounds of the convent, we separated into pairs and began to walk down a narrow path. To my good fortune, I was paired off with Deborah.

"So, how are you truly, Deborah?" I asked her.

"And by that you are implying if I feel remorse over learning that Samuel Lucas loved me after all."

"You still do not care to be direct, do you?"

"No, for it is a waste of time."

"Very well then, yes, that was my fear."

"I am fine, truly Lizzy. I will not deny that a part of me will always think fondly of him, yet I have been quite resigned to my life. Though I do not wish to have seen him one last time. For our ending was so romantic—when you consider it from an objective point of view. We wrote to each other through intermediaries and announced our true affections. That is the stuff of legend, Mrs. Darcy. And it shall follow that our paths were perfect. He shall wed and I shall remain strong in my journey. We are in our perfect places. And yet, I am curious about him. Is he the same as I last saw him? Does he now have a beard, or longer hair? All of these questions and by seeing him once, I shall know. Therefore, it is a wish that I both do and do not want to be fulfilled."

"Well, Deborah, I know not what to tell you."

"No one can tell me anything, for I am in a position that few are ever in."

"Were you telling the truth about how nuns usually fell in love once?"

"Our faith does not turn us into stone. Oh yes, we all had our moment, and if a nun has not, then I feel sorry for her."

"Why?"

"Because she will never know how to feel the effects of being in love. It is a beneficial experience, for it teaches you much about yourself. Therefore, if a nun has never felt affection of that kind before, and learned the lessons one gets from it, then she came to the convent with her life missing many experiences that would have made her stronger."

"Then you are something we need never worry over, Deborah?"

"Oh, worry over me if you like. I find it to be quite flattering if you do."

"Very well. We shall worry about you from time to time."

"Thank you, Mrs. Darcy. That is a great comfort. And speaking of worries, that woman there who is standing with Jane is Charles Bingley's sister?"

"Yes," I sighed, "Caroline Bingley."

"Then I worry for you. Did she come here meaning to wound Lydia, for it appeared that she was attempting to do so?"

"Yes, I believe she was deliberately attempting to do so. And it is sadly her nature. She is a woman who has the impulse to insult those who she feels to be in her way, sadly."

"And how does she view Lydia to be in her way?"

"Miss Bingley decided to single out Henry Darcy, even before she met him, as the perfect choice for her to marry, since my husband did not choose her."

I then proceeded to tell her the history of Caroline Bingley, and she sighed. "Well, I was correct. Just, Lizzy, trust your judgment. There is something about her that needs reformation. Until then, be aware of her. That is all that I shall warn you of."

❧

The next day, in mid-afternoon, I was taking a walk through the gardens of Canterbury, for I was told that most of the gentlemen were off to enjoy a drink at a tavern. So, I was surprised when I heard Henry Darcy's voice through the trees. Yet I halted when I realized that he was not alone. It was a female voice, and it was none other than Caroline Bingley's.

"I confessed to not wishing to attend the tavern because I needed some time in solitude," Henry Darcy said—I can assume he was explaining why he was out alone. "Yet why are you not with the ladies this afternoon?"

"I felt that I needed time alone as well, and I find it quite unhealthy in regards to one's autonomy to always be in the society of others. It seems to me to show an abominable sort of co-dependence and neediness. It shows a person can never be content alone and must always require the company of others to define them."

This was hypocrisy if I ever heard it. Caroline Bingley was the sort to always be seeking the company of others to define her self-importance and stroke her vanity. She was, in all frankness, using her skills to find a common ground between her and Mr. Henry Darcy, perhaps in hopes of making him feel a bond to her. It also showed that Caroline Bingley did not reproach arts and allurements used to entice a man, and only objected to them if those arts were not her own.

"I wonder," Miss Bingley said, "why your future wife does not wish to join you?"

"Oh, she is meeting with my mother now to discuss the decorations for the wedding."

"Oh, I see, but I confess myself to be a very different sort of woman. If wedding plans were to arise, I would see to it that the time I kept to focusing on them was left to a minimum so that I would spend more time on the man I loved. And thus, showing him that I cared little for the ceremony and more for him."

What a disgusting woman!

"However, Mr. Darcy," she continued, "since we both find ourselves in need of a walk just now, might we take this way together?"

"Oh, very well."

Behind a tree, I saw them link arms and walk along the wood. I kept my distance enough that I was not seen, but close enough that I could still hear.

"I must also compliment you on your house and estate, Mr. Darcy, for I daresay I have never seen its equal."

"Thank you, but I have been told that Pemberley is the most ideal looking of seats to hold. Canterbury was actually inspired from the designs of Pemberley."

"Oh, that makes all the sense in the world! For I see the

comparison and it shows the good taste of your family—to aspire to such grandeur in architectural design shows that your concepts are noble and regal ones. Such superiority of mind!"

"I admit that I can take no credit for it. Canterbury was here long before my time and it shall be here, hopefully, long after."

"Yes, I am certain that it shall. May no evil befall it. And yet, seeing it in such hands as yours, I predict that it shall always be fruitful and affluent."

"You flatter me."

"Indeed, I do not. I simply admire your ability to oversee the estate. And now, being so close to obtaining happiness in marriage, your joy must be almost complete."

"Miss Lydia Bennet and I are already married in my eyes, and we have only to wait till we undergo the ceremony for society and God to recognize it."

"You call her Miss Bennet? Why so? Wait then, do you not know? *Miss Bennet* was wed before now to a Mr. George Wickham."

"Oh, I know of it, yet I always simply think to call her Miss Bennet instead, and we speak little of her previous marriage."

"Oh, then I might be more knowledgeable than you on that score, if I might be so bold. Such a *colorful* story it is, and meant for a good read in a novel, I daresay. It is the fruit of passion, I suppose that led to it all. While at Brighton with her friend, the militia was camped there and Lydia took a fancy for an officer in the regiment, named George Wickham—who I'm certain you did not know was no more than the son of the late Mr. Darcy's steward at Pemberley! And somehow they fell into an interesting sort of love where they eloped with each other...only the elopement took quite a while to actually happen."

"Because my fiancée fell for a libertine who lied to her," Henry Darcy finished, "and they lived in London, where she would find out that he was paid and pressured into wedding her? Is that how you were to conclude your narrative, Miss Bingley?"

"Oh, well..." Caroline mumbled, perturbed at his already knowing the story, "I see that I was not more knowledgeable than you."

"Not in this case. Miss Lydia has informed me of her past and the phantom that haunted it before. She has the wonderful notion that honesty between husband and wife are the best qualities to have to lead to a perfect state of matrimony."

"Yes, that is very admirable," Caroline Bingley replied, with no energy or emphasis to her tone. "Very admirable indeed."

"Yes, it is. Would that all people were like her, Miss Bingley, and they understood that any deceptions used to influence others is never a virtue, but a vice of the worst kind. And I must confess that when she and I met, I found her not to my interests at first. Yet it has been many months now that I consider her one of the handsomest and most worthy women of my acquaintance."

Caroline Bingley was hushed at this. That much was clear and was left to all the satisfaction of having forced him to say what gave no one any pain but herself.

I took that as an opportunity to reveal myself. I walked down the lane and met them, to which Caroline declared herself tired and Henry proposed that we walk back to the house. He linked his left arm in mine, with Caroline on his other, we pressed on with him and I talking all the way back while Caroline kept intentionally quiet.

๑๚๑

Later that evening, we ate dinner, and the men told us of the ships they saw make berth along the river. I watched Caroline Bingley all the while. She was subdued most of the meal, but I was still decided as to my next step. Her foul machinations had reached a new height of incivility, and this time, it would not go unchecked. I wouldn't be able to return from what I was planning to do. Yet Caroline had made herself my enemy long ago and now there was nothing else to do but reciprocate the feeling.

Therefore, that evening, when we all retired to bed while the men decided to spend the night in more discussion, I told my Mr. Darcy to stay with them rather than join me. He did not understand my pressing him, at first. But I told him that I would explain later, I followed the ladies up the steps, and was luckily able to catch up to Miss Bingley before she reached her bedroom.

"Miss Bingley?" I said, happy that we had that great hall all alone. She turned, and while she smiled, her eyes were cold, showing her disdain for me.

"Mrs. Darcy, what can I do for you?"

"Actually, you can do very much," I confessed, "And while one should always be civil, I find now that I cannot. Therefore, if what I say is about to distress you, then please understand that I must confront the matter."

"I do not understand what you are about to speak of."

"Yes, you do, for you are not an idiot, just cunning. You know as well as I that I overheard some of what you said to Mr. Henry Darcy while you were in the wood. You know that I must have, for I did come upon you, and above all, you know that I know what you said about my sister."

Caroline Bingley's face grew stern.

"Eavesdropping is a very bad habit, Mrs. Darcy."

"And ruining another woman's happiness because of misplaced jealousy is worse."

"Pardon me?"

"You heard me, Caroline. I am neither blind nor deaf. I am very aware that you despise me because Mr. Darcy chose me over you. For too long, you let your jealousies overwhelm your judgment. Yet I did not care, for it hurt me not at all. But now you have acted with the malicious intent of hurting my younger sister. That is where you have made a grave error. And you shall repent that you did."

"Is that a threat, Mrs. Darcy?" Caroline sneered.

"Yes, it is." I smiled.

Caroline's eyebrows raised in alarm, yet I would not be deterred or moved by a desire for peace—no, I would hold fast to my resolve and continue on.

"Caroline, that was a vile and cruel act that you just committed. How dare you try to sully my sister's name in the hopes of ruining her chances with such a gentleman?"

"How dare you speak to me so?"

"How dare you be so evil and downright insolent?"

"Everyone has the right to know who they are marrying."

"And he already knew, making no one look foolish and improper in the end—except you. Your own venom backfired and now you have poisoned yourself. And that poison that is within you may buy you many friends in the ton—for it is women like you, who for some reason, always have friends—yet it shall never buy you happiness. And do you not see that it will never buy you a husband?"

"Some men still remember what a proper lady is," she snarled. "And you Bennet women only seduce them."

"We seduce them because they find us attractive—which is something you are not and never will be."

Caroline flinched at this.

"Men are not so dim that they do not see the schemes you used to try and bait them—and it is a useless scheme at that which shows how blind you are—and you repel them, Caroline Bingley. They run from you, do they not? And you still do not see the reason as to why, for you are too proud of yourself to see clearly. Yet mark my words, Caroline, I know what you have done. I have informed my husband," I lied, "and Mr. Henry Darcy knows it now as well. What are the chances that he has not told Lydia, and his parents of your conduct, and his siblings? What are the chances that Caroline Bingley has just made herself a most disgusting woman in the eyes of everyone?"

Caroline Bingley's face grew cold, yet I saw the fear in her eyes.

"Yes," I continued, "that thing you care for so much—your reputation. And yet, for all your concerns of it, you seem very quick to make a mockery of yourself."

"It is something you Bennets are good at yourselves."

"Whatever our faults, pureness of heart is something we possess when you cannot even boast of that. Therefore, I shall do you a service."

"What could you do for me?"

"Do not ever descend to such cowardly revenge and hurt my sisters or I in such a paltry way—or any way at all—and I will make sure this misstep in morality of yours will not be made public. You have made many friends because of your schemes, Caroline, and it has blinded you from all the enemies you have made in the process. Do you really want everyone to be your enemy here?"

Caroline swallowed and looked down.

"And please remember, Caroline," I began, "that you cannot hurt me here. And if you were to ever attempt to sully my reputation, there will be many repercussions the likes of which you will never see coming."

Caroline was quiet at first, and then she looked at me coldly. "Is there anything else you need, Mrs. Darcy?"

"No, and—oh, but there is one more thing. During the process of your obligatory reformation, treat your brother's wife better. Miriam deserves your love, and not your condescending tone and scorn."

"Well then," Caroline said, and then she did not finish her speech, for she turned her heels and disappeared into her room.

Though she did not promise me anything, I knew that she would submit to my requests. The fear of being in a room of enemies all throughout her stay in Pennsylvania was too much of an intimidation for her not to feel it most keenly. And I knew the largest fear on her part would be of Cousin Emilia, and also Henry Darcy's sisters. That many women looking down on her with disgust would be too much for her to take, and therefore, at the present, Caroline Bingley was overcome and defeated. For I have often learned that the only thing that could intimidate a woman who was not used to being intimidated was a combination of women who were even more of a biting force than she was.

Caroline Bingley may not have been intimidated by me. Yet she was terrified of the Darcy women.

⚜

After supper and our congregating in the sitting room for conversation, we all retired to bed.

When we had done so, and while in the privacy of our guest room, I told Darcy everything that had transpired between Caroline and me. When I was done, I asked him if I was wise in my actions, or if I had been foolish.

"Oh, you my dear are a force to be reckoned with," he smiled, "And while I can imagine how you may feel disconcerted now, for one always feels so after a heated debate—you were in the right. Caroline Bingley will always be unpardonable, yet she needed to know her limits. And would you mind if I were to speak with her myself?"

"Oh, dear, you do not have to do that, for I wouldn't want you to debase yourself."

"On the contrary, I must do it. Not for the sake of just Lydia and anyone else who might find themselves at the mercy of Caroline's jealousies, but also to save you."

"What do you mean? Oh! Are you referring to the fact that she might slander me in some way, out of revenge?"

"Precisely. I do not want her to return to England thinking she can accuse you of the worst things. Lizzy, I do not put it past her to spread gossip—even the harmful kind that could ruin you."

"Such as?"

"Adultery, for example. She might find it to her benefit to think if she makes you appear unfaithful, then I would have no choice but to forsake you, all for the sake of my pride and appearances."

"She would not be so malicious, do you think?"

"She just tried to ruin Lydia in her fiancé's eyes."

"Yes, but it was based on facts, whether she was right to spread them or not."

"And when facts do not work, believe me, she will bend her mind toward fiction. I have known her longer than you, Lizzy, and she is open to anything if it will help her achieve her goal. I believe she still has some heart but being too much amongst the ton has quite ruined her, almost. And as you have seen, there is only one thing to save Caroline Bingley."

"Confrontation?"

"Yes, and also to show her actions and words will come with a price, and ultimately she will be the one to pay it."

I walked up to Darcy and kissed him.

"Darcy, what would I do without you?"

"Much, but I'm happy you still love me all the same. And not to worry, I shall wait till after the wedding to confront her. It shall be done before we book passage to England, for she can do no damage here."

"You are wonderful."

"Oh...you know I love when you praise me."

"I know you do, and I am happy that my confrontation with her is at an end—yet I am also glad that I followed through with my resolve, for it was a conversation that I did not fear to have. Not in the slightest."

14

TWO BROTHERS

Colonel Fitzwilliam was in the cellar, getting his musket ready, for the men were planning on hunting that day to bag birds for their dinners later that week. While he was preparing his piece, he heard footsteps behind him.

"Darcy, if you are requiring me to move faster, then I am moving at a fast pace, and it is you that is impatient."

"Hello Richard," Lord Fitzwilliam said.

"Oh!" Richard said, turning to his father, "I did not expect you, Father."

"I knew that cornering you would work."

"How so?"

"Oh, do not be coy, Richard. You know precisely why I am come to talk with you."

"You want to join us for our hunt?"

"Richard?"

Richard sighed, put down his musket, and prepared himself for the onslaught.

"Very well then, if we must speak of this, then go on then, Father."

"And we shall. Richard, am I correct in understanding that in all the time that you have been here, you and your brother still have not confronted what occurred between you both?"

"He knows where I am," Richard sneered. "If he wants to see me, then he may see me."

"He is probably waiting for a warm reception. Or for you to make the first move to show him that you will forgive him."

"No," Richard objected, "it shall not be that way. Father. You were not there to see it. Henry, my own brother, rode onto Pemberley and, before Kitty and Elizabeth, challenged me to a duel for anyone passing to see. It is bad enough he intended violence upon my person, but in the presence of two ladies who did not deserve to see that or be put in harm's way by being so close. Therefore, if he wants reconciliation, then he must find me. He must be the first one to make that shift."

"I can understand your anger, Richard."

"With all due respect, Father, no, you do not understand. You do not understand what it is like to have your brother want to commit such violence upon you, over a woman that you gained fairly."

"He was heartbroken."

"He had no right to be."

"I know, and you are right, Richard. I do not know how it felt for you, and I am sorry that it has occurred so. I know that he was in error, and it is hard."

"And so, I repeat," Richard urged, "that if he wishes to reconcile, I will make no start to him, nor will I let you be his voice. He wants forgiveness, then he must seek it out actively."

Richard turned from his father, finished assembling his musket, and left the cellar.

"Family is a damned nuisance," Mr. Darcy said as he and Colonel Fitzwilliam reloaded their muskets and walked through the trees with Henry Darcy, Joseph, Mr. Bingley, Mr. Hurst, and Mr. Bennet.

"Oh, you do not need to tell me," Colonel Fitzwilliam replied. "I know my father meant well, but Fitz, it is not something so easily forgiven."

"I know it is not. What your brother did was reckless and rash—not to mention heinous. You are right to demand that he seek you out and earn your forgiveness. And make sure to hold to your purpose. For the only way for Henry Fitzwilliam to learn his lesson is if he has to choose to undergo his penance rather than being instantly pardoned. Hardness is best in moments like this."

"I hope I may cling to it, Fitz. You know my nature. I cannot stay obstinate for long."

"I know you can't. That was always my talent."

That evening, when they finished their day of shooting, and the servants carried the bags of pheasants to Canterbury, Cousin Thomas and Emilia looked at their catch and approved of it.

"Well, if you are to earn your keep," Thomas said with a laugh, "you are doing a right job of it. And besides, the whole family is dining here once more, so thank you for your success! For we shall be out of meat by morning."

"Which reminds me, Mr. Thomas," Mr. Bingley said, "Where do your children stay since we have taken their rooms?"

"Oh, they are staying in Victoria's home and Joseph's as well, which has many guest rooms. We see Samantha less because she and her husband have to take the ferry ride over the river to visit."

The gentlemen entered the house and went to the billiards room. While there, Colonel Fitzwilliam had learned that his brothers, Henry, and Acton, who had gone into the center of the city earlier to look around, had returned.

The next day, Mr. Bingley and Miriam took a visit to see Miriam's parents. Cousin Thomas told Colonel Fitzwilliam that he learned of his desire to ride a horse, and the Colonel asked him if there was a mare that Kitty could ride with him. Thomas believed they had one and instructed the Colonel to go down to the stables to inspect the horse and see if it would be to Kitty's liking.

He made the journey to the stables, observed that they were nicely kept, and told the stablemen about his purpose in coming. After they showed him a magnificent stallion and he looked on it with approval and a desire to test it, he was then shown the mare, which was a beautiful brown with some white on its nose.

"How does she ride?" he asked the stable boy.

"She has been broken in," the stableman replied. "And if you are choosing her for Mrs. Fitzwilliam, then I promise she will be a good beast to choose."

"What is her name?"

"Andromache."

"Andromache?" Colonel Fitzwilliam smiled. "After Hector's wife from the Trojan War?"

"Yes, that one."

"Well," Colonel Fitzwilliam said, turning to the horse, "you were well named. A loyal and devoted name, may you be that yourself, for you'll carry a devoted woman on you."

"Still talking to the horse before you ride them, brother?"

Colonel Fitzwilliam froze over and then turned to see Henry Fitzwilliam approaching him.

Colonel Fitzwilliam did not move or make any action toward his brother yet let him come at his own speed. When Henry finally stopped a few feet away, Colonel Fitzwilliam turned to the stable boy.

"You may leave us alone at present, and we shall call on you when you are further needed."

"Very good, sir," the stableman said, and then he left the two brothers alone. When only in each other's sole company, the brothers looked on each other, at a loss of what to say at first. At length, Henry decided to begin.

"Father told me that he has spoken with you."

"Oh, so it was you who had sent him? Wonderful Henry! You could not even come yourself, at first."

"Richard, this is not easy."

"Yet it was easy to challenge me to a duel over Kitty."

"I...Richard, I am sorry for that."

"As you should be. And you should say you are sorry to Kitty as well."

"I am not certain I can do that still."

"What?" Colonel Fitzwilliam said, enraged. "You surely cannot feel resentment for her still when she did nothing to lead you on?"

"I know she did not now, I see it, but the heart is strange, Richard. It cannot be commanded so. And logic sometimes is its enemy."

"You cannot use the foolishness of the heart to shield you just now."

"I am not. I am simply explaining."

"And Henry, are you certain that it was love you felt for her, and not obsession? A passing infatuation that was solidified and given more weight when you discovered that she was taken from you?"

"Richard, I wrote to Darcy every two weeks in hopes of seeing her."

"Truly? It was that often?"

"Yes, and I grew to be angry that he was not accepting my invitations. That is why I had arrived at Pemberley without getting permission. I felt that they could not deny me a visit if I was at their doorstep."

"Then, you really did have true designs for Kitty."

"Yes, I did."

Colonel Fitzwilliam looked at Andromache as she stood in her stall, and he wondered how his life could grow to have become so complicated. When he did imagine himself finally falling in love, he did not expect it to be so complex and with such strain attached to it. Marriage to Kitty was always blissful—until his damned family would get involved.

"Then," Richard sighed, "it is quite possible that you still have feelings for my wife?"

Henry did not reply at first, realizing that it would be best to speak up, he carried onward.

"Yes," Henry breathed, "yes, I do."

Poor Colonel Fitzwilliam! And poor Henry Fitzwilliam as well!

Both brothers hung their heads slightly, not knowing what to do in the matter.

"You must understand," Henry continued, "she was the first woman to ever speak nothing but truth to me—while also being kind."

"Yes, I know," Richard said, "that is her way."

"And you know the women we were raised around. Ladies of the ton seem to be made of falseness and deceit."

"Yes, making Kitty an anomaly to us."

"And with Fitz getting Elizabeth," Henry continued, "and she and Kitty being so much alike, you must understand that it had a marked impression upon me. All the happiness that Darcy has found in Elizabeth, it seemed that it would be my turn. And from her standpoint, I thought I could appear as the very same fate her sister had been given, but now offered to her. A rich man who fancied her and could give her a great estate. It therefore hurt my vanity when I turned out not to be the dream she chose."

"She might have, had it not been for me, Henry."

"Precisely," Henry sighed, "And that is why I despised you, Richard, for the thought did cross my mind often that if only she had never met you, she would have considered me. She would have preferred me—if she had been given the time to. You were given the time, Richard. You were given all the time in the world, while I was not."

Colonel Fitzwilliam and Henry looked at each other, each feeling different emotions at the time.

"Do you hate me for confessing this?" Henry asked.

"I cannot find it in me to hate you, Henry. I simply cannot trust you."

"No, no you cannot."

"You must stay away from Kitty."

"I know and I shall. When I say that you cannot trust me, I do not mean that I will do anything to seize her."

"I would kill you if you were to attempt it."

"I know, Richard. All that I am saying is that you cannot trust my feelings for her to end so easily. They will linger within me, Rich, and I know how I am. She is the first woman that I have come to feel for in so long. Being fickle in that way has never been my talent. On the contrary, it was yours."

"You accuse me of being a rattle?"

"Richard, you were a rattle. You once had the power to shift from dalliance to dalliance without need for emotional attachment."

"I never hurt any woman, nor sullied a reputation."

"No, but you enjoyed many a woman's company. And therefore, for you to find your destiny in love before myself, do you not see that it also seemed so unfair for me?"

"No, Henry, I do not see it so. For you are the heir to Matlock, you shall also inherit the title and become an Earl. I live by my wits, while also father still has to send me some currency every few months just so that I can maintain giving Kitty a good living. So, what if I enjoyed some fancy ladies here and there? I was a man who did not have the luxuries that you did. And you are no saint either. All that I am saying, Henry, is that you were given everything—so do not begrudge me for obtaining one thing."

"And as I said, the heart is senseless."

"Then try and always be under the power of your mind and not under the influence of the tenderer organ."

"I shall always wish you well, Richard, and happiness with Kitty. I am just asking for your forgiveness for how I acted, and to pardon me, for I still have not been able to overcome this pain as of yet."

"I will forgive you, Henry. I must. As long as you apologize to Kitty."

"I shall."

"Very good then. Well, Henry, your past mistakes have now been pardoned. Now we are friends again, for we were always brothers."

"Thank you, Richard. Thank you very much."

Henry nodded to Colonel Fitzwilliam and then left the stables.

That night, Kitty and Colonel Fitzwilliam were in their guest room, and they had just ended their acts of intimacy. With his body spent, Colonel Fitzwilliam rested his body on top of Kitty's and then ran his hands down her thighs.

"I love you," she whispered.

"And I love you," he said, kissing her, and then moving his lips along her neck, down her chest, then taking her breasts in his mouth and suckling them tenderly. As he did so, he put his hand in between her thighs and began to stroke her most softly as she covered her mouth to keep her moans quiet. When he had finished, he looked down on her fondly.

"I am the most selfish woman in the world," she confessed.

"Why so?"

"Because I never wish to share you with anyone," she admitted. "I just wish us to be able to push the outside world away and remain in here, making love and then holding one another."

"Tell me that you adore me." He chuckled, nibbling her stomach.

"Richard, that tickles!"

"I know, now tell me that you adore me."

"You know that I do."

"Yes, but I should still like to hear it."

"Then I adore you."

"Good, continue to always do so."

He raised himself up and rolled her over, kissing her along the back of her neck, down her spine and over her bottom, pressing his lips deeper and deeper into her while she sighed out in ecstasy. When he had done, Kitty climbed on top of him and made him roll over as she began to give him a massage.

"That feels nice," he sighed.

"Well, I should not just say that I adore you," Kitty laughed, "but rather, I believe I ought to show it as well."

She moved her hands over his back gently and then ran her hands through his hair.

"Richard," she whispered.

"What is it, dearest?"

"Henry came to me today, and he apologized."

"Oh, good."

"I knew it! He came to me out of your doing."

"Yes, he did."

"Did he apologize to you for attempting to harm you?"

"Yes, he did."

"While I am moved by his desire to seek penance for what he has done, and while I should have felt pity for his distress, for it is my doing, I forgave him because I must have—but not because I wanted to. I still harbor resentment. You had just returned from fighting in the war, you were still recovering, and he could have killed you."

"Yes, he could have."

"This means that his actions, if successful, could have been lethal to you. I cannot forget that. I could have lost you."

"Yes, but do not fear. I am here," he said, wrapping his arms around her, "and you shall never be forsaken."

"You had better hold to that promise," she warned.

"I hold to it, Kitty."

"Very well, yet I do forgive him. I just apparently have resentfulness in me, and I can never forget it. He has lost my good opinion, and I fear I might not have the heart to give it again."

"You sound like Darcy." Colonel Fitzwilliam laughed.

"Do I really?"

"Yes, it is quite comical."

"It shall not happen often. This I swear to."

"Good. For it would be strange if you did so. I would not want to be wed to my cousin's twin."

"Richard, I really am sorry to be the cause of such strife between you both."

"You were worth every moment of it, Kitty. And you need not apologize, for it is not your doing. Besides, we have quite reconciled, and though there is still tension and mistrust between Henry and I, at least there is now peace between us two brothers. Therefore, set your mind at rest, my love. And your heart."

Colonel Fitzwilliam and Kitty kissed once more and then fell asleep in each other's arms.

15

LADY CATHERINE'S SECRET

I t was the eve of the wedding, and Cousin Emilia needed to run a couple of errands before the big day. My parents had decided to spend a day together and eat at the City Tavern for lunch. Kitty, Georgiana, Anne de Bourgh, Miriam, and Lydia had gone on a long walk, and Caroline and Mrs. Hurst were asked to join Samantha, Victoria, Ester and Molly into town and buy some ribbons and new bonnets. Therefore, all that was left to accompany her was me, which I enjoyed greatly.

"I had no idea that your daughters had taken a liking to the Bingley sisters," I began, "so Caroline and Louisa have become a great favorite of theirs?"

"Not particularly," Cousin Emilia replied as we rode in the carriage. "They occupy their time because they know that, while I am on steady enough terms with Louisa, I detest Caroline Bingley."

"Oh!" I replied, never ceasing to be amazed at Emilia's frankness.

"I am not afraid of being open with you, Elizabeth," she explained, "for I know that you know my reasons. My boy, Henry, told me about what Miss Bingley attempted to do. And I know that you are aware of it as well."

"I have spoken to Miss Bingley on the matter," I said, "Hopefully she shall hold her tongue in the future."

"Yes, but I am afraid that I might not. I have grown fond of Lydia, or at least the Lydia that she is now. She has confessed to me that she was different in the past, however as a woman who has raised seven daughters, that is the nature of us women. We are not born angels, but it becomes a skill, which if we are fortunate, we acquire over time. My daughters had their bad moments, and one even did attempt to elope."

"Did she?"

"Yes, I shall not tell you which one, but the only reason she was not successful was because we caught her in time and were able to prevent the deed. Such mistakes ought to be forgiven, for they are not done out of malicious intent or are crimes of coldness, but are errors committed out of love and belief that one is braving the contempt of the world for doing what one judges to be right. It is the way of being young. And being young is something we all need to be forgiven for at some point. And you know me, Elizabeth. Despite his flaws and faults, I love Henry very much, and for him to finally have a woman who appears perfect for him, well, it shall make me feel complete. Therefore, for Miss Bingley to attempt to ruin that—unfortunately for her, she has forced herself onto my bad side."

"It is refreshing to even know you have a bad side, Emilia." I chuckled.

"Every mother does, believe me. And the efforts of Caroline Bingley would all come to nothing, because with my will set, nothing is going to stop this wedding from occurring."

"Thank you for that, Emilia." I sighed. "It is nice that your heart is so large."

"Some of us are tied to a profession and for me...being a mother will always be my occupation. Yet with Caroline, it is also a matter of foolishness. Why would she be so blind as to do anything to make me at odds with her, when she knows that I have no fears of even facing more formidable foes than her, such as Lady Catherine de Bourgh?"

That last sentence sparked my interest very much, and I had hoped that Emilia's desire for openness would not close any time soon.

"Emilia, that is something that always amazes me. Your complete lack of fear of Lady Catherine."

"We are not in England, and so her power has no hold on me, for she has none."

"Oh, so that is all?"

"Partly. I also know her main secret."

"She has a main secret?"

"Everyone has a main secret, and I am just the lucky sort to know hers."

"Then if you are in each other's confidence, I shall not inquire about it."

"I never said she and I were in each other's confidence. And perhaps this is something that you should know."

"Is it proper for me to know it?"

"It might explain things better for you, and it is best that you tell your husband as well, for I believe this might also affect him. Yet you must promise to keep the secret within yourselves, because Thomas has promised not to let it spread. I know your husband is good at being clandestine, yet you must promise to be so as well."

"I promise I will not utter it to anyone else but my husband, and him being of such loyalty and devotion, he will not spread your words."

"No," she said, looking at me carefully, "He will not."

"I promise," I said, "I will not either. And you tear at my curiosity by holding me in suspense."

"Oh, very well. I do not fear Lady Catherine because I know what fuels her."

"What is that?"

"She is a woman who always wishes to win, because she remembers how at one time, she never won."

"Pardon?"

"Lady Catherine is a woman who has suffered the knowledge that she was not the chosen one. She was not the sister who the late Mr. Darcy married. And by the late Mr. Darcy, I mean your late father-in-law."

The surprise at such a statement was overwhelming, to say the least.

"Emilia, are you saying that Lady Catherine once had an affection for my husband's father?"

"Yes. You see, Lady Catherine was the older sister of Sarah Fitzwilliam, but it was Catherine who had fallen in love with the late Mr. Darcy when they were young. However, he fell in love with Sarah instead, and they married. Lady Catherine spent her whole life probably saddened and bitter over that, wondering why she was not the sister who was chosen. That is why she feels that she has to control all under her, and why she attempts to dictate all marriages, because that is her way of attempting to finally be the person who won in the end. It is insecurity that fuels Lady Catherine, and she mistakes it for strength."

"I can scarce believe it." I sighed. "Lady Catherine was in love with Mr. Darcy's father. Yet she got married herself."

"Do you honestly believe that was a love match?" Emilia smirked. "Oh, bless me! Not at all, for heaven forbid Lady Catherine ever do the right thing in regards to the art of matrimony. She married him for his title and estate, and he wed her for her money. I'm quite certain that they were miserable together, for they never looked happy at all. That is another reason that she cannot abide to see others happy without her, I suppose. For she feels it wrong for anyone to be higher than herself, or not having her share in the conversation."

"This changes many thoughts of mine," I said.

"Yes, it should. Well, now that you know some of the history behind the woman, what do you think now?"

⁂

"I think I was greatly used!" My Mr. Darcy said, angrily pacing back and forth. We were in our guest room, and as soon as I had returned to Canterbury from my outing with Emilia, I found Darcy and told him of what Emilia confessed to me.

"Darcy, lower your voice," I cautioned. "And what do you mean when you say that you were greatly used?"

"I mean that the guilt of the parents was pushed upon me. Elizabeth, when I proposed to my cousin, Anne, it was because all my life I had been pressured to do so. My mother and father had always hinted at it, though they also acknowledged they would forgive me if I did not wed Anne. However, their preference toward Anne was always keenly stressed, and it led to me wishing to satisfy them and make them proud of me."

"Yes, you have told me so."

"Well, now it all makes sense. They probably felt guilty of marrying when Catherine did not want it and loved my father, so they put their alternate path on me. And my Aunt Catherine probably also stressed this upon them, and they gave in. My marrying Anne would make up for their marriage. That was at the expense of Catherine's heartbreak. I was sacrificed."

"Oh, Darcy," I said, standing up and embracing him, "You must not think of it that way."

"Yet what way am I to see it?"

"You do not even know for sure if that was the reason behind their intent upon you marrying Anne."

"Do you think I am wrong?"

I thought on the matter, and while there was a slight chance that he was in error, his argument was sound and made sense. It did seem the logical outcome of three people who were trying to use their children to end any grievances they had within themselves.

"A part of me knows you probably are not wrong. Yet you shall never know, for that is a matter between your mother and father. Let them be at peace, Darcy. For you loved them, did you not?"

"Yes, very much."

"And they loved you, didn't they?"

"Aye, they did."

"Then be content with that. And let this knowledge not impede all the good memories you have of them. Yes, this is a moment where you have all the right to remember the past in the way that it always gives you pleasure."

"Perhaps you are right."

I kissed his hand.

"And I am happy that you did not marry Anne."

"Dear lord, I almost did! Yes, that was a foolish thing that I should never have been asked to fulfill. Anne has proven to be a good woman, when allowed to come into her own, yet she still was not for me—nor was I for her."

"Very much so. Though, if what you say is true, Fitzwilliam, I am sorry that you were put in that position."

"Yes, and there is nothing for it now."

"Except to promise me something."

"Yes?"

"When it comes to William and Caiden, when they grow, we just do our best to steer them towards the right sort of women *because* they are the right sort of women. And not because of blind favoritism."

"I hope that we can commit to that, however the only thing I can promise is that we shall never force onto them an arranged marriage."

"Yes, for it is not as if we are royalty and confined to such foolish traditions. Yet in regards to your Aunt Catherine, why do you think that minor detail is such a dirty secret of hers?"

"I can only think of one thing. It makes her look vulnerable. And vulnerability implies weakness. And above all else, she might have considered it to look as if she failed. And whoever wants anyone to see their failure?"

"'Tis true."

"Though now I do not think I shall ever look at her the same."

"Yes, I can see that. You now are left to wonder what your own aunt was thinking when she looked at your father often. Altogether it is a rum business."

"Yes, an egregious one."

"However, Emilia and Thomas know even more about her. I wonder how it feels for Lady Catherine, to be in a place where she has no power."

"It must feel hard, but it is a lesson that she should have undergone long ago."

"She must be craving getting back to England. Yet until then, she is confined here—and though ignorance is bliss, I must confess myself happier in knowing Lady Catherine's secret."

"Yes, for it now solves another riddle to her complex nature. And it answers many questions."

❧ 16 ❧

A DAY THAT SEEMED WOULD
NEVER COME

The next day came, and it was the day of the wedding. As Cousin Emilia had promised, she made sure that nothing would keep it from happening.

All of us Bennet girls were rushing around Lydia's guest room, helping her get prepared. She was wearing a lovely gown that had a long train and embroidery around the bodice.

"Though I do not mean to complain," our mother cried as she helped Lydia put on the veil, "There is a shocking lack of satin."

"But Mama, I have never been partial toward satin," Lydia replied. "And please tell me that you like my gown?"

"Oh dear, of course I do," my mother said. "It is just so hard. You are getting married."

"I have gotten married before, mama," Lydia laughed.

"Yes, but I was not there to see it, and now I get that chance. Now, I can correct the first experience. Oh, to think! That we should get a second chance to fix the previous incident. Fortune has been very good to us."

"Yes, better than I could have ever expected." Lydia sighed, and then she looked into the mirror at herself. "I cannot believe it.

Henry Darcy is truly the perfect man for me. Could any of you have foreseen it ending in this happy way?"

"I can and I did," Jane replied.

"Oh, that I could make him happy! I hope that I can."

"I'm certain that you shall," Mary said.

"Did you just compliment me?" Lydia laughed.

"I do it...sometimes."

"Well, it is slim pickings with you, but I shall enjoy your good opinion when you bestow it."

Lydia looked at herself in the mirror one last time.

"Finally, I shall be free of the name Wickham for good. I shall be free, and I shall be made anew."

"Yes." I sighed, "I hope that you shall."

⊗⊛⊗

Together, all of us were assembled in Christ Church, which was located on 2nd Street. Our families from England were on one side, the American Darcys along with their friends and neighbors were on the other, and Henry Darcy was standing at the altar while the reverend stood behind him.

Then the church pianist began to play and at the end of the aisle Lydia appeared on the arm of our father, with a bouquet of flowers in her hands. As she walked down the aisle, she smiled at Henry Darcy, who, if I was not mistaken, breathed out a sigh of relief when he saw her.

As Lydia walked, and our father beside her, I wondered how much this scene was altered from her wedding to Wickham. Surely there could have been no one present for that ceremony, and the posting of it in the papers was not even written properly. It did not mention her family, or where she was from, but was short and stating just that she was married to Mr. George Wickham and that was it. And I was certain that the difference was not lost on her, for this ceremony was quite the opposite. Here she had followed all the correct measures and behavior of a woman in love and now she was experiencing the benefits of it.

"She looks beautiful," Kitty said beside me. "She was never ugly by any means, but now, with such genuine happiness, she glows."

"Yes," I acknowledged. "Yes, she does."

The wedding commenced in the traditional manner, and all occurred without mishap. However, out of curiosity, I looked down the aisle of pews and I beheld Miss Bingley standing next to Mrs. Hurst, who stood near Mr. Hurst, Mr. Bingley, and Miriam. As I looked at Caroline, her eyes were like ice, and then she looked down at her hands and began to pick at her nails. Mr. Darcy had indeed spoken with her. I wanted to laugh, for she displayed all the signs of a woman who was thwarted once more. In that, she and Lady Catherine were not so different.

The reverend had Henry Darcy place his ring on Lydia's finger and then, after they exchanged vows, he pronounced them husband and wife, allowing Henry to kiss his bride.

Henry Darcy leaned down.

Lydia got onto the tips of her toes.

And then they kissed.

Upon doing so, Lydia Bennet Wickham could now be released enough to shed her last name and simply be known as Mrs. Henry Darcy.

Such an amazing thing it was!

When they finished kissing, they turned to the crowd, and we all clapped.

Except for our mother, who cried.

And except for Emilia, who fainted.

Yet it was all well, for Cousin Thomas caught her before she hit the floor.

After the ceremony, we went back to Canterbury, where the

wedding luncheon was served, and the guests came to offer their congratulations for the happy couple.

As I looked on Henry Darcy as he stood next to Lydia, I saw that they truly were bonded in a powerful way. For she turned to him often and he would return her gaze and there was pure affection in their eyes. They loved looking at one another and being close. It was the look Kitty and Richard had for each other, and I could only wonder if they also mirrored Fitzwilliam and me.

During the feast, I was able to draw near Lydia, who was getting another piece of cake for Henry Darcy, and she laughed when she saw me.

"It turns out the man I married has quite the sweet tooth."

"Fitzwilliam has quite the sour one," I acknowledged.

"Then it is nice that there is something different about them," Lydia said, "for they are too similar in other ways."

"Yes, they are. Lydia, I must offer you my congratulations. And while we did not get the chance to see your first marriage, we were happy to have been there for the second one."

"I am happy you were not present for the first one." She groaned. "It was a sad sight, and I smiled through the whole ordeal to save my face and because I was a fool who loved Wickham. Now I am no fool and he is gone, therefore there is nothing for me to do but see the situation for what it was."

"Do not vex yourself with memories of it just now."

"You are right, I should not, but as I wed today, I could not help but compare the contrast between both of my weddings. And it is that contrast that makes me trust that I have done right this time. Of course, upon entering the married state, no one can ever be sure of the domestic felicity they will encounter, but I still feel that life with Henry will be a pleasant one—and a passionate one. It may not appear so, but he is very deep and filled with desire between that firm exterior. He is like the rocks beneath the earth, he is."

"You speak like a woman in love."

"I am. And I wish to always be. Yet I still marvel at all of this. How could I, whose life looked bleak for so long, be granted a second chance? Oh Lizzy, it is too much. And when you stop and reflect on it, our lives have taken so fortunate a turn without us having to resort to the one thing I feared most."

"And what was that?"

"None of us had to marry Mr. Collins!"

I guffawed over the truth of that statement.

"Now please enjoy my wedding day, Lizzy," Lydia sighed, "for I feared this to be a day that seemed would never come."

Lydia then left me to find her husband and give him his last piece of cake. I turned and saw Mr. Darcy looking at me, and even amongst the crowd, he cut a defined figure. He was where my road led me. May Lydia's fate bear the same bliss.

FIRST NIGHT

When night fell, Lydia and Henry Darcy retired to their bedroom, where they both were still in their wedding attire.

"I believe," Lydia said, "that this is the first time that I have ever been in your room."

"It's been mine since I was a child. Another perk of being the eldest is being the one to get the best room."

"I would not know of that," Lydia said and smiled. "I got my sister's hand-me-downs often."

They both then began to stare at each other with affection mingled with wantonness.

"It is all so strange," Lydia sighed.

"What is?"

"I have been married before, and therefore I should not be so frightened, but I am. Being here now, I do not wish to disappoint you."

"You shall not, Lydia," he said sincerely. "Now will you not come to me?"

"Oh dear, I am so sorry," Lydia gasped, then she rushed to him and jumped into his arms. "I cannot believe my luck."

"Nor I with you."

Henry Darcy lifted her up and carried her to the bed, then laid her on it and began to tear her gown off her.

"In a hurry, are you?" Lydia laughed.

"Woman, you haven't the slightest idea!"

Little by little, he removed all of her garments and she was left in naught but her stockings and the garters that held them up. As she lay on the bed, Henry looked down at her.

"Do I please you?" Lydia asked shyly.

"Lydia, you are beautiful. Most beautiful."

Henry undid her garters and pulled off her stockings slowly. Then he settled down on top of her and kissed her passionately, undoing her hair as they embraced.

"You forget yourself!" Lydia laughed in between kisses.

"How so?"

"You still have your clothes on!"

Lydia rolled on top of him and then began to unbutton his vest and undo his cravat. Henry looked up at her and marveled at her tenacity as she worked her way down and removed his boots, stockings, and his shirt. Finally, she began to unfasten his trousers and when done, she hurled them across the room and stared down at him.

"Henry, you are stunning."

"Never have I been called so," he whispered. "Am I truly?"

"Yes, you are." With a burst of passion, she laid on top of him and they kissed. Then Henry leaned up, running his hands down her body while she remained atop him. He moved his lips down, kissing the inner parts of her neck.

Lydia moaned from the touch of his tongue along the edge of her collar bone, then his lips moved downward. He kissed her breasts, and Lydia gasped, running her hands down his back. Deeper and deeper his kisses became as she felt her nipples in between his teeth and tongue. Then he rolled her over and continued kissing her stomach, her thighs and he moved in between them, lowered his head down and began to tease her in her most intimate of places.

Lydia placed her hands on Henry's head, holding it down as her back arched and she had to use all her self-control to keep from crying out in exhilaration. Never had she felt such intense satisfaction before, and it was all new to her.

Deeper and deeper his mouth entered her, and she felt herself rocked in between wave after wave of emotional ecstasy until her chills ran down her spine and her body had reached its peak. When feeling her body release, Henry raised himself up and looked down at her.

"Are you ready?"

"Henry, of course I am!"

"My spirited wife," he purred.

He lowered his body down, spread her thighs, and entered her. At first, he moved slowly and deliberately, hoping to enjoy every inch, and then his movements became more rapid. Deeper and with more speed, he rocked within her, amazed at the feeling of completion that he found from being in her embrace.

"Lydia, you feel wonderful."

"I am happy to please you. And please do not cease yet."

"Oh, I am not so easily spent."

Moment after moment went by and still, he found his desire not fully quenched as they were in each other's embrace and moving around and in one another. Then finally his body began to quake, his desire reaching satisfaction as his seed finally escaped him and he had reached his peak. His body stiffened and released as he fell on top of her, overcome by exhaustion and happiness.

"I want to believe that you are now fully satisfied," Lydia whispered in his ear after their third time of making love.

"Have I overwhelmed you and made you tired?" Henry chuckled, lying on top of her while she wrapped him in her arms.

"Actually, I could go a couple more times."

"Lydia, are you serious?"

"Very serious. From the little I have learned, when we women are not afraid to admit that we have immense carnal desires, we can last longer than men."

"Oh, that cannot be true!"

"Oh, but it can. Very easily. Believe me, Henry, a year into our marriage, I will still have the strength in me to want to engage in this activity every night, and you might not always be up to the task."

"Every night?"

"Oh, you haven't the slightest idea of a woman's true appetite. Since we are now husband and wife, I do not fear speaking indelicately. For we are in the middle of the carnal act, therefore I think you will still find me lovable if I am honest."

"Yes, now continue."

"Women are not fine and delicate creatures, but as human as any man—only our desires actually run deep always. You think yourself dissolute and carnivorous when it comes to pleasures of the flesh, however we are more so."

"Are you? I doubt that the minds of women are nearly as naughty as that of men."

"It is, sadly. Sometimes even more so."

"Then this means that you really did enjoy our night together?"

"More than you could ever know."

"I doubt that."

"No, you do not understand—it is terrible of me to say so during our wedding night, but the mind is what it is. I cannot help but compare it to my first wedding night to Wickham, Henry."

"You are thinking of him now?"

"I cannot help it. My mind is comparing the two and being with you in this way has made it all the plainer to me just how insufficient he was as not only a husband but also as a lover."

Henry raised himself up and looked at her.

"What do you mean? Explain further."

"Wickham was as selfish a man as there ever was, Henry, and he only cared for his own desires being satisfied, not mine. During our moments of intimacy, he only sought pleasure for himself. He did not care to please me or thought about what I would like him to do to me. Yet, on our first night, you did things—activities—that overwhelmed me and were precisely what I always desired. You thought of me in ways that he never did. You were generous, Henry. You...you were perfect."

"Then..." Henry smiled. "I was the best?"

"Oh," Lydia exclaimed, "shut it!"

"No, I must gloat now." Henry sighed, very self-assured. "You just confessed that I was the superior companion. Admit it again—and stroke my vanity."

"Very well, but don't you dare get too proud of yourself."

"Lydia, I already am too proud of myself."

"Oh, very well then! Yes, you are the superior one, Henry, in every way."

"Ah!" Henry sighed, laying down and reveling in his glory. "I, therefore, am the ultimate."

"You are this close to me smacking you, Henry."

"No, I am not, woman. You clearly adore me, and it is plain now more than ever."

"Yes, I adore you, but Henry, take care, my love. For when has adoration for a man ever stopped a woman from smacking him?"

"Oh, your vehement point really astounds me, my dear."

"Then let it intimidate you into wishing to do something that I beckon you to."

"You shall use your power over me to bend me to your will?"

"Oh yes, Henry Darcy. Very much so."

"Very well. Proceed."

"You must promise me now that we shall never go more than a week without engaging in this most intimate activity."

"You are requesting that we make love in this manner often?"

"Yes, it is the one thing that I will ask you to promise me to do."

"You desire me that much?"

"Yes, but do not take advantage of me for it."

Henry chuckled and looked down at her. "Was I that amazing?"

"Henry, cease these self-congratulations," she said in exasperation, nibbling his ear.

"No," he said with such proud firmness that all Lydia could do was laugh.

"Very well, then, keep to your resolve. Yet you must promise me, Henry. In truth, I want you often, and I do not enjoy the concept of going too long without your touch."

Henry saw the seriousness of affection in her eye and then he smiled.

"Then I will have you promise me something in return."

"What is your request, sir?"

"That we never go less than enjoying one another in this manner twice a week?"

"You will promise me that?" Lydia grinned. "You must give yourself to me at least twice per week."

"Yes, I shall. It is a great task and sacrifice for me," he said in jest, "yet I am certain that I can fit you into my very busy schedule."

Lydia pinched his buttocks and Henry growled.

"I love when you make jokes." Lydia said. "As long as you know that it is a joke you are making."

"I am not so certain. Between running an estate, attending matters of business, eating, and sleeping, how could I possibly have time to satisfy the carnal desires of my beautiful wife? Honestly, woman, who do you think you are, to demand me to engage in acts of intimacy so often as to spare time for you at least twice a week? How can you be so selfish?"

Lydia rolled on top of him and kissed him passionately.

"You may joke, Henry, and I may let you, but when you climb into this bedroom, never forget that I will always have my way with you."

"I am your plaything?"

"A husband can become so on occasion."

"So can a wife."

"Henry?"

"Yes?"

"I do adore you."

"I know," he replied, growing serious, running his hands down her breasts, and pinching her nipples, "And I adore you as well."

"And I do not want to share you with the world. I want you all to myself."

"Take heart, Lydia. You shall never lose me, and I will always come back to you."

"I know. You, Henry Darcy, are a good man. And never forget that you are."

"And you, Lydia Darcy, will always be in the depths of my soul. You are the foundation to which I feel all strength and security. Never turn from me Lydia, never stop loving me, for you are the reason I feel safe now, when I did not before."

"Never will you be forsaken, Henry. Never from me."

Lydia and Henry kissed once more, then fell asleep in each other's arms, content in knowing their first night as husband and wife had come and gone in the most perfect of means.

❧ 18 ❦

TO NEW YORK

The next day Cousin Thomas announced at breakfast that he and Emilia had another present for the newlyweds, and it was in the form of their honeymoon.

"We know that you cannot stay away from Canterbury for long, Henry," Thomas said, "for you shall have to return here in due time to run the estate with me and begin overseeing the business transactions we have with the East India Company."

"The East India Company?" Mary asked. "You are involved in trade?"

"Yes. How do you think we are to live so comfortably? We may come from old money, yet my father and his father before him always thought it wise to have a constant source of income coming from elsewhere."

"Very wise."

"Oh yes. Well, Henry, you know you are indispensable to us, yet I know a month is enough for your time at leisure. Therefore, your mother and I have paid for a full month trip of yours in the very best part of New York City."

"New York City!" Lydia cried. "Really?"

"Yes, we thought you would like that."

"This is wonderful!"

"You will love New York City," Kitty said.

"You have been there before?"

"Oh yes," Kitty replied, "The last time we were in America, we went to New York City for a time."

"You did?" Colonel Fitzwilliam asked.

"Yes, oh Richard, you would love it there."

"And this year," Emilia said, "there has been talk of them improving the city."

"I wish I could have gone with you, Kitty," the Colonel said.

"Oh, you need not worry, my dear," Kitty cooed. "We shall go there one day."

"Well, is there any way that you wish to attend now?" Lydia said, "that is, if you would be fine with it, Henry?"

"Oh, you wish them to journey with us?" Henry Darcy began.

"I did not mean to ask them without consulting you at first," Lydia assured him. "Forgive me, I was too eager."

"Well, I am not opposed to it," Henry Darcy replied. "And since Kitty has gone, she can show us much, while the Colonel can have his chance at seeing New York. Well, what do you both have to say to this scheme?"

"If you would be satisfied with our joining," Colonel Fitzwilliam said, "then I would very much love to attend, and as is our duty as your companions, we promise to give you newlyweds your time alone when needed."

"Oh, we get to go back to New York City!"

"Yes, you do," Georgiana said, demure. We all looked at her and her thoughts were obvious.

"Call it my many years of being a sister," Molly said. "Yet I think you wish to also go, Miss Darcy."

"Oh, no I would not dare invite myself."

"Georgiana," Lydia asked, "do you wish to go as well?"

"I…"

"Oh, say yes!" Helena said. Over the last few days, she had gathered enough comfort with us to actually wish to sit with us during meals. "It is so clear—clear that—that you want to."

"Would you all mind?" Georgiana asked.

"No, we shall not," Lydia said.

"However, Georgiana, we had hopes that you would return with us," my husband uttered, "so that we could return as a family."

"You can if you all just grow wise and all decide to go," Ester said.

We all looked at each other.

"Oh well, it is very obvious, is it not? You are a family who loves to do things together very often. So why do you not all go to New York, and therefore Lydia and Henry Darcy will have more time with you before you all depart for England? Remember, this is the last chance that you will have before you will see each other for years at least. Especially since this bloody war is on the rise."

"While I miss my sons," I admitted, "I admit to agreeing. We shall not see Lydia or Henry Darcy for years after this."

Mr. Darcy looked at them all, seeing that even if he did not wish to go, too many imploring faces were looking up at him.

"Cousin Thomas and Emilia?" My husband asked.

"Yes, Fitz?"

"Your children are relentless in their ability to influence my cousins and sisters, aren't they?"

Everyone laughed as he admitted defeat.

※

"So, you are all going away to be happy in New York!" Mrs. Bennet cried.

"Mrs. Bennet, do not think I shall let you go as well," Mr. Bennet chided. "You are coming back with me to Longbourn."

"And why so, Mr. Bennet?" she groaned.

"Because this is a time for our children to be unified, and we have done all that we can for them. Also, I was very much hoping we would return and enjoy the quiet of a home together, enjoying each other's company."

Cousin Emilia cooed at that, and mother blushed.

"Mr. Bennet, you have quite changed."

"Perhaps I have, and I make no apologies for it. Yet as for my other children, they are welcome to join this jovial lot if they also wish to go to New York."

"Well," Jane said, "while I do not wish to be away from my students for long, I admit to being far from objecting to another holiday in New York. And this way, I shall be a good companion to Georgiana in case any of the couples wish to travel through the city with only themselves as company."

"Oh, that would be splendid," Georgiana said.

"And what say you, Mary?" Mrs. Bennet said to her middle daughter. "Shouldn't you like to go to New York City?"

"That is where I must draw the line, Mrs. Bennet," Lady Catherine said. "For we must return to Rosings Park, and I have been long wishing to request that I employ your daughter, Miss Mary Bennet, to be my daughter's companion back on my estate."

"What?" Mrs. Bennet gasped.

We all turned to Lady Catherine, then to Anne, and lastly to Mary.

"This idea is quite sudden, is it not?" Georgiana asked, surprised.

"Oh," Mary said, "I had no idea that you valued my company so."

"Yes," Lady Catherine said, "Anne has spoken well of you and your company while we have been here in Philadelphia. And I have come upon the brilliant scheme that it is time Anne has a companion that is her age."

"It was not her idea at all," Samantha whispered beside me. "Our mother suggested the idea because she saw that Anne fared better when she was in our company, and therefore saw that Anne was simply lonely."

I looked at my mother, who looked suspicious. If it were any other wealthy woman who owned a great estate, then she would have thought Mary's good fortune to be a blessing. However, since it was Lady Catherine, and she despised the woman, she probably did not trust this scheme—or at the very least, did not like the idea of Mary being in her company.

"Oh," Mary said, "thank you very much."

"If you are quite content with the idea," Anne said, "then I think you would make a great companion for me."

To say that I was surprised would be an understatement, at the very least. I suppose that I was so involved in observing Caroline Bingley, while also making sure that Henry and Lydia were truly in love, that I did not notice a bond that must have been growing between Anne and Mary.

"Well," Mary said, "Miss de Bourgh, you are a very good sort of woman, and I would be thrilled to be your companion."

"Well then," Mr. Bennet said, his eyes sparkling, "this is a very interesting turn of events. Upon my honor, I do so love being surprised! And recently, nothing much has challenged me."

"My dear," our mother said, "I give you full permission to joke about this later, yet right now we still are in the midst of the moment, so it is too soon."

"Oh, forgive me. I see that I have anticipated everyone."

"Well," our mother smiled, still wary of Lady Catherine, "I thank you for employing my daughter to be Miss de Bourgh's companion, and the honor is most keenly felt. However, as her mother, I must be promised that she shall be treated well."

"Of course, she shall be," Lady Catherine boomed. "I am not the sort of woman to disrespect someone in my employ."

"Thank you, Mother," Mary said, "and thank you Lady Catherine." Then Mary turned to the rest of us, "While I would have loved to have gone with you all to New York, I think it nothing but the best of luck to be Miss de Bourgh's companion."

After breakfast, we all were packing our items. Mr. Darcy and Mr. Bingley were writing letters to their connections in England to tell them of our prolonged holiday, and I took that time to see Mary in her room. When I entered, she was half-way done in her packing when she looked up at me.

"Hello, Mary," I began.

"I know why you have come."

"Directly to the point, I see?"

"Yes, for I know that we are all busy today. Now come in and tell me your woes."

"My woes? That is awfully dramatic for you, Mary."

"I know that you are surprised with me being asked to be Anne's companion."

"I confess that I was surprised."

"It is not your fault," Mary assured me. "Very often when she and I took trips into the city together, you were not present and therefore did not see how I tended to her."

"Tended to her? Then Mary, are you implying that you were attempting to become her companion?"

"Oh, no! That was a happy accident. It was more so like we both developed a connection. I suppose that it is due to us being so similar."

"Are you?"

"We both know what it is like to live in the shadow of greater people and therefore not know how to have your own voice."

I faltered at her confession.

"Mary, I had not known that you felt that way."

"I know you did not, and that is not your fault, either. But being in a house with Jane, you, and then Mr. Collins choosing Kitty over me, well, let us just say that I have, for some time, suffered from feeling insecure often. And with Anne, she has felt it as well. Therefore, when together it felt very easy to gain a sense of camaraderie, and a friendship developed."

"Yet will it not be hard for you to be at Rosings when Mr. Collins is at Hunsford and you will see him in the presence of his wife?"

"It might, but Mr. Collins' decisions do not affect me the way they once did. I shall take my post as a companion, and I shall like it, I believe. And this way, I can also be of use."

"What do you mean?"

"Elizabeth, as vain as it is to confess this, my pride needs something to stir it. I need to feel of importance in this world. So far, I do not feel as if I belong anywhere. Maybe this will be the first step."

"Oh, Mary..."

"And this way I shall be able to help you all."

"How so?"

"I know how Lady Catherine used to perceive our family. And how much she deemed us inferior. However, if I do my duty well, if I become a valuable asset to Rosings, only think of how her opinion of our family will change? She shall open up to you more and even invite you all to Rosings Park. I shall help the family make peace. We shall resolve much."

"That is a noble ambition, Mary," I said, "yet I do not want you to do this out of desire to be doing a duty."

"Let me do so, knowing it is a duty. Elizabeth, do not worry about me—you are kind to do so—yet still do not fear. With my duty, hopefully, I shall have my goodness now. And that is a comforting thought."

"Then if you wish to undertake this, Mary, I am happy for you. And I thank you for thinking of us."

"You are very welcome. I do believe that I am beginning to understand what family ought to be like at its best."

"That is very good then."

"Yes, yes, it is."

The next day, Lord and Lady Fitzwilliam disembarked with their sons Acton and Henry Fitzwilliam, who wished to also return to England. Mrs. and Mr. Hurst also left—and yet Caroline Bingley wished to remain for reasons that we did not understand. Later on, I would come to find out that she could not leave. For upon returning to England, Mr. and Mrs. Hurst were invited to a holiday in Brighton with another family in the ton and they were not even stopping at London first. The invitation had not been extended to Caroline, and therefore Caroline had no choice but to remain in our company.

Our parents left with Mary, Lady Catherine de Bourgh and Anne as well.

That left the company of Colonel Fitzwilliam, Kitty, Jane, Georgiana, Lydia, Henry Darcy, Mr. Bingley, Miriam, Miss Bingley, my husband, and myself. We were able to remain at Canterbury until all travelling arrangements were finalized.

As we sat down to tea after the rest of our family departed, I turned to my husband and gave him a look.

"What is that face for, my love?"

"From the funny realization that I have come to, which is that our family is so co-dependent that none of us have ever had a honeymoon where we did not take our family with us."

Mr. Darcy reflected on my words and then he chuckled.

"You are correct. For our honeymoon, we brought Kitty, Georgiana, Bingley, and Jane. Then Colonel Fitzwilliam and Kitty brought Georgiana and Lydia. And for Lydia and Henry, we now have a miniature army."

"Yes, yes we do."

"What is wrong with us?"

"Darcy, I haven't the slightest idea. Yet in regards to ever being normal, I believe our family never shall be."

"Perhaps not so, or maybe it is because everyone in my family has labored so long under the weight of propriety that we are now broken. And so, we do not even put up a fight and allow much to run amuck. When Colonel Fitzwilliam and Kitty had locked themselves away in Aginfield, to be honest with you Elizabeth, I barely even felt angry about it for more than one day."

"Nor I. And while they acted so rashly and were reckless to a fault, I suppose you could argue that decorum pushed them too far, and their internal need to rebel had therefore taken too much into effect. I am not justifying them, yet only explaining. And with my family—well, propriety had often been thrown to the wayside and forgotten."

"Yes, but reflecting on all past actions, there is barely one outcome that I regret. We brought Bingley to America on our honeymoon, and he met his future wife. We brought Kitty to Pemberley and now she and the Colonel are also wed. When they went on their honeymoon, they brought Lydia, and now she is wed to Henry Darcy."

"And now we are joining them for their honeymoon in New York. What a character study our family would make."

"And what does the past, in our case, do if not foreshadow things to come, or at least it seems so."

"What do you...oh, you mean our journeying up North."

"Precisely. If our family continues to follow this train of action, then what will this next journey bring us?"

"Hopefully, nothing but gaiety and still waters."

"You know what it is to be with me, my dear. Still waters run deep."

"Yes, they do. Yet I believe we are entitled to a moment of peace."

"Many are entitled to it. And those who are most entitled never receive it."

"Very well. Let's look forward. To New York, Mr. Darcy!"

"Aye, Mrs. Darcy, back to New York."

19

THE MOST BEAUTIFUL, IDEAL, OVERPOPULATED, CRIME INFESTED, MISERABLE AND OVERALL PERFECT CITY

O ur journey to New York City felt surprisingly short, and I was glad of it. When we arrived, we found ourselves of the fortunate sort. We did not have to rent rooms in an inn or a hotel, but Cousin Thomas had rented out a beautiful villa on the outskirts of the city. He had been friends with the owner, a Mr. George Adams, but Adams had journeyed to Italy on business (and also pleasure) and took his family with him. This made his home available to be rented out and Cousin Thomas had forwarded him the payments before his departure. This made us able to spend our holiday with the lovely villa—which was quite large and was called Arruin. It sounded like a name that came from a romantic medieval novel, classic literature of some epic kind, yet none of the servants knew of the title's true origins.

When we had arrived, the house was already prepared, and the servants welcomed us. The head housekeeper of the household was a woman named Mrs. Barbara Hale.

"Welcome to Arruin," she began, "And Mr. Adams has left you all a present of wine and spirits to commemorate the newlyweds."

"That would be us," Henry Darcy said with Lydia beside him. "And thank you for this warm reception."

"Very good, and this is the rest of your family?"

"Yes, it is." Henry then introduced us all to Mrs. Hale, who ushered us inside, had the footmen take our luggage, and she already had tea and cakes prepared for us.

"I have also had hot water drawn if any of you wish to take a bath," Mrs. Hale continued, "And your rooms have been fully prepared if you wish to retire. For you must all be tired from your journey."

"Thank you very much," Lydia began, "yet if you do not mind, we would love an introduction to the city, and then the next day be given the tour of the house as opposed to now."

"Is this your first time in New York City?" Mrs. Hale asked.

"For some of us, yes," Mr. Darcy said, "yet for some of us, this would be another visit to the wonderful city."

"Your coming is at both a wonderful time and a hard time."

"Are you referring to the imminent war?"

"Yes, I am. And I must warn you not to ever go out without some servant guard of some kind, for New York will always be the beating heart of action and passion when it comes to revolution of some kind."

"Oh, is it?"

"Yes, New York City was the center of the rebellion during the Revolutionary War. And some New Yorkers are still alive from that time and remember it. And some, even especially, were alive or born when the British seized this city in 1776 and used it as a military base till 1783. After the revolution, many of them ceased to be angry over the ordeal and looked on British tourists as exotic novelties that were refreshing to meet. Yet now, due to political upheaval, some wounds are being re-opened. Yet you need not worry over any verbal abuse or physical attacks from the populace —especially in the social sphere you shall move in. The middle and upper class circles do not shed blame on innocent tourists, and at most will only wish to debate with you on your stance of naval impressment."

"I can assure you that we are against the impressment," I urged.

"Very good. Acknowledge that and the New York Elite shall love you, and then hold you as an emblem for all good English society. Also, there are some British officials stationed here in the city who are still doing their best to negotiate terms and form an alliance between both of our countries."

"There is hope for peace?" Kitty asked.

"No, there is not," Colonel Fitzwilliam answered before Mrs. Hale did. "Before we left England, I heard from certain individuals who were acquainted with Parliament officials, that it was all falling to calamity."

"You are correct, sir," Mrs. Hale replied. "The British and American government officials know that it is hopeless. If you ask me. They are simply holding out in hopes that a miracle will happen."

"If only it would."

"Miracles, unfortunately, are not in season this time of the year, no matter the holidays."

"However, I make your arrival seem decidedly bleak," Mrs. Hale said. "Forgive me, you shall love New York City. It is only that I wish of you to be aware."

"Yet," Henry Darcy offered, "would it not be beneficial—or at least prudent, for me to say only that we come from Philadelphia where we are recently married? Many of the Philadelphian upper-class still hold a bit of a proper accent and sound British there, therefore they shall think our family simply holds the accent but are still Americans."

"Oh, that would be a marvelous idea," Mrs. Hale said. "I know that it does not seem honest, but when one thinks on it, it is not so much a lie, is it? You, sir, are clearly American, and if the rest of you would not mind, it would be best if you all simply claim to visit us from the Canterbury estate in Philadelphia. In that way, you do not lie at all."

"That is fine with me," Colonel Fitzwilliam replied. "For while I have always wanted to see the city, it was our decision alone that has led to us coming during a time of political strife. And we are the family of the Philadelphian Darcys, which is a bond that should secure us very well." Then he turned to the rest of us. "Are you in accordance with this scheme as well?"

"I am for it," Kitty added. "I love being from our country, but I do not wish for our time here to be dampened by national tension."

"And we are not forsaking anything," Mr. Darcy concurred, "we are just simply saying what is true, and that is that we have come up from Philadelphia to join our newly wedded family who live there. Yes, I shall be content with that."

The rest of us agreed, and I thanked Mrs. Hale, because she could very well not have told us any of this, out of a desire to be pleasant. But she found the necessity of news to be of more grave importance. She was clearly that of a woman who understood that which was vital to say would always be valuable to our stay there.

Like all the rest, she felt saddened that we had to come to New York during a time of conflict. Yet I did not regret it, for we had come once, and this would be our last chance to come again for years.

Mrs. Hale showed us our rooms and our individual servants were already preparing our dinner clothes for us to change into our evening apparel. As Fitzwilliam and I finished helping each other dress—for husbands and wives shared rooms in this villa, we discussed what Mrs. Hale told us.

"I am not by any means discouraged," Darcy said, "For I still did wish to come to New York."

"I am simply happy that Mrs. Hale is not of the frivolous sort who did not think to advise us. She is a good housekeeper, clearly."

"Yes, she is."

Such conversations as the one we had with the housekeeper are not often written of, because when telling one's story, such details are usually meant to be overlooked. Yet I always felt that those discussions people do not speak of are sometimes the ones that many need to remember most. And while some would have me not speak of war and strife altogether, all I can say in return is that while living through a period where it is the best of times and equally the worst of times, these were the topics we spoke of most —for it was our lives—and the times that we lived in.

"I do so wonder what she is thinking of us, though," Mr. Darcy continued.

"She does not seem to be judgmental, but only frank for the sake of saying what is important."

"No, I am referring to our state of coming. You observed her reaction to seeing all of us, I am sure."

"I did."

"Precisely. She was amazed at seeing so large a party for a couple of newlyweds. She must think we are an oddity to travel with each other so."

"I thought we discussed this in full already," I said. "We are an oddity."

"Yes, we are. Still, I wonder."

"Something else surprises me."

"Such as?"

"Henry and Lydia."

"What do you refer to in regards to them?"

"I understand why Lydia was interested in the idea of us all joining her. Yet I am surprised that Henry enjoyed the idea as well."

"Perhaps he is finally learning to like us very much. Even Jane."

"Yes, perhaps so."

We finished dressing and went down to dinner, where we met the rest. While we all sat down and the first course was served, we began to tell all who were new to the city of our adventures there before.

"You shall love it," Georgiana concluded when she had finished telling us her view of New York. "For it is the most beautiful, ideal, overpopulated, crime infested, miserable and overall perfect city that I have ever seen. Oh wait, it is the second one. London shall always be the first."

20

WHERE IS GEORGIANA?

The next day, we rode our carriages into the city and began to walk through the center of it, enjoying everything all around us.

Henry Darcy, who had been to New York a plethora of times, began to point out historical sights and give us information about them.

"It was in Brooklyn and Harlem Heights that George Washington's Continental Army of the patriots tried to hold the city in 1776," Henry began to explain, "but it was soon lost to the Redcoats."

"Why did our armies choose to hold their base here?" Kitty asked.

"New York was strategically important to both sides, and the British were smart. They knew that it would be best to seize the city as soon as the war began." Henry then smirked at us. "My mother even has a story about how during the British Occupation of New York, there was a British soldier who was quite taken with her."

"Really?" Lydia smiled. "She never told me that one."

"From what I remember, my mother was quite the beauty in her youth, and my father says that it was most vexing that he had to push through so many men just to get to her. For you have seen it, she has an infectious way about her. And during that time, she had been staying with some of her family here in New York. Then the British seized the city and one soldier, a Colonel named John Forster."

"Colonel Forster!" Jane blurted out. "John Forster?"

"Do you know him?"

"Well," I gasped, "it might be a popular name, but we know a Colonel John Forster in Hampshire. He has married a young woman, however, but he is well into his sixties now."

"The age does match," Henry replied. "Yes, it could very well be the same person. She said that he was a very charismatic man who loved women, especially when they laughed."

"Dear lord, that is him to the very life!" Lydia said. "That is Colonel Forster, and he has not changed a bit."

"Upon my honor," Mr. Bingley said, "is it not extraordinary how small the world is? For us to have met and lived in the same neighborhood of one of your mother's past beaus."

"Yes, I shall write to her of that, for now I am most amazed if it would be the same person. If you do see this Colonel Forster again, then remember to ask him if he knew an Emilia Hemmings. For that was my mother's maiden name."

"Emilia Hemmings? Indeed, we shall, for this is a wonderful mystery."

"And yet," Jane offered, "if it was indeed the two of them that courted at one time, how did it end? Was it the war that had separated them?"

"Oh no, and it was not a love made out of pressure. My mother said that Colonel Forster was the perfect gentleman always, and that he did not fancy having to hold the city in a siege, but was ordered to, as were the rest who served alongside him. My mother enjoyed him, but she unfortunately did not fall in love with him. As a result, she ultimately refused him."

"Oh dear!" Miriam said, "He must have been hurt very much."

"And greatly offended," Caroline Bingley added, "for her to refuse him when he was a solid Englishman with a bright future, that seemed outrageous."

"By no means, Caroline," Miriam replied, "for if she had not followed her heart, then she never would have found Mr. Thomas Darcy, and therefore, it can only be concluded that love was the right course of action for her to take."

"Most discerning, Mrs. Bingley," Henry said.

"Thank you, Mr. Darcy."

"Oh, dear, that will not do, for there are two Mr. Darcys here again."

"Yes, there are," my husband said. "And unfortunately, there are also two Fitzwilliams. My first name and Richard's last."

"Oh, dear lord," I groaned, "What a tangled web of names you all have."

"Yes, therefore we must all choose which name to go by."

"Agreed. Would it suffice if you simply go by Henry? Richard goes by Richard only, and I go by Darcy?"

"That shall do."

"Agreed."

"Oh," Caroline Bingley said, a brilliant smile on her face, "to be on first names with you all only increases the feelings of intimacy and being on the inside of a circle of comrades. I must confess to finding this all quite agreeable."

"More agreeable than my mother-in-law choosing love over security, I see?" Lydia smirked.

"Oh, do not find my words to be offensive," Caroline cooed. "It is only to show the concept of gratitude." Caroline then looked at Darcy and Henry. "To show a man that one respects his title, name, breeding and adore him as well, enough to acknowledge that it is right to accept him for his virtues, for waiting for an even more happy ending sometimes is fatal."

"But it proved not so for Mrs. Emilia Darcy," I added, "therefore you are correct in some cases, yet I daresay that my sister is happy that she did not, for Henry never would have been born."

"And that," Caroline smiled, "is the main source behind why Mrs. Emilia Darcy, I admit, was correct in her desires to wait."

'Caroline Bingley,' I asked myself. *'What are you up to? What are you hiding?'*

We continued to walk through the streets, and we saw some impressive buildings, but Mr. Bingley and Henry got into the discussion on textiles.

"It is a pity that trade shall become hard," Mr. Bingley said as we walked. "For I hear that New York does much textile trade to Manchester and other English industrial cities."

"It does."

"Our Uncle Gardiner has done much trade between New York and England," I offered.

"Oh yes," Kitty added, "when we worked at our uncle's factory in Cheapside, he told us that New York ports were most vital to the Southern planters here in America, for they would send their crops of cotton to the East River Docks, where it was shipped to the mills of Manchester or other places in England. Then he, along with other textile manufacturers, would ship their finished goods back to New York."

"Precisely, Mrs. Fitzwilliam!" Mr. Bingley said. "I do that at my factory as well, and you are most attentive for remembering the method."

"But..." Henry began, "you worked in a factory?"

"Well yes," Kitty faltered, "Elizabeth and I did it while we would visit our Uncle Gardiner in London."

"Oh, forgive me," Henry assured her. "I did not mean to sound as if I cast your actions in a negative light. On the contrary, I am just surprised and intrigued. Gentlewomen never wish to excel at such work. Or even make an effort, along with believing that work is not respectable, when in essentials, it is quite the contrary."

"We sometimes believed otherwise."

"That is most extraordinary." Henry smiled. "And I confess that you Bennet daughters are continually surprising me." He then looked at Lydia fondly. "I really must learn to stop underestimating you."

"Well," Richard said, "while you do so, Henry, I merely must reply with frustration. Kitty, you never told me that you worked in a factory! And you too, Mrs. Darcy, do you both keep things from me?"

"Oh, we are sorry, Richard," Kitty said. "This all occurred before I met you. Even before Elizabeth and Darcy married."

"Indeed, yes," I concurred. "We did it to occupy our time, and also to find a sense of..."

"Self-importance," Richard finished, "and to define yourself."

"Well, to be honest, yes."

Richard grinned and pressed Kitty's hand affectionately.

"You both must tell me about your experiences there. Kitty. I want you to always tell me things from your past. I want to know everything."

"Everything?" Kitty asked. "Are you sure? For parts of my history are quite dull."

"History can often be dull, yet as with such extracts as the one you have just given me, I am learning that there is still much about my wife that I do not know."

"I am surprised that I never thought to tell you of it before. It was while we worked there that Elizabeth and Darcy re-met after he left Hampshire."

"What?"

"Oh yes," Darcy said, happy to know how to contribute to the tale. "I was accompanying Mr. Bingley."

"I had some business in the factories," Mr. Bingley explained. "And I wished to establish a connection to their Uncle Gardiner."

"Yes, and there we were, innocently entering, and we came upon these two beauties. I did my best to remain indifferent, but that was when I began to fall in love with my wife."

Miriam looked moved by the story, and Caroline Bingley looked cold—bitter.

"Then, Darcy," Lydia said, "you were already hopelessly lost. For we Bennet women always shall have this tendency to be caught in the boldest of actions and then look for the beauty of it."

"Yes, you all do believe in doing things differently."

"I feel too traditional now," Miriam said.

"Tradition is not an evil by any means," Jane said. "It is just simply something that we Bennet women are allergic to."

Everyone laughed as we walked on.

Soon we arrived at a most pleasant flower shop.

"A woman cannot help but be a woman." Caroline Bingley sighed. "And would anyone mind if we were to step in and take a look at their assortment? I highly doubt that it shall be anything superior to the shops in London, yet one must still be curious."

"Flowers in one country can be as lovely as flowers in another," Jane replied, "therefore, I am delighted to step within. And do you not recall, Elizabeth? We often went into our garden and cut flowers or dried them out in our greenhouse."

"I recall it very well." I laughed. "Our mother was against us planting and growing them ourselves, however."

"I know," Lydia said, "it would have been most fun to have

done so, I think. It would have given me an occupation of some kind."

We all stepped into the shop to take a look around the Hothouse, and the flower assortments were lovely. However, I still could not help but wonder at Caroline, for to go into a Hothouse and look at flowers implies that you would want to purchase some. Yet I never recalled her to be of the sort to care about them—unless she wanted someone to buy her them.

"They are quite lovely, are they not?" Caroline began looking at Henry and Richard.

"Yes, they are," Henry said.

"The beauties of nature," Caroline said. "For what are men compared to rocks and mountains! Or flowers at their most beautiful sight. I do think I shall purchase some for Arruin. It may not be our home, but I believe that only through flowers does a woman truly know how to make a house her home. Even if the home be temporary."

We walked around the Flower Shop some more and then, after a quarter of an hour, I noticed that we were missing one in number.

"Fitzwilliam?" I asked him.

"Yes dear?"

"Where is Georgiana?"

21

A PAIR OF FINE EYES

As Georgiana had walked through the Flower Shop, she had begun to sneeze. Realizing that she must have been sensitive to one of the flowers in the flowerbeds, she felt that she only needed air, but did not want the others to leave the store simply because of her growing allergy. Her nearest companion had been Caroline at the time, and she asked her to tell the others that she was stepping out of the shop temporarily to recover. Caroline had asked her if she wanted her company, but Georgiana assured her that she wanted to be alone, and that she need not worry on her account. For she was simply stepping out onto a public street where nothing would happen.

Caroline allowed this, not caring one way or the other, and Georgiana was content with that. There had been a time when Caroline smothered her with false flattery and compliments that were so obsequious that Georgiana was often overpowered by it, and it made her most uncomfortable. However, now that her brother was married to Elizabeth, all compliments ceased, and Caroline was indifferent to her.

Georgiana quickly left the shop and emerged into the open air.

As her allergy reduced and she began to feel immediately healthier and more like herself, she heard a voice preaching from a distance. She looked down the road and then she saw a large group of people crowded around a man who stood on a crate. From the distance, she could not fully hear all his words correctly, and she could not make out his face, however she found herself curious about him.

Feeling that there was no harm in walking down the straight street where she was in the sight of many, Georgiana began to walk slowly to the street preacher.

As she grew closer, she noticed the man who stood on the crate was actually quite short and was also a little meek in build. Yet his height was barely noticeable, for he seemed to have a great energy about him, and it allowed him to look larger than what he was. The man's face was ageless, which showed that he could be in his twenties, or in his forties even. But it was hard to tell. His clothes were a little old and dingy, his skin was peach, and a little red around the cheeks. His hair was a little long, falling down to his ears, was a dark brown, but his eyes looked brighter. However, she could not see their color fully from where she stood, so she moved closer. As she did so, his words became clearer, allowing her to listen.

"...And while the city is repaired, re-modeled and re-worked on," he began, "What more of the rights of all who still are being oppressed?" The crowd cheered. "Our government officials speak of change, but here we still are, drenched in the same injustices that plagued the previous generations! Yes, we cry out about the injustice of impressment, but why had it taken so long for the government to even notice that this oppression was even going on? How many of our women's husbands, children's fathers, or sons did not come home, and the government did nothing?" The crowd cheered once more. "And why? Because for so long, it did not matter to them...it did not matter because these sailors were simply poor. And we poor still do not matter to them!" The crowd began to raise their fists and shout various cries of anger at this. "Only when it became a national hindrance, only when our strength was finally impaired, did we begin to do something. How late we were to do so? Very late. And that same willingness to turn a blind eye and let an oppression commence is something that we do on our own shores. Here we let tyranny reign. Here we let slavery still commence! As of now, we do nothing but allow it here! How dare we let the plantation owners still ship their cotton here so that we can manufacture it and continue to 'once again' turn a blind eye! Here we stand, still a society that has not given women the right to vote. Do you have it?" The women in the crowd shouted "No," at this.

Georgiana found her heart lifted at the mention of women's right to vote, for never had there been mention of it before—or at least never in the circles that she moved in. Could it really occur? Could women be given the right to vote on political matters and officials? It seemed like such an abstract idea, but one that she felt could open up new thoughts for her. She focused on the rest that the man had said.

"No, women still cannot be offered any representation of any kind," he continued. "They are not allowed, but for what reason? What denies a woman the right for legislation, and to suffer disenfranchisement? What makes a person of darker skin unable to be free? We who have lived under the declaration that has stated 'All men are created equal'. Why does not that include women and are not slaves humanity as well? I shall tell you why. It is because—"

The man's eyes fell on Georgiana, and he stopped suddenly. Feeling his eyes rest upon her, Georgiana grew tense and found that she could not move a muscle, nor could she turn her gaze away from his face.

Blue. His eyes were a striking blue.

The seconds that they looked upon each other, it felt like an eternity to Georgiana. His eyes were full of life, energy, and passion —a passion that was the likes of which she had never seen before.

Then he blinked and turned to the crowd, continuing to speak to them.

"It is because we are allowing this oppression by again turning a blind eye. It is because we need to look at the words of freedom that our forefathers had written and see that all men created equal really means all 'people' created equal!"

There were mostly cheers in the crowd, but some left, not caring what he spoke of. For either they did not support the idea of women voting or slavery being abolished. Yet the rest of the crowd remained while he finished.

"And until we do this, until all are given freedom, equality, and the rights to their pursuit of happiness, we are not all that we can be! This is a dream long stored in our minds, our thoughts, and most importantly, in our souls!"

With his last word, he rested his eyes on Georgiana and his gaze lingered on her even longer than before.

The crowd cheered one last time, but through their sounds, Georgiana heard her name being called.

She turned and down the street, she saw her brother looking for her.

Feeling as if she had fallen out of a dream, she tore her attention away from the speaker and then began to rush down the street, back to the Flower Shop. As she walked, she saw a reflection along the glass of a shop window. Behind her appeared to be a person following her.

It was him!

The speaker who she had listened to.

Slowly but surely, he was following her and at first Georgiana grew nervous, yet it was not fear. At first, she was determined to not look back at him, yet her curiosity grew too great.

Still walking onward, she turned her head slightly and no more than five feet behind her, he was still following her. Their eyes locked once more, and he smiled at her.

She sighed out in apprehension. Yet her heart raced, and she was nervous. A part of her wished to turn and speak to him, however another part was frightened. He did not appear to be dangerous, but he was still a stranger, and she was wise enough not to consider speaking with him. And yet, she wanted to.

She tore her eyes off him once more and continued to walk forward. His reflection, however, would not leave her be, for every store she walked past, his image was there.

Eventually she reached Darcy, who turned to her, shocked.

"Georgiana! Where have you been?"

"Oh, I went for a walk down the road, just to get more air."

"You could not find it just by standing where we could all see you? And who is that?"

Georgiana turned and no more than seven feet from them the man had stopped and looked on them coldly. Georgiana could tell he was disturbed at the idea that she was not available, for it would appear to him that she was married.

"I have not made his acquaintance," Georgiana replied. "He was giving a speech down the road, and I merely listened to it."

From out of the door rushed the rest of the company, including Elizabeth.

"Georgiana," she said, "we were quite despaired of not knowing where you were."

"I..." Georgiana began, and then she saw the man out of the corner of her eye. Looking dismayed, the man turned to leave, and something grabbed hold of Georgiana's instincts. She did not want him to believe that she was married, nor did she wish for him to be forlorn. A part of her knew it would be wiser to let him believe so, and safer, yet she could not explain it—but she was curious about him.

"I am fine, brother!" she said, loud enough for the man to hear, and certainly, out of the corner of her eye, she saw him stop and turn partly, eyeing her intensely. "Truly, I am well now. A brief walk was all that I needed."

"Well still!" Darcy reprimanded, "you must never be out of our company again, for what if something had befallen you?"

"I thank you for your concern, brother, and I am sorry to have caused you all worry."

"Why do you continue to call me brother?" Darcy asked. "What do you mean by it?" Then Darcy looked over Georgiana's shoulder and still saw the man. Realizing what must be happening, he ordered them all to continue walking onward and took Georgiana in one arm, then linked his other with Elizabeth's, and the party walked down the road.

Georgiana every now and again turned back, and she still saw the man standing there, watching her as they left. They had no way of communicating, of seeing one another and learning who the other was. Therefore, as they turned the corner and the man disappeared from her sight, she felt a sudden loss, for she would never perhaps see him once more, or his pair of fine eyes.

22

GEORGIANA

As we turned the corner, I noticed Georgiana's eyes linger for too long on the man who appeared to be staring at her. When we turned onto the next street and she could no longer see him, she looked down at her hands and was blushing.

Darcy, ever the observer, also noticed.

"Georgiana?" he began.

"I promise that I did not speak to him at all," Georgiana countered, "I merely was walking down the road and he was giving a speech about equal representation, as well as support for the abolition."

"He was an abolitionist then?"

"I suppose so, yet he spoke of other things as well. I was simply intrigued."

Darcy looked at her suspiciously, not liking the interest she had taken in this man. From what I had seen, he was not ugly nor handsome. He was very short and did not have much about him that was remarkable, yet there was a certain manner about him that did linger in a person's mind. He appeared to be of the sort who was kind, but also passionate—and I noticed that simply by seeing him once.

However, he spoke and Georgiana clearly was affected by it, and he might have even possessed wisdom about him. I could not tell. Yet he seemed to be of the sort who looked younger than what he was. His face appeared boyish, but I could see a few wrinkles on his brow and around his eyes. The man could not have been less than in his mid-thirties. Although it was not something that affected my perception on him, for Georgiana was now in her mid-twenties and such an age difference could only help rather than hinder her.

A man in his thirties was one who normally overcame his youthful tendencies and had begun to learn from his mistakes. Yet what was an impairment was his attire. The man was dirty, ragged, and clearly of a meager income. This did not make him lesser than anyone, but it frightened one into believing he might be a fortune hunter or was the sort to prey on the wealthy maiden to enjoy her for company. As such, he could only wish to risk her virtue and be done with it.

Darcy, however, was not as docile on the subject as I, and spoke his words plainly and sharp.

"Strangers cannot be trusted, Georgiana," he stated firmly. "They bring harm with them."

"Yes, I know...it is just...if I run from every stranger, how shall I ever increase my circle and get a better acquaintance with the ways of the world?"

"We have many in our own circles who you are acquainted with."

"Yet that is precisely the matter. They are all in my circles. Why can we not speak to those of the lower classes?"

"They can be dangerous."

"Our class can be dangerous as well, we have learned."

"Georgiana!" he snapped. "I do not wish to discuss this matter at present. Therefore, only understand and do as I instruct."

Georgiana quieted immediately, and I felt embarrassed for her.

"That advice, Mr. Darcy, is very sound and valid," Caroline Bingley said. "For every brother should wish to protect his sister from corrupt influences."

Mr. Darcy did not respond, yet Caroline Bingley had grown accustomed to his silences, and still took it as affirmation of him agreeing with her. We walked on and most of us felt regret for Georgiana being so publicly set down by Darcy. I looked up at him, wondering if I should speak with him when we returned to Arruin. Yet was it my place to do so? This was his sister. All that he said was from a place of protection and caution. Also, what did he say that was not true to an extent? Yes, those in the ton could be very dangerous, yet the danger that they displayed was known to us. And as my father always said, 'The evil you know is better than the evil you do not'. Strangers were often dangerous, mentally and physically. Yet here, within our circles, Georgiana was safe. And protected. It was difficult indeed, and distressing, for I did not know what to think.

We walked on and Mr. Bingley and Colonel Fitzwilliam changed the topic of discussion to news about the theatre.

༺✦༻

That night, we all sat down to dinner, and there was a lull in the conversation. Georgiana had been a little dejected since we had returned. While I worried that she had remained silent for the whole supper, as soon as no one was speaking, she decided to offer a topic.

"Have any of you ever wondered why women are not given the right to vote for anything?"

Darcy, Richard, Bingley, and Henry looked at her, startled by the abrupt query.

"Oh," Bingley began, "well, I have not thought about it."

"It is not something one ever considers," Henry replied.

"And why not?" Georgiana asked. "Why should it never be considered? It seems to be a very interesting subject."

"We shall discuss it later if you like," Darcy began.

"Why later? We are not speaking of any other topic at present, therefore why can we not talk of such subjects?"

"It is supper," Caroline said, "and is the honeymoon of your sister-in-law, Georgiana. Such serious talk you want over our meal?"

"I do not mind it," Lydia said, "for it is an interesting subject, and one that does incite curiosity."

"And what is serious should not mean it should not be spoken over a meal," I said. "Conversations should not simply be restricted to light banter."

"Thank you," Georgiana said, "I just merely wish to inquire what everyone's views on it are?"

I looked around, and the men all looked at one another with apprehension. It was clearly a subject that they had never been forced to confront.

"Well," I began, "while it is a new movement, I confess to enjoying the idea of being allowed the right to vote."

"As would I," Kitty added, and then she turned to Richard. "What of you, my love? What are your thoughts?"

"My thoughts mean little," Richard said, "for there is no activity now, no movement to begin to rectify women's rights on that score, that I cannot think on something that has no likelihood at present of ever coming into existence."

"Precisely," Henry agreed. "There are no actions to be done at present to change the way of living, therefore one cannot be ready to give a just opinion."

Lydia looked at Henry with alarm and Kitty gazed upon Richard in the same way. I turned to Darcy, who was silent, and I could not believe all three of them.

"But Henry..." Lydia began.

"I believed," Kitty said, "that simply because there is no action to change an injustice, it does not signify that one should not speak of it. For only by speaking of it can a movement to alter it begin."

"That was what I was wondering," Miriam nodded.

Charles looked to Miriam, and nodded to her, smiling gently. He knew it unwise to join the argument, but he also did not want to show her that he was unsympathetic to our condition. Unfortunately, I cannot say the same for the rest of our husbands. They did not wish to agree nor disagree with us.

"And this is why I am resolved to carry my point through," Caroline said. "For this is always the result of such serious debate. It leads to one part of the table being against the other."

"A disagreement does not nor should not mean that there is a conflict, Miss Bingley," I said. "It only means that one's opinions are different. Peace can still reign over those who are resolved to think differently and wish to speak of different matters. Mr. Bingley and Darcy disagree with each other often, do you not?"

"Precisely," Mr. Bingley laughed. "It seems that Darcy and my whole friendship actually relies on us never agreeing about anything."

"'Tis true, how does our close bond remain so?" Darcy replied, "For we are even at odds at movement speeds."

"Yes, I love to do much quickly as a hare, and you love to do it at the speed of a tortoise."

"Did you just relate one another to a tortoise and a hare?" Miriam smiled.

"Yes, I believe we did. And who do you think shall win the race?" he asked the table. "Well, if we ever were to race, that is."

"A hare naturally would win," Lydia said. "Unless there is a chance that I missed something vital here."

"No." Charles said, chuckling. "There is no hidden meaning, unless I missed something as well."

"I do not know, Charles." I offered, "a hare may be fast, but a tortoise is still determined. And from what I recall, hares can get easily distracted. What if you were to be running this race, and you had come upon a fellow hare, and you took a fancy to her? You would not finish the race, because you would have stopped simply to woo her."

"You forgot, Mrs. Darcy, I did find her!" He smiled and turned to Miriam, and together we all laughed.

The conversation turned lighter, and we all spoke of small and quaint things that we enjoyed about our outing.

☙❧

The next morning came, and I was walking along to find Jane. I passed a room where I heard voices. The room had been the library and within it, I heard Darcy speaking with Georgiana.

"You thought I would forget that you promised to speak with me when we left the flower shop?" Georgiana began.

"No, I simply did not think that you would want to further our discussion."

"Of course, I did. I wished to speak of it at the moment before you became so angry with me and curt in public."

"I did not mean to be sharp on you, Georgiana, but you were not seeing that we should not have spoken of it at the time."

"Well, we have a moment now."

"Georgiana, I am not a fool. That man followed you."

"I can assure you that I had not spoken to him."

"And I can assure you that he wished you did."

"How could you see that?"

"I am a man and so is he. And we all can read each other quite easily. Georgiana, he wished to pursue you."

"Well, then, I was still in public."

"Georgiana, are you implying that you would have spoken to

him if he had accosted you? Even when you have not been introduced?"

"We are not in high society where it would have mattered."

"A change in location should not deter you from following decorum."

"What harm would have come to me if I had let him speak to me?"

"He is a stranger."

"I know he was. And yes, I know that strangers can be dangerous."

"Then you know my fears. And the last time that I took my eyes off you, you..."

"I what?"

"It is nothing."

"It is something clearly. What were you beginning to say?"

"It is nothing."

"It is not nothing. You always tell the absolute truth, Fitz, so do not lose your courage. Even if you plan to hurt me."

"I never intend to hurt you."

"Yet sometimes you do. Therefore, what is stopping you now?"

"The last time that I took my eyes from you," he finished, "You had almost eloped with Wickham!"

"And..." Georgiana faltered, "you think me capable of making the same mistake again? You think me that foolish?"

"No, it is just...Georgiana, you are too trusting. People of your sort can be easy to manipulate. Also, you were about to let a stranger approach you on the street. You were about to breach propriety again."

"Therefore, what you are saying to me is that you do not trust me? Or my judgment."

"I love you, Georgiana, you know that, but sometimes...no I do not always trust your judgment."

There was a deafening silence between them, and my heart went out to Georgiana, for that must have been painful to hear.

"You think you are perfect, Fitz?" Georgiana snapped. "You had many faults of your own when you were courting Elizabeth."

"I know, and that is why I do not trust men that I do not know. Because we can be capable of anything. I was once."

"But I wonder, is that it?" Georgiana began. "You are not our father, but you have no choice but to be so to me now. And it makes you like this, doesn't it? This protective? Yet that would not be the only problem here, is it?"

"Georgiana, are you speaking nonsense?"

"No, I am simply speaking the truth. You do not just blame my judgment for Wickham, however, you also blame yourself. If I had not been alone when it occurred, then he never could have preyed upon me. If you and father had taken better care of me, then I never could have fallen into his influence. And now you feel guilty. Now you want to make up for what happened to me by being extra cautious. The truth really is that your guilt is what shackles me now, and you would have me be alone for it and keep the world at bay!"

I took that as the time to walk away and cease to listen in on their argument.

That day we all spent at home, for the next day would be spent out for a day of dining, along with the theatre in the evening.

When we had retired for the evening, I lay in the bed after having made love to Darcy and I felt his fingers stroking my back, absentmindedly.

"Darcy, where is your mind now?"

"I was just thinking of many things."

"Do not conceal to me, my dear. You are thinking of Georgiana."

"Yes, indeed I am."

"And what are you feeling?"

"I am feeling lost. I do not know what to advise her with. I know what I ought to say, and I have said it, however, who am I to judge anyone? A person will always follow your actions more than your words. I have too many actions to my name."

"You are doing your duty and trying to protect her. And given her history, it is not your fault that you are being cautious. I understand what you are feeling, yet I understand what she is feeling as well."

"Why can she not see that I wish to keep her safe?"

"Oh, she sees it. However, sometimes safety gets dull for a woman. Think of it, Fitzwilliam. She has looked on her life and has felt locked away like a jewel in a case. Safe yes, but now she is curious about the world and wishes it to be larger. That is why she was fascinated by that man, because he must have had an effect on her where she felt that she was no longer stuck in one place."

"I do that?"

"Darcy, you are her guardian, not her friend. You are supposed to do that. However, she is a young woman, and the emotional need to see what is out there in the world is also something that she will never overcome. It is something she feels that she has to do."

"How are you so certain that this is what she feels?"

"Because, I suppose, that was what I felt when I first saw you."

"What?"

"Think on our tumultuous acquaintance when we first met. Think when I saw you in the park there, weeping, in pain. When I looked at you, my world had felt so small and cluttered, and it was. I did not fully notice it until I saw you there, and something about you made me wish for it to grow larger. We met at the ball, yes, and it had a lasting effect on me, but it wasn't until I saw you sitting on that bench that I realized something."

"What was that?"

"My world did not involve you, and therefore, it was not large enough for me to be happy in it. That is why I could never hate or despise you—why I could never turn from you fully, because your very existence showed me that I needed to enlarge the world I walked in."

"You saw all of that by me sitting there?"

"Your face showed much emotion. Emotion that I do not see often. It showed pain, agony, truth, wisdom even, and the ability to be moved by something. Till then, yes, I had seen my sisters cry, as well as myself, but I never saw anything that allowed the sort of emotion that you possessed. In your eyes, I saw loss, and that sadness made me unable to look away from you. Fitzwilliam, I do not know why I felt so deeply for you at the moment. All I can say is that I did."

Darcy looked up at me, kissed my lips, then my neck, my breasts, my stomach, and then in between my thighs. I covered my mouth as he did so, afraid of the sounds that would escape it. Deeper and deeper his kiss became, with an urgency that I never wished to be without. I never wanted such bliss to end, yet it did eventually, and he raised himself up and rolled me over. He kissed the back of my thighs, ran his tongue over my bottom and then laid on top of me.

"Save me, Elizabeth. What must I do?"

"I do not know. All we can do is make sure to look after Georgiana, and if you wish, I shall talk to her."

"Yes, my dear, do."

"Very well, I shall speak with Georgiana."

23

A WELCOME ADDITION

I did not get the chance to speak with Georgiana, however, because the next day, we were greeted by the arrival of two faces that were wonderful to see.

"Forgive us for not sending a card in advance, but when it comes to family, who needs that?"

It was Henry Darcy's sister Samantha and her husband, Mr. Eastbourne.

"Henry!" Samantha continued, hugging her brother. "You know you are not really upset for us coming to visit so swiftly?"

"Not at all, Samantha," Henry smiled, "For I know that you will always follow your own way."

"Yes, I shall."

I had forgotten that Samantha and her husband lived in New York City, and it was a most welcome arrival. For Samantha was robust and lively, and Mr. Eastbourne was also a jovial sort. Therefore, their appearance in our sitting room at Arruin was delightful.

"We arrived in the city two days ago from Philadelphia. Mother and father will be expecting you to write to them already, Mrs. Darcy. Oh, forgive me, Mrs. Henry Darcy."

"Why should they want me to write instead of Henry?" Lydia questioned, cheerfully.

"Oh, they know that Henry is terrible at sending letters."

"I am getting better," Henry argued.

"Are you?" Lydia grinned, "Oh, Henry, it is nice to know that you are bad at something."

"How so?" Henry blurted out.

"Because being married to perfection is very boring."

"Oh, how nice to know. Well, while we are at it, I also forget to cover my mouth when I burp or sneeze. I am grumpy in the morning."

"Oh, I already learned that one," she said, laughing.

"What nonsense," Samantha cried. "Henry you are grumpy all the time."

"Well, then it clearly is the Darcy way."

"To have a propensity to grumble about everything?" Richard offered. "Yes, it could be said so of some. Yet as Darcy over there has said, every disposition leans towards some particular evil."

"Quite so," Darcy replied. "For if Henry's tendency is to grumble, then mine is to scowl."

"And what is Richard's vice?" Kitty asked and turned to her husband. "Colonel Fitzwilliam, I must know your vice, for it appears that if I do not, then you are boring."

"Have you ever known me to be boring?"

"It is always possible that my perspective of you shall change."

"You wish me to comply with you?"

"Oh yes, my dear Colonel!" Kitty grinned. "I shall be wicked and use every bit of influence I have over you. Tell me, I implore you."

Richard leaned close to her, and their noses were inches apart.

"My bad habit is that I have this tendency to always do what my wife wants."

"Oh Richard!"

"Yes, my dear," he said, and then kissed her in front of all of us. We all looked down, for it was not suitable to commit such an act in the presence of others. Only Samantha and Mr. Eastbourne laughed.

"Oh, don't blame me," Richard bellowed. "It was obvious she wanted me to kiss her, and I warned you what my vice was."

"Ah, see how my husband blames me!" Kitty sighed.

We all laughed delicately, except for Samantha and Mr. Eastbourne.

"You need not worry," Samantha said. "In New York, you'll see women and men kiss on the street often. So, the rest of you had better get used to it."

We all began to laugh more comfortably.

"People really do that?"

"The middle and lower classes, yes, but on the street, even the affluent families can be spotted doing so. Therefore, do not stand on ceremony here too often. Or it shall become very apparent that you are not from around here."

❧

Samantha and Mr. Eastbourne stayed for the mid-day meal, which proved to be for the benefit of the men in our circle, and for us a little as well.

"I shall not get to join you on many outings unfortunately," Mr. Eastbourne began, "for many of us political officials shall be required to attend the trial."

"What trial?" Kitty asked.

"Oh, the Trekenna Trial. Have you never heard of it?"

"We have not."

"Oh, I know you are just arrived, yet it has been on the tip of everyone's tongues even in the streets, so I thought you would have been aware."

"This is the first we have heard of it," Henry began, "so don't be too long in telling the news, Eastbourne."

"Ah, there is your grumpiness."

"Now you are taking longer."

"Very well. The Trekenna Trial had begun earlier this week. It is in dispute of a slave trade ship, the Trekenna that made berth here in New York a month ago. When the ship came into port and began to unload their slaves, there was an alarm sounded, stating the slaves were illegally apprehended."

"All slavery should be illegal," Georgiana stated boldly, and we all turned to her. Seeing that all eyes were on her made her falter at first, but then she continued, "It has been abolished in other parts of the world and therefore I wish for it to be so here. So, it is so strange that it is not."

"And that is where the illegality has entered the matter," Mr. Eastbourne continued, feeling encouraged. "Some officials have claimed that the ship, Trekenna, had passed through Scottish territory along the ocean, which meant that as soon as the slaves had been unloaded on those shores, they were, by law, of the abolition, free men and women. Unfortunately, while there are some British officials who claim that the Trekenna was specifically placed on the island's records as making berth, it has made little impact. Also, with the anti-British sentiments felt around the city at present, their words are not being heeded to so much as we would hope. The trial was on break for three days while the defense desires to find more tangible proof of the slaves' right to liberty. However, the defense looks bleak."

"And you will witness this when it occurs?" Colonel Fitzwilliam asked. "I confess that finding out the particularities of this trial interest me. And I wish that despite the conflict going on now, the people did not turn from the influence of the British officials. Despite our flaws, we at least have fought hard to assist the abolitionists in bringing such an injustice to an end. Mind you, the Trade is still going on in Britain, but in Scotland, it is fully abolished. If they made berth there, even for a second, those slaves would be free."

"As the grandson of a slave owner," Mr. Eastbourne said, "I agree with you in this matter. Well, then, I have an idea. If you are so much inclined to see the trial, then I am certain that I can use my influence to secure you seats next to mine in the courtroom."

"You can do that?" Darcy said, perking up. "You could really do so?"

"Yes, I can."

"And it would not be hard for you to attempt and achieve it?"

"I promise that it will be of little matter," Mr. Eastbourne said, "We shall merely be in the crowd of other officials, yet this way you can know all the particularities of the trial, and if the ladies wish to know of it all, you can inform them."

"That would be delightful," Georgiana said. The rest of us agreed, except for Caroline, who looked bored.

◊◊◊

"Tonight, you shall attend the theatre?" Mrs. Hale began, "and I simply wish to know what time you all plan to return so that we can have hot water drawn for you."

We gave her an approximate time and then we left for our dinner with Samantha and Mr. Eastbourne, who offered to join us at the theatre if it was not sold out.

We all dressed in our finest, were punctual and left for the Valisren, the finest Dining Hall in New York City. After our meal, we made our way to the theatre.

All throughout our meal, Georgiana inquired after the trial and

Mr. Eastbourne was happy to know that she took a keen interest in the matter.

I was often very close to them and could chronicle all that they spoke of, which was quite curious. Georgiana always had an interest in many things, yet this new interest had now become too direct, and it puzzled me.

However, overall, our company had become much livened with the appearance of Mr. and Mrs. Eastbourne. I had worried that our disagreements over the night before about women's rights for representation in the government or parliament to vote would carry over into the next day. However, with these two now attached to our company, they served as a distraction, and we all were set to rights.

To our luck, there were more seats in the theatre available, and they were only three seats behind our row.

The show that we had come to see that evening was called *The Rivals,* and it proved to be a wonderful comedy of manners.

"I do so love this play," Mr. Darcy said beside me as the play reached intermission.

"As do I."

"Yes, and the Eastbournes accompanying us does actually lighten the mood."

"They do indeed. Yet I never knew that you would have taken such a keen interest in this trial."

"Oh, I must confess that I am quite curious on the matter."

"And is there any other reason?"

Mr. Darcy eyed me keenly.

"Mrs. Darcy, what do you really wish to ask me?"

"I am wondering if the reason you are wishing to see this is because of your desire to have justice win out—the way it did when you came to that Freed woman's aid in Philadelphia all those months ago."

Fitzwilliam looked down and then he sighed.

"I confess that I do think of it sometimes. The memory still lingers within me."

"As it should. We saw something that cannot be unseen and felt the effects of it." I bit my lip and then continued on. "There is something else that I still remember."

"What is that?"

"The woman when we took her in our carriage. One of her children, the daughter, her eyes when she looked up at me. After the slave catchers left and we had gotten them into safety, her eyes were filled with emotion. Yet she did not know how to voice it. It was pain, sorrow, fear, but a glimmer of hope was in the dark brown of her pupils. I thought she was beautiful."

"I remember her a little, yet it was the boy who I remembered more." Darcy sighed. "He was almost as dark as night and his face looked like one that did not know how to react to such tragedy. He was too young to have endured what they did. And then I looked on his features and thought what he would have looked like when he grew up? Then I thought, what would have happened if he had been captured? Their family would have been separated, he would have been reduced to the worst of fates. And then I saw him in my mind's eye: one year he got older, then another year and another and another. Then before me was a grown man with the saddest of expressions. That is what could have become of him if that family had been torn apart."

I took his chin in my hands and kissed his cheek, knowing that even if the elite were around us, no one would care to gossip—for as Samantha had pointed out, New York was a different world altogether.

"My dear, your mind thought on something very profound."

"Yes, it did. And it scares me, Lizzy."

"It should. Yet I must warn you."

"Warn me? Of what?"

"Of the fact that we are in a time when justice does not always prevail. For justice is not always blind. If you go to that trial, there is a chance that those slaves shall not be freed. There is a great *great* chance that you will see oppression win. And you must prepare yourself for that."

"I shall return home angry, then."

"I know."

"Yet I must see this trial, Elizabeth. Something in me must see it."

"Will you promise to tell me all about the details and particularities of when you return?"

"Yes, I shall."

"Then very good. For I wish I could be going myself."

Yet that was the point of it all! I was not allowed to be able to witness it. No woman was. The intermission came to an end, and we all sat in our seats, but my mind was occupied. If women had been equal to men in our society, I would have been allowed to have seen it firsthand. I felt as if my mind had been channeling the sentiments of Georgiana at present, but I did ponder it.

However, I knew I could rely on Darcy to tell me all the details and would conceal nothing. Therefore, if I was not given the rights due to society, at least I was given equality in the security of my home and within our family. Looking down at Samantha and her husband, I could also easily recognize that Samantha and he were on equal footing with each other as well. And such tendencies to be level with one another made them a welcome addition to our party.

They brought liberty of discussion and offered us new perspectives—yet if I had known then what such knowledge would lead to, I would only regard their appearance as another beginning to a new adventure in the chronicles of our lives.

24

HOW THE MATTER WOULD UNFOLD

Georgiana went through the halls of Arruin to find Kitty in hopes that she was alone. To her happiness, Kitty was sitting in the library reading, and she came upon her.

"Kitty, are you quite alone?"

"Yes," Kitty said, closing her book, "for the men are out shooting and Elizabeth, Lydia, Miriam, and Caroline have joined them."

"Where is Jane?"

"She is in the sitting room, sewing."

"Good, for I needed to speak with you." Georgiana sat down and began her request. "I need for you to join me on an outing to the flower shop we had gone to before."

"But why so? Your nose was sensitive to something there, do you not recall?"

"Yes, of course I do. However, I am wishing to know what it is. Oh, think of it, Kitty, it is best to know what one is sensitive to, for it shall help me if I ever come in contact with it again."

"Georgiana, do you really think it is necessary?"

"Yes, I do."

"Well then, I should be happy to ask Richard to join us tomorrow so we can go together."

"And have me feel as if I am only an awkward third piece that interrupts your moments spent with him? Kitty, if I go with you both, I shall only feel in the way, and sometimes that hurts me."

"Oh, dear Georgiana, I do not wish for you to ever feel like you do not fit in the company, yet I can see how you might feel so."

"Precisely. Can we not just have the carriage drawn, and Nicholson join us so that he might accompany us? If we leave now, we may return even before the men return from their shooting party."

"Oh, very well, but Jane shall join us."

"Oh, I do not wish to bother her."

"You were not afraid to ask me?" Kitty laughed. "Why do you think Jane would be against it? Don't worry, she shall not feel like we are imposing upon her at all, and she quite liked the Flower House."

Kitty stood up and left to put on her bonnet. Georgiana did not wish for Jane to come, for Jane would not naturally be as compliant as Kitty in this situation. Yet she knew it would not do to not tell Jane.

Therefore, there was nothing for it but to tell Mrs. Hale where they were going. The carriage was drawn, and Nicholson and another coachman drove them to the heart of the city. They stopped at the Flower House and entered it.

To Georgiana's happiness, Jane loved flowers so much that she grew wrapped up in gazing at them and also decided she wished to make a purchase. While she was busy and asking for Kitty's advice, Georgiana told them that she was going to check at the front of the shop to see where her allergy had sprung from. Kitty eyed her suspiciously but acquiesced and she walked back to the entrance of the shop. When she noticed that they no longer were paying attention to her, she slipped out of the front door furtively, and then she beheld Nicholson.

"Nicholson," she began, "I am feeling suddenly sneezy again, and I just wish to take a brief walk."

"Oh, Higgins can watch the coach while I escort you, Miss Darcy."

"Oh, you need not do that, for I am just going down the road, straight ahead. All I ask of you to do is to watch me so that I am always safe. Also, I do not want you near me when I am sneezing, for I do not wish to give you anything."

"Oh, thank you for thinking of me, Miss. But are you sure that you do not need me to escort you?"

"All you need is to promise you shall watch me."

"I can promise that Miss Darcy. Mark my words."

Excited to finally detach herself completely, Georgiana began to walk down the road. She looked left and right, trying to not look as if she were looking for someone in particular, but only gazing at everything as if she were a tourist.

Every face that passed her, she looked at keenly, in hopes that it was him. Every man of her height, with brown hair and tattered clothes, she gazed at him, but was disappointed each time. She knew that it was unlikely she would find him, for he would not live on that street. Yet she had hoped that maybe he might be speaking to a crowd again of some kind. She walked on and then arrived at the spot where she had seen him last, but it was empty.

Very easily she could recall him standing on a barrel, with people around him listening to his every word. Hypnotized by him. From what she could recall, he had a natural ability to move people with his voice and captivate them. It was a power that she did not understand, for she could never fathom how to do such a thing. His confidence was extreme and prominent, to say the least.

He had to have some training of some kind, for he spoke so eloquently, and his accent was not colloquial, nor was his manner.

If anything, his clothing contradicted his speech, which was elegant and well thought out. He had no common way about his vernacular.

However, a strange thing began to happen. His face began to lose shape in her memory. And while she remembered the outline of his form, his features and details began to become forgotten. She could not recall how his cheeks were, his nose, his countenance was thin, but she could not recall if his arms were too short or long for his form, or if his legs were lean or average. It was a strange thing, but it seemed as if her memory did not want to remember him fully —as if she wanted to release him, for it was clear that it must be so. Therefore, all she could remember was his dark brown hair, his voice, his striking blue eyes, and the brilliance that they contained.

"Georgiana!"

Georgiana turned around and Kitty was approaching her.

"What are you doing here?" Kitty continued.

"Oh, sorry, I went for a walk. I was just..."

"Looking for him," she finished.

"Kitty," Georgiana began.

"Georgiana, you know that I am not a fool, so do not think you should treat me as so. I knew that you were up to some scheme when we left Arruin, yet I felt it best to go along with it. Yet you have me not in your confidence."

"Forgive me, Kitty, for abusing your faith. Yet I did not wish to tell you, because there is clearly nothing to tell. He is not here."

"Georgiana," Kitty said gently, "while I understand the intrigue that may come when meeting a man for the first time and feeling a spark, I sadly have to admit to agreeing with Darcy in this situation. This is not a man that you know, therefore it might only be the mystery that draws you, and therefore it is best that you did not see him again."

"I know I am being foolish. And why did I even believe that he would be here?"

"You are not foolish. You were just being romantic. Curiosity is a healthy thing, yet I am happy that it ended where it did, for strangers can be a danger—" Kitty suddenly ceased speaking and Georgiana looked up to see her looking at something that was behind her.

"What is it?" Georgiana asked.

She did not reply, and somehow, her expression said it all. Georgiana grew still, feeling the presence of someone behind her. Slowly, she turned around to face the individual.

He was there.

The man who she had seen giving the speech.

Their eyes locked gazes where her brown ones met his blue ones and they both stood there transfixed. As she beheld him, she noticed every line and detail of his face, committing it to memory and quickly the image she had of him, which had been very unclear before, was now defined and fixed in her mind's eye.

She quickly folded her hands in front of her, nervous as she noticed that his hands were flexing slowly over and over, showing that he might be as apprehensive as she was. She knew that Kitty was still behind her. But she could not be bothered at the moment, and completely forgot to offer to introduce them—especially since she had not been introduced to him as well.

"Good day," the man said, his voice firm and soft, deep, and light.

"Good—good day," Georgiana replied.

At last, we speak to each other. At last, we have spoken our first word.

"Forgive me," he whispered. "We have not been introduced I know."

"No, we have not," she whispered, her voice feeling suddenly hoarse.

"Yet, if you do not mind..."

"No, I do not."

"Georgiana?" Kitty said behind her. Georgiana closed her eyes, actually annoyed with Kitty being there for the very first time ever, and she turned to her.

"Yes, Kitty?" she asked, unable to hide her impatience.

"Georgiana, this is not wise."

"Kitty," Georgiana said, approaching her and taking her hands. "When you committed acts of rashness, did I judge you? No, I did not. And I allowed it in the end. Please, allow me this. And stand apart but watch over me."

Kitty looked at the man over Georgiana's shoulder, and then she relented.

"Very well. After all, who am I to judge anyone?"

Kitty stepped back, and Georgiana turned back to the man, who stood fifteen feet away from her. Seeing that she encouraged his attention to her, the man took a few steps forward.

"I thought..." he began, "I thought that I would never see you again."

"As did I," Georgiana said, rooted to the spot. "I thought you would not return as well and—"

"Kitty and Georgiana!"

That time, Kitty and Georgiana's eyes shut in annoyance as they turned to see Jane coming toward them, carrying some flowers wrapped in paper.

"What do you both do there?"

"Oh, we were just looking around," Kitty explained.

"Were you?" Jane said, seeing the man behind them. "Well, Georgiana, I am happy to see that your sensitivity has abated. Now it is time that we return."

"Oh," Kitty objected, doing her best to help Georgiana, "but should we not walk the streets a little? We might enjoy turning down a different avenue and see—"

"Kitty, you know that we are expected. We should not make everyone feel apprehensive over us. And it would be most inconsiderate."

Kitty turned to Georgiana, and they both knew that there was no chance that Jane would allow them to continue to remain. Therefore, they had to follow her. Georgiana turned to the man one last time, nodded to him, and then followed Jane. Every now and again, she looked behind her and the man at first simply gazed fixedly at her, then he began to follow after her.

They all reached the carriage and Georgiana turned to see the man as he began to run toward them as they entered it.

"Where can I find you?" he cried. "Where do you live? You must tell me?"

Nicholson beheld the man with contempt as he shut the carriage door and got into the driver's seat next to the coachman.

"Georgiana," Jane warned, "Whoever that is, you must not tell him, please. Drive on, Nicholson."

Nicholson and the coachman urged on the horses and the carriage began to roll onward. Georgiana looked out of the window, and she saw the man running up to the window.

"Please," he said, "you must tell me!"

His head reached the carriage window and with a burst of nerve, Georgiana leaned forward and whispered in his ear.

"Arruin estate in Greenwich."

The man smiled at her, and then the carriage increased its speed and left the man behind. Georgiana leaned her head out of the window and watched him until he disappeared into the distance.

"Georgiana," Jane said as the carriage continued on the way to Arruin. "I know that I am not related to you by blood, yet in the absence of your brother, I still must do what I can in his stead. While I believe that we all have it in us to be good, too many circumstances have shown me that I had been too idealistic in my thoughts in the past. And I will not let my tendencies toward being a dreamer keep me from being realistic in this circumstance. It is not wise to speak with people you have not the good fortune to be acquainted with. They are dangerous and you must refrain from doing such things to harm yourself."

"I was safe, I can assure you, Jane."

"I do not mean to reprimand you, but you must understand our desire to keep you safe."

"Maybe that is the problem with me. I have always been too much protected of late."

Jane looked at Kitty and she was at a loss of how to respond, then she continued the matter.

"Georgiana, please tell me. Did you tell him anything about our whereabouts? For to give a stranger such knowledge would be dangerous for us all. Therefore, please tell me that you did not do so."

"I..." Coming to a decision, Georgiana then thought it best to lie. "I told him nothing. We are quite safe."

"Very good. Thank you, Georgiana."

Georgiana felt bad for lying, as well as feeling bad at the reality of Jane's words that she had caused a great risk. Yet she could not take back her actions, therefore, all that she could do was see how the matter would unfold.

25

WORDS THAT MUST BE SPOKEN

For the rest of the day, Georgiana spent it in wonder, excitement, and alarm. She either brought on a great intrigue to herself, or she brought on a great danger to them. However, she knew that between her brother, Richard, Henry, Mr. Bingley, and Jefferson, there was no chance that harm could come to them, truly. For all were men who were equipped at fencing and firearms. Arruin was a safe haven, to be sure. Even if she had been foolish, no ultimate harm could come to them.

As night fell, Georgiana was preparing for bedtime, when she felt a knock on her window. She turned, and she realized that it was rocks that had been hit against the glass. She walked over to it and her breath grew heavy.

Down below was the man from the street. In the moonlight, she saw him faintly, but just enough to see that he was smiling gently. He waved up at her and she waved down. Georgiana then opened her window and poked her head out of it.

"Good evening," she whispered.

"Good evening," he replied. "I am sorry, but...I have written you something."

"Have you?"

"Yes, I simply...please do not be afraid."

Georgiana thought only briefly on the matter, and then realized that she would be in no danger, for that part of the villa was enclosed by a gate. He could not harm her, for they were parted by the barrier, but still able to see and speak to one another.

"Give me a moment," Georgiana said, closing the window. She went to her closet and pulled out the loveliest over-gown that she had that was sheer and tied beneath the bust. It flattered her figure because all she had was a sleeveless under-gown underneath. Then she put on a coat. Making sure she looked presentable, Georgiana put on her slippers and began to tiptoe along the hallway, down the steps, out of the house through the servants' entrance, and then she entered the garden that was enclosed by the gate. There, on the other side of it, stood the man, looking back at her.

Feeling suddenly bashful, she quietly approached him, unable to stop shivering. She reached the gate and looked into his eyes, which were level with hers.

"You found me," she whispered.

"Yes, I did. Thank you for telling me how to do so."

"Oh," she smiled, looking down.

"Are you cold? You are shivering."

"I am not. I am simply nervous."

"Are you?" he whispered, his blue eyes twinkling in the moonlight.

"Yes I am."

"What is your name?"

"Georgiana."

Though she had immediately felt intrigued, she knew it was not wise to give her last name just yet.

"And what is yours?" she asked.

"I am Jason. Jason Friend."

"Your last name is Friend?"

"Yes, it is."

"That is a wonderful last name to have. If you can own to it."

"I want to believe that I am so."

Georgiana raised her hands up against the gate to lean on it. To her utter amazement, he raised his hand against it as well. Slowly and surely, he drew his hand closer to hers and then their fingertips touched. Amazed at his courage, she could not draw away. She only looked at their hands touching and smiled bashfully.

"It is improper for a man and woman to ever touch, unless it be during a dance."

"Are you scandalized?"

"No, I am simply wondering why I do not care to follow such a rule at the moment."

Their heads drew closer on both sides of the gate and their eyes gazed deeply into the others.

"You are not from New York," he said, "I can tell from your accent."

"You have an accent as well, though."

"I was originally from England."

"I am from England!"

"I can hear it. And here, so far from home, we find each other."

"Yes, we do." She sighed. "I...I remember your speech on the street."

"Do you?"

"It was spellbinding. How did you learn to speak like that? You had the people intrigued by you. Even those who opposed your beliefs could not find anything about your delivery wanting. I could never perform to strangers."

"My words are all I have. For I have no other talent."

"It is a talent not many of us possess. It made me remember you."

He drew closer to her, and their noses were almost touching through the gate opening.

"Every day since I had seen you," he said, "I kept coming back to that street, in hopes that I would find you."

"I came there today in search of you."

"I began to understand. And I... to be there today when you did, it was all too much of a miracle."

"It felt so. I could not believe when I turned around and saw you standing there."

"As I could not believe that I saw you looking for me. Then you felt it?"

"Felt what?"

"The sensation—that we had to see each other once more."

"Yes...yes, I did feel it. I cannot explain it."

"We are not foolish."

"Are we not? We do not even know each other."

"Sometimes, in regards to affection, or passion, one glance is all it takes."

"We should be sensible." Georgiana chuckled. "And yet, I find that I cannot be so."

"Then do not be."

Jason reached through the gate fully and covered Georgiana's hand in his own.

"Are you still giving a care to our hands touching?"

"No, I never cared, actually. And I quite enjoy it."

"As do I."

Jason then reached into his pocket and pulled out a piece of paper.

"This is what I wrote for you. Read it when we part."

"Very well. But what does it say?"

"You shall see."

"I shall," she said, intertwining her fingers with his. "Jason, do you really believe all those things?"

"What things?"

"Those things you spoke of. Of the abolition, helping out the poor, and women's rights for equal representation?"

"Yes...yes, I do."

"That is a marvel. Some amongst my own acquaintance do not believe so."

"They are afraid to open their eyes and see. And I cannot blame them, for it is difficult. However, the only way for the world to change is if we speak about it."

"That is why you preach on the streets?"

"Yes, for there will be many who will disagree with me. That is the way of the world. Yet if I can make at least one of them walk away asking questions, if I can put the dilemma into their mind, then I have succeeded, I feel."

"You sound as if you know that you are going to fail."

"Revolution often leads to failure."

"And yet you still have hope?"

"Yes," he whispered, moving his face even closer to her. "For some of us, it is not about our destination, but the journey along the way."

"I wonder if I could be so brave."

"You dared to listen to me speak. Then you came to find me, and then you have come down to me again. You seem to already be so."

"Or I am intrigued."

"By me?"

Georgiana looked down.

"I should not confess that."

"I would like it if you did," he said, reaching through the gate and touching the bottom of her face with his fingers, caressing it gently. "Really, do not be afraid."

"You—you intrigue me. You are a mystery while also seeming so familiar. I feel as if I have seen you in some way before. As if you are a face that I know, even though I know it not."

"Then let me see you again. When can I find you alone? Can we walk in the park Thursday during the afternoon?"

"My family always is around me. They shall not let you close."

"Then how shall I find you?"

"Tomorrow, my brother and the rest of the gentlemen are going to attend a trial. Can you come here then, and we can speak on the outskirts of the estate? The fence will still separate us."

"Unfortunately, I cannot come tomorrow, for I have to see to my work," he said, avoiding her eyes. "Yet is there a chance that I can come tomorrow night, then? We can speak in this way once more."

"Very well. I would like that."

"Yes. We can do so at first, yet I shall want to see you more. If you will let me, I shall want to."

"I shall want to, as well."

"Then till tomorrow night, I shall think of you."

"And I of you."

"Yet, how did you know where my room was? You threw rocks at the right window."

Jason looked sheepish.

"Forgive me, I did what I had to do."

"And what did you have to do?"

"I have been watching the house for two hours now, and I saw you through the windows."

Georgiana blushed and looked down.

"I did not mean to seem so...obsessive. I just simply wished to see you."

"I understand. And I am happy that you did."

He cradled her face in his hands, and then Georgiana moved away from the fence, still looking at him.

"And," she began.

"Yes?"

"I like your eyes."

"And I like yours as well."

Georgiana turned from him and entered the house. She went to her room quietly and without being detected, she glimpsed Jason's form still down on the street. He still looked up at her and then when she blew out the candle, he turned and walked down the street, his hands folded behind him and every now and again turning to look back up at her. When he finally disappeared, Georgiana spun around in the room, elated and filled with joy.

He had come for her, and he had spent hours to achieve his objective. To do so and to search for her in the way he did had to display some sincerity on his side. He was partial to her, and she wanted to believe that all his words spoke a truth of his heart. Yet she did her best to remain rational and understand that he could still very well not be earnest or have any honorable intentions. He could only wish to use her. Therefore, she must still be put on her guard.

Then she remembered the letter he wrote to her, and she groaned inwardly, and relit the candle by her bed. Taking off her slip, she slid into bed and then began to read his missive.

I do not know your name, but for so many hours and minutes, the memory of your face has haunted me. From your eyes, brilliant with sentiment and benevolence, your smile, which cannot be forgotten by any with a warm heart—and your form, light, lovely and there shall never be a word that can do it justice to define its elegance.

And your beauty. When I was giving my speech, to turn and see you, my words failed me, all thought left, and I almost forgot myself, for all that I desired was to walk toward you—to be in the presence of such loveliness would be something that I never thought I would glimpse.

Then you spoke. You did not shun me, nor reject my desires to become close to you—you opened yourself to me. And you must do so now. You cannot deprive me of the chance to be in your presence, for your smile, face and voice are like that of the sun to a man. You shine down on me and make me desire to come closer to you, for until I met you, I now see that I was left in darkness.

I cannot turn my mind from you. I wish to win your good opinion, seek your admiration, and may you look kindly on me. May you see me as the man worthy of a courtship to such a regal woman as yourself. Let me know you, woman, who lives in Arruin. Let me attempt to convince you to think I deserve you. Even though you are like the light from the sky and greater than us mortals, still allow me to believe that even the sky is not beyond the reach of man. I am Jason Friend—if I can, I shall do my best to make you adore me. May I succeed.

Georgiana closed the letter and lay back against the pillows. His words were all that she desired; they were not ostentatious or flamboyant, but simple and seemed to be filled with truth. His words were not like that of Wickham's! And that was an encouraging thought.

She was happy that she had allowed him the chance to see her again the next night, for she felt as if it could not come soon enough.

They had so much to say to one another, and to feel and to do, and though they had barely met, she could not deny the strange connection she felt to him. When a woman dreams of falling in love, it always seems as if there is a stable vision of that man: tall, well-made, with a deep voice and handsome features. Yet reality can be quite different, and simpler than people would believe. Jason Friend did not fit into any dream she had. He was not tall, muscular, with a sensuous voice or marked features. Yet she found herself to prefer the reality to any dream that she ever had.

Jason Friend had confidence, ease of manner, and an artlessness that she could not help but find alluring. He was the beauty that storybooks could never explain because he was without definition. He was...simply real. And the reality of him made her heart stir, and every word that they uttered together rested within her, making it hard to sleep. For she felt a giddiness that always comes with attraction. And that she had been so bold as to agree to see him again, it made her both proud and scared of herself. She was no different than Elizabeth, Kitty or Lydia—what was in the nature of them all to throw caution to the winds in hopes of fortune making sure everything turned out for the best? For they all had it.

However, she rolled over and finally fell asleep. When she woke up the next day, it was as if no time had been lost. For she awoke to thinking of the night, when she would see Jason once more, and they would speak all the words that must be spoken in the name of attraction.

26

VICTORY OR DEFEAT

The next day, Darcy, Richard, Henry, and Charles joined Mr. Eastbourne for the Trekenna trial, while Georgiana, Jane, Kitty, Miriam, Lydia, Caroline, and I remained home, either sewing, reading, or catching up on our letters. None of these activities truly were to the enjoyment of Caroline Bingley. She wished for us to go into town and partake in Fabric Row while also shop for gowns. But all of us wished to remain, in hopes of being present so that when the men arrived, we could find out the results of the trial for that day.

"Why does this trial concern you all?" Caroline whined. "It does not affect nor pertain to any of us."

"That does not make it of no importance," Miriam replied. "And now that we are alone, Georgiana, I have been wondering about our rights for equal representation in the government or parliament. Would it not be a pleasure to vote?"

"Yes, it would," Georgiana agreed.

"And not just for high officials," Kitty added, "yet for lesser matters as well, it would be a pleasure."

"Darcy and Henry are correct in one way," I said, "which is that it cannot be achieved in our lifetime. Yet perhaps that should not be a reason to not speak of it. For only by speaking of it can the matter become a problem in our society and the matter be brought forward to the public eye."

"Then should it follow that we should abandon all hope just because it may not be achieved in our lifetime?" Georgiana sighed. "No, I do not believe it to be so. Rather, it might be a struggle that would be better to endure, knowing that after our lifetime, it may come into effect."

"Such a heavy discussion," Caroline Bingley said, "and it is not as easy to speak it."

"What do you mean?" Miriam asked.

"I mean that you are all not the first group to think of a noble cause. I have seen it occur before and people revolted or held conventions to discuss equality of some kind—and it is always met with them being censured, despised by the rest of society, or worse, even physically attacked. The world and its reactions are like a wave that can destroy all in its wake. Believe me, let the world be and do not oppose it. Or the wave shall come crashing down on you and all those around you."

"I never knew you feared the world, Miss Bingley," Lydia confessed.

"I do not fear the world." Caroline groaned. "I just fear ruin."

The rest of us looked at each other, and while I detested admitting this to myself, but Caroline's point was a valid one. At what point does the sacrifice a person makes to face the censure of the world become a bane so terrible that the person regrets ever taking a stand? If we were to decide to hold assemblies, conventions at public forums, who would stand with us? Who would risk rattling the ton and society's cage that we all revolved in? And what would that risk be? We would be ridiculed everywhere we went and then it would reflect on our family—our husbands would be slighted for it, for they would be guilty by association. Would their love for us turn sour? Nothing kills love more than hate, and I would never want to be the source of disquiet or degradation for Darcy.

Therefore, to fight or not to fight? If one ever wished to take a stand, this would be the painful dilemma that one would have to make. I sighed out, not worried at present, for these were all just words we were speaking, and ideas that we had only recently come upon. For none of us were in a state where we could do anything, even if there was a chance to.

Yet if we were in a position where we had to make a decision, if it came to that, what would our choice be? For with every woman who sat there, the answer to that query would be quite different, I assumed.

⚜

Eventually, our husbands returned with Mr. Eastbourne and Samantha. Once they were all in and settled, Mrs. Hale announced to us that dinner would be served in half an hour. Therefore, we all congregated in the drawing room and inquired eagerly about the trial.

"It was incredible to witness!" Mr. Bingley said. "The defense for the Trekenna Crew did not have the better attorney, yet they won out in the end."

"The Trekenna Crew?" Jane asked. "Then that means that the cargo will remain slaves?"

"Yes, unfortunately."

"I am not so certain, however," Mr. Eastbourne objected, "for all it takes is some more push on the offense side of the case and they shall state a re-appeal and call for another trial."

"It is possible, then?" I asked.

"Oh, yes," Darcy said in reply, "Especially considering all the witnesses they have who stated that the Trekenna Ship did pass through British and Spanish territory. Also, they have records kept from the island registries that the Trekenna made berth on the Scottish isles."

"Then how can they still hold the crew and dismiss the case?" I gasped.

"Because they want to," Henry Darcy replied firmly. "Bigotry is sometimes so powerful that it will allow their minds to overlook honest matters of the law. Also, the defending attorneys argued that the registries could have been forged."

"Indeed," Mr. Eastbourne said, "the only way in which they will hold the registries as valid is if they have a seal of some high political official of some kind. Be they Spanish or British. Yet no attorneys on the side of the offense have such means to support and solidify the evidence."

"If there is a re-trial," Richard added, "Then the defending side of the captured cargo needs to still be headed up by the main attorney. Whitfield was his name, was it not?"

"Yes," Darcy added, "He was a very good speaker."

"Did you know the attorney?" Georgiana asked Mr. Eastbourne.

"I cannot say that I do. Yet one thing is certain, he is a great speaker, which is something to be said, for he is not tall or broad in stature and naturally should not create intimidation. He uses his voice to gather effect. What I do know is that he is English and is of good family."

"He is English, but he is here?"

"He's lived here for a couple years now. I know that much through reports, but that is all I know. And to be honest, I do not recognize those attorneys out of the courtroom. For with those powdered wigs while they work, their looks change in the social setting."

"I always hated powdered wigs," Richard said.

"We know you do, Richard," Darcy chuckled. "And I do not

blame you, for they do look quite dreadful. I never saw the appeal to them."

"I understood the concept of wigs when cleaning habits were rare," Lydia acknowledged, "yet now that the Shower Bath is now coming into effect and we have improved our concepts of sanitation, I see no need for them unless one is growing bald and therefore the wig is a necessity."

"Fashion can be foolish." I laughed. "Just look at the Elizabethan Era."

"Oh, that is true," everyone agreed, and then we all proceeded to revert back to the trial.

As we spoke more on the matter, Georgiana took more of an eager interest in the details of what occurred. What the attorneys said. If the slaves were present at the trial. Which they were not, but they were held in a nearby house.

I turned to Darcy, and he noticed this as well. I could not tell if he was eyeing her with wonder, respect, or apprehension. It was hard to tell if Georgiana's reason for taking a sudden and eager interest in the matters at hand were out of a desire to care about political affairs, or if the man she had seen in the street had influenced this marked difference. It was not the principles that Darcy feared growing in his sister, but rather it was a possible attraction that he had no control over.

However, like the Trekenna Trial, his finding out what was truly within her would result in either victory or defeat, and Darcy was never one to enjoy defeat.

❧ 27 ❧

DUTY AND DESIRE

That night, Georgiana looked out of her window when the rest of the villa seemed to be asleep. When she saw Jason's familiar form in the shadows on the other side of the fence, she put on her over-gown once more and crept out of the house, approaching it with speed.

"You've come back," she sighed.

"Of course, I would," he replied. "How could I not?"

"I...I read your letter," she whispered, placing her hand on the gate again for him to take in his own, which he did gently. "It was lovely."

"It was how I felt," he said, looking deeply into her eyes.

"Then that is how you see me?"

"When I saw you watching me as I spoke, I no longer was able to recite the words to the people, for I had never seen anything like you before in my life."

"Yet this is too much praise," Georgiana whispered, "for how can I live up to such an image of me? I am human, like any other, and my flaws might make you think ill of me."

"We are all human. Yet if you are frightened, tell me your flaws then?"

"I get angry sometimes."

"As do I."

"I grow too passionate sometimes and I wish to be heard."

"As you have seen, so do I."

"And I never wish to ever clean anything or learn to cook."

"Really?" He laughed.

"Yes, yet it is not out of the desire to never be self-sufficient or because I look down on it. I just despise learning things because I have to go through much failure first. And I am afraid of failing at things—it is my greatest fear."

"Why so?"

"Because it can make one ugly." Georgiana smiled. "It is quite bewildering, for when people see you fail at something, they do their best to never forget it. When people see you embarrass yourself, they always look at you as such, and they never release you from that image. I wish failure did not make us humans gruesome to each other, yet it does. That is why I did not ever play the pianoforte in public till I was fourteen years old."

"You play?"

"Yes, since I was a child. However, fear of making a mistake led to me never wishing to display my talents until I was certain that I would never fail."

"So, you have fears...we all do."

"For too long, those fears kept me from living."

"Did it?"

"Yes, it did."

"Then why do you not fear me?" he asked her, cradling her chin in his hand. "Georgiana?"

"I do not know," she confessed. "I just look into your eyes and see a man who is kind. Who is understanding. Even though I do not know you—I feel as if there is goodness in you."

"Then never be afraid, and you could never be ugly. Even if you failed at something, you would never be so."

Georgiana and Jason leaned through the gate, getting closer and closer, until they kissed.

⚜

Georgiana knew that she had taken a large risk and was being quite foolish. Yet all thought escaped her as their lips pressed against each other's and the feeling of intimacy and desire eclipsed them both. He also reached his hand through the bars and grabbed her waist.

Minute after minute passed by.

Their kisses still continued, and Georgiana had never felt such bliss in her life. After almost a half an hour had passed, she knew that she had to cease and return into the villa before her absence might get noticed.

Before they parted, they swore to meet again the next evening at the same time, and they kissed one last time.

"Georgiana," Jason whispered.

"Yes, Jason?"

"I hope I have not frightened you with my kisses, yet I could not help myself."

"I could not either."

She smiled at him once more before she ran inside the house, and he left the exterior of Arruin.

⚜

As Georgiana lay in bed, her mind wandered to the memory of George Wickham. It was cruel to think of him at the moment, yet she found herself compelled to. Inwardly, she began to compare the kiss of Wickham to that of Jason Friend, for yes, she had allowed

Wickham to kiss her before their elopement. At the time, she had thought it the most wonderful experience she had ever encountered. Yet her situations where she had been kissed from a romantic view were very much limited, therefore she had nothing to compare it to. Until now. Jason's kiss was so overwhelming, encompassing, and passionate that now she saw Wickham's kiss for what it was: cold and empty. He was neither a sincere lover, physically or emotionally.

She could have been in error and Jason could very well be another Wickham. However, she still chose to have hope that he was otherwise. Not all men are evil by any means, and only generalizations made them so.

Therefore, as her eyes closed and she gave way to sleep, she felt content that she had finally kissed a man who might be worthy of it.

She had waited long enough to do so.

The next evening, they re-met, and then the next and the next. Each night Georgiana and Jason learned more and more about each other, while also enjoying the intimacy of allowing oneself to fall in love.

However, on the seventh night of them meeting so, Jason grew frustrated.

"Georgiana, I cannot remain this way."

"What way?" she asked, her brow furrowing, for she feared she had upset him in some way.

"Stealing words and kisses during the night only. I wish to be allowed to take you out during the day, where we can walk along the streets, and I might have us partake in a mid-day meal. I do not wish to be a shameful secret any longer."

"You are not a shameful secret. Just a secret."

"And that is not what I seek. Is there some way that we can meet and walk through the park, or I may take you to a tavern that I know you shall like?"

"Jason, we might get caught in some form."

"I know, yet I wish to show you the city. I wish to be near you more. Do you not wish to be near me as well?"

"Of course, I do."

"Then please try...for me."

Georgiana looked into his eyes and saw the look of longing and request, and her heart immediately softened toward him.

Outrageous! I can deny him nothing it appears! No wonder Kitty allowed Richard to lock themselves away in Aginfield. When in love with someone, they can convince you to partake in any amount of foolishness.

"Very well," Georgiana said. "Tomorrow, after 1 o'clock, may we meet in the park?"

"Yes, we may." He smiled. "Georgiana, that makes me happy."

"It does for me as well," she smiled, though not having any concept of how she would be able to succeed at doing so.

She wished that this all had never happened to her, for it made everything confusing for her. She wanted to keep their rendezvous a secret, out of safety. Yet if they did so, then how could they reach the desired effect of growing into a courtship?

She also was aware that she should end their meetings, yet the other part of her wished to continue them in earnest. Torn between choosing between duty and desire, she began to learn the painful theory that either path she chose she would gain something and lose something as well.

28

WHEN ALL THAT IS RIGHT TURNS
INTO ALL THAT IS WRONG

"You wish of me to what?" Kitty exclaimed, and then she lowered her voice.

"I cannot help but do so, Kitty," Georgiana said. "I have no other ideas."

It was the next morning and after breakfast, Georgiana had told Kitty about Jason Friend and also about her plans to meet with him that day.

"You want me to join you under the pretense that we only wish to go to the park," Kitty said, repeating the request Georgiana asked of her. "So that you may meet this Jason, if he is who he says that he is, and then remain in the background and serve as your chaperone."

"Yes. Please Kitty, I cannot tell anyone about him."

"And why not? I'm certain that your brother would not be against you being courted. Especially since you are old enough to be your own woman now."

"You have seen it yourself, Kitty. Jason is clearly poor."

"Yet if he is so, then how do you know he is not a fortune hunter?"

"He did not know that I was wealthy when we first met."

"Your clothing was well-looking enough."

"I dressed plainly."

"But not poorly."

"He is different, Kitty. Believe me."

"Georgiana." Kitty sighed. "You know as well as I do that I did not marry for wealth, but from what I recall of this Jason Friend, he was decidedly poor, to the point where your worlds are very different. I may have lived comfortably, yet I also lived modestly enough. You are used to all the best in life. And you are planning on seeing a man who still dares not introduce himself to your family. Therefore, what do you expect to achieve by it?"

"I do not know, Kitty. Yet are you telling me that you expected all to end well for you and Richard?"

Kitty did not respond at first.

"And if it did not appear that you would have gotten a secure future from his attentions, would that have stopped you from still allowing him a few moments with you? Tell me the truth, Kitty. Would you always have obeyed your duty?"

Kitty looked away and turned around, considering it all.

"No," she admitted, "I would still have allowed him to take liberties, even if there was no chance of us becoming one."

"I know that you would have. And therefore, I know that you see how I am feeling. And I can't help but feel this."

Kitty turned back to Georgiana.

"Very well, Georgiana. What would you have me do?"

"Just be my chaperone and tell everyone that we are going to the park together—and mention nothing about Jason."

"Georgiana, look at me and tell me the truth. Is this man truly worth it?"

"Yes, I cannot help but think so."

"We shall get into all sorts of trouble when this is discovered, and we all get caught."

"You have been in trouble before."

"And doing so again does not suit my pallet."

"Yet you will do this, for me."

"We are friends. Therefore, of course I will."

༄༅།

Kitty and Georgiana announced that they were going on a trip to the park where they had hopes of enjoying their small company.

This did not get taken amiss, and they took the carriage, driven by Nicholson and another coachman, and traveled to the park. Immediately as they arrived, Georgiana climbed down from the carriage, and Kitty had to move fast to keep up with her and signal to Nicholson that it was again his time to escort her as she followed behind Georgiana.

Very soon upon them entering the park, Jason appeared, carrying a bouquet of roses.

"Miss Darcy," he began, "you look even more beautiful during the daytime."

"Thank you, Jason." Georgiana smiled. "You brought me flowers?"

"I wanted to do this properly," he said, "And roses seemed to be worthy of you. Unless they are not enough."

"They are exquisite," Georgiana said, taking the flowers, then she noticed his eyes move past her and rest on Kitty and Nicholson, who was a little further behind.

"Forgive me, Jason, but I could not come without a chaperone."

"I understand," he said. "I am just going to have to be careful of what I say."

"No, you shall not," Kitty said, looking at the park, but not at them. "Good day, Mr. Friend. I am Kitty Fitzwilliam, and I will do everything in my power to act as if I am not present. You are perfectly allowed to forget that I am here, yet mark my words, I still am a chaperone. So, if you do anything that is inappropriate or abusive, then I must warn you that I am stronger than I look, and our coachman Nicholson is perhaps stronger than you."

"Thank you, Mrs. Fitzwilliam." Jason smiled. "And I am pleased to meet you."

"Meet who? Remember, I am not here."

Jason and Georgiana looked between each other and smiled.

"I like her." Jason laughed.

"I knew that you would."

They both continued to walk on while Kitty remained a few feet behind and was joined by Nicholson.

"Mrs. Fitzwilliam," Nicholson said.

"Yes, Nicholson?"

"Mr. Darcy and Colonel Fitzwilliam are not aware of this meeting, are they?"

"No, they are not."

"Yet, I fear they shall find out inevitably."

"Oh, I know they will find out."

"Then we shall get into trouble."

"I know that we shall get into trouble."

"Yet, you are resigned to this?"

"Nicholson, I see what you are feeling, yet there comes a time when one has to accept getting into trouble for family."

"Oh..."

"And if you are worried about losing your post and position when this all comes tumbling down around us, do not fear. Georgiana will simply say that she blackmailed you into serving us in this manner."

"Oh! Thank you, Mrs. Fitzwilliam."

"You are very welcome, Nicholson. You are very welcome."

They both walked on, allowing a small enough distance in between themselves and the secretive couple.

As they walked on, Georgiana and Jason did not know what to

say at first, for it had been the first time that they had a chance to speak in daylight.

"Thank you for the flowers," Georgiana began, "They are lovely."

"I am glad that you liked them."

"Yet they look expensive."

"Do not worry." He smiled, "It was no trouble."

"Yet I am sorry for all this secrecy. My family is simply trying to protect me."

"I understand. Though I would very much look forward to the idea of walking with you without fear of us breaking some rule."

"Yes, it does feel unnecessarily scandalous—for it should not be scandalous at all. I suppose that is the double-edged sword of wealth. To be wealthy is to have liberty of one kind but are also severely restricted. At least we women are."

"Yes, it is hard that you all have so many regulations to tie you down."

"Yes, it is grossly unfair. And Jason?"

"Yes?"

"Did you really mean it when you mentioned that women should have proper representation in politics?"

"Yes, I did."

"Before I heard you speak of it, no man I ever met in my social circles ever mentioned it. It was mostly as if none of them wished to."

"Have you no family to speak of it with?"

"I tried to. Jason—they did not want to listen. They have quite let me down in that way. I thought better of them than that."

"I understand your frustration, yet when it comes to men who have never thought of the idea, it is hard for them to reconcile with it at first. New ideas frighten people, even the ones who we expected to be made of stronger parts."

"Yes, but I cannot help but see them differently. And Jason, you were not born hearing of such noble principles and beliefs, were you?"

"I see your point. No, I was not."

"Precisely. Yet you still think on these things. Just because my brother and cousin did not ever hear talk of the topic does not excuse them entirely, for why did they not ever think on the matter themselves? Was it content for them to never do so? Were they ignorant of the injustice? Or did they choose not to pay attention?"

"It is a frightening thing, is it not? That no matter what reason a person has for turning away from an injustice, the reason will not be sufficient enough to exonerate them from allowing to remain ignorant. For it is too often the way it is with the Trade. Many believe that because they were born and raised with the belief that it is a necessary and natural system, that they are opposed to the Abolition movement. How many a time a man has turned his head and chooses not to see that it is wrong for a people to not be free?"

"Yes, that is such a tragedy."

"Yet I confess, Georgiana, I am amazed, for you are the first woman that I have ever met who wished to speak of social upheaval as opposed to me reading you poetry."

"Oh, that would put pain to it! Who at first devised the power of poetry in driving away love?"

"I thought that poetry was the food of love."

"Of a fine stout love it may, but if it is a weak inclination, then I am sure one poor sonnet will kill it stone dead."

"Then what do you recommend, to encourage affection?"

"Dancing," Georgiana replied. "Even if one's partner is a street speaker."

They both laughed at that.

"Yet to be proper," Georgiana continued, "and allow us to speak of things that young lovers ought to speak of. Then might I begin with a compliment? You look as if you would be a fine dancer, Jason."

"I want to believe so, for I do love the amusement of dancing actually. It is very strange, yet I have never understood why other men have such a distaste for it. What do they have to groan about?"

"My brother hates dancing."

"You speak of your brother often."

"Oh, forgive me, it is just that he has been my whole life practically. He has saved me in many ways and limited me in others. Yet one thing is certain—I owe him much."

"And he is Mr. Darcy of Pemberley?"

"Yes but...wait, I do not believe that I told you that he was the master of Pemberley."

"You did not have to. I know the estate too well. When I lived in England, I actually lived in Kent for a time. I never met any of you Darcys, but we heard of you often."

"Did you?"

"Yes, you are a popular family. With a legacy of history behind you, do you not?"

"Yes, our greatest ancestor was Prince Henry D'Arcy of France in the 16th century, during the French Renaissance."

"And how does that make you feel? Being descended from royalty."

"It feels daunting. Coming from such a powerful legacy, what am I in the shadow of it?"

"You are much, Georgiana. Believe me. You are much."

Jason then began to chuckle.

"And what is it? Why do you laugh, Jason?"

"I laugh for that particular reason. When hearing of your family for so long, and knowing that you came from such an incredible ancestry, I never would have thought that I would get the chance to woo one of you."

"And how does that make you feel?"

"Daunted," Jason grinned bashfully, "For I do not believe I could ever deserve you."

"Yes, you could. I acknowledge that we are living in a dream now but let us not think on the reality this moment. And let us not talk of me just now. Let me know more of you, Jason. Or let me know about all that New York has to offer, and your experiences here."

"I can tell you always more of my adventures in America than my upbringing in England. My upbringing was actually quite simple, boring and without any real joy. I was born and raised mostly in Surrey, had a modest education that was good enough. Yet I had no real talents except for at talking, as you see. I was not born brilliant or special—I was only born passionate. Then I came to New York, and that was where the adventure began."

"You like it here more."

"Definitely not so. I like it equally to being at home, no more and no less. Yet being an Englishman in America after the Revolution has been gone and ended decades ago is actually much easier than you think. It is only this blasted war now that has gotten in our way. Yet before it, it was quite a lovely situation to be in. And did you know that New York City served as the capital of the United States from 1785 to 1790? It was a city that played a very active part for the rebellion, and after the Revolutionary War ended, the city recovered quickly, and by 1810, last year, it had become America's most important port for trade. Also, this year, infrastructural improvements have been made. The Commissioner's Plan has taken effect, where it established an orderly grid of streets and avenues for the undeveloped parts of Manhattan. They are north of Houston Street."

"You really do like this city, don't you?"

"I cannot help it, for it is full of life. It seems as if it is a city that never sleeps fully, for there is always something or someone on the move. Mark my words, someday, that is what shall be said of it."

"Well, it reminds me of London a bit."

"It many ways, they are similar."

"Before we came here, we came from Philadelphia, and I quite liked it as well."

"Oh, I have been there as well, and I liked it also. I had some blinds made there for me."

"Window blinds?"

"Yes, there was an upholsterer who was known for making Venetian Blinds for windows. I saw her model that she had for them, and I commissioned her to make me a pair for my parlor. My parlor is ghastly, but the blinds still look brilliant. What is most amusing is that she is a woman who claims to have sewn the first American flag."

"What?" Georgiana blurted out.

"Yes, I heard the story from one of her children who she told it to, and she is of the right age and personality for it. To have made it requires having some spunk to her—she eloped with her first husband."

"Did she? The woman who sewed the first American Flag eloped with her husband?"

"Yes, it truly brings a whole new light to some things that society looks down upon, does it not? Her name is now Betsy Claypoole, but when she eloped and also made the flag, she was known as Betsy Ross. Yet do not tax yourself on remembering her name. The poor woman shall never gain any fame or renown for her history."

"Betsy...was that short for something?"

"Yes...Elizabeth."

"That is my sister-in-law's name."

"Good name."

"And it is still a good story," Georgiana said, feeling a great comfort in knowing that her mistake in eloping with Wickham had been once done by a woman who made a national emblem. It simply made her feel...not alone.

"Yes, it is a good story."

Jason and Georgiana walked on, talking of England, America, and other topics, which once they exhausted, they began to speak of places they wished to see. Jason wanted to see Spain, for he heard the landscape was lovely, and Georgiana had wanted to see Greece and Turkey, for she had always had a secret love for ancient Greek Mythology and the land that it sprang from.

After an hour, however, Kitty came forward and announced that it was time to depart. Jason and Georgiana held hands and Jason quickly kissed her on the cheek and walked them back to their carriage. After they entered the carriage, they all drove off while Jason watched them leave.

When she could no longer see him, Georgiana turned back to Kitty, who looked obstinate.

"Georgiana," she said, "We are very much going to get into trouble."

"I know! Is it not hilarious?"

"No, it is not hilarious."

"This is coming from the woman who took a horse ride at night to Aginfield."

"Oh, shut it."

"No, you shut it."

"No, you shut it"

"No, you shut it."

Outside, as they rode on, Nicholson sat next to the driver and they both looked at one another, rolling their eyes, for they wished that both women would not put them through this again.

And of course, the next day, the two women were off once more, and they were putting Nicholson and the coachman through their adventures again.

They arrived back in the park, Jason was waiting, and he met Georgiana with eagerness. Kitty remained behind again, walking behind them with Nicholson. She was certain that Jason was harmless, yet she still felt it correct to do her duty and while the couple talked, Kitty analyzed them.

It was clear that there was a great affection on both sides and that they enjoyed each other's conversation but were also comfortable when it came to being silent around one another. Kitty wanted to believe that he was not a fortune hunter. Yet even though he appeared sincere, it was impossible to be sure.

Ahead, Jason and Georgiana walked and began to speak of Greece, Turkey, and Spain, when Jason made the mistake of beginning to hold Georgiana's hand.

"Oh, dear me, I am sorry."

"It is fine," Georgiana said, "There is no one else around us, besides my chaperones, and therefore it is not scandalous. Besides, we have done worse, have we not?"

"Yes," he said and grinnedwickedly. "And I am not ashamed to admit that. I do so like holding your hand."

"I like it as well."

"Release my sister's hand this instant!"

Kitty, Georgiana, and Nicholson froze as they all turned, and Mr. Darcy was stomping across the grass and glaring down at them. "Release her, or I shall run you through, sir!"

Behind Mr. Darcy, Henry Darcy, and Colonel Fitzwilliam appeared, followed by Mr. Eastbourne.

"Fitzwilliam," Georgiana rushed out, "I am so sorry, but please let me explain."

"Kitty!" Colonel Fitzwilliam cried, "what is the meaning of this? And how dare you!"

"I am sorry, Richard," she cried, "I was just trying to be there for Georgiana, and you must not blame Nicholson, for he was just following orders."

"And you!" Mr. Darcy bore down on Kitty. "Are you content to always be at the center of controversy in this family, Kitty! I am at my wits' end."

"Neither of you blame her!" Georgiana exclaimed. "I blackmailed her into coming, and she was incessant on having Nicholson join us as a guard to protect us. Neither of them is to blame. Only I am so."

"And she is not alone," Jason said. "This scheme was of my devising, I took advantage of your sister's affection for me and exerted my influence—Kitty, Georgiana and all the rest among us are blameless. Therefore, cast your wrath upon which it is due. I am Jason Friend, and I am to blame."

"Pardon?" Mr. Eastbourne interrupted. "What did you say your name was?"

"My name is Jason Friend, and I—"

"You are lying...it cannot be..."

Jason looked at Georgiana and he saw a look of disbelief in her eyes. He had felt remorse for lying, yet now she would be thinking the worst of him—and she was.

"Your name is not Jason Friend?" she whispered, eyeing him dubiously.

"I am Jason and sir you must be—"

"You are not, sir!" Mr. Eastbourne said. "And why are you wearing those rags, for you are of higher birth."

All in the crowd turned to Mr. Eastbourne.

"Eastbourne?" Henry Darcy began, "what do you mean when you—"

"I know your face, sir," Mr. Eastbourne continued on, "Why are you demeaning yourself?"

Jason looked down at his feet, unable to lie.

"It is necessary," he said finally, "if you will but hear my excuse."

"Yes," Mr. Eastbourne said, irate. "For an explanation is surely due."

"What are you speaking of Mr. Eastbourne?" Georgiana cried.

"Yes, what do you speak of?" Colonel Fitzwilliam reiterated, confused. Mr. Eastbourne looked around and noticed all the men looking at him with puzzlement.

"Am I the only one who sees it?"

"What do you see?"

"Oh, well, I have been paying closer attention to the trial for a longer timeframe, when you had only seen it once."

"For God sakes, spit it out Mr. Eastbourne!" Mr. Darcy roared.

"That this is the attorney who argued the Trekenna trial, in hopes of liberating the captured Africans. This is Jason Whitfield, of the Whitfield family in England."

All eyes turned to Jason, who avoided their gaze and then gathered the courage to look upon Georgiana.

"I did not mean to deceive you," he began. "I had wished to tell you myself, yet I did not know how to confess it. And please understand, you were the first woman who liked me for who I was —and not from what station I had in life. Not many women of the ton would ever do that."

"Then..." Georgiana stuttered, "I do not understand."

Jason turned to Mr. Darcy, who was over a foot taller than him, it seemed and looked boldly in his eyes.

"Mr. Darcy, I know that I have not the right to ask anything of you, but I must. Please, let us not quarrel or rage under the spying eyes of the whole world right now where all can look on and laugh at us. But rather, let me speak to you in the confines of Arruin, where I can explain my situation, and you may judge me if you may."

Mr. Darcy looked around at everyone and then forced himself to acknowledge that to let their business continue to be displayed in a public place was bad form indeed.

"Very well," he hissed. "You shall sit in my carriage, but mark my words, while we travel, you shall adhere to the saying 'as silent as the grave'. For if you dare attempt to speak to me, I shall hurl you out of the carriage, while it is moving."

"Fair enough."

"Very well." Darcy turned to Georgiana and looked at her coldly. "I shall not deny that you have disappointed me terribly, Georgiana, and I am sorry for it. Now you, Kitty, Colonel Fitzwilliam, and Henry shall sit in your carriage while *Mr. Whitfield* here, Mr. Eastbourne and I journey in the other."

Georgiana agreed quietly, then they all entered the carriages and were off to Arruin.

"Georgiana," Colonel Fitzwilliam said, "did you really blackmail Kitty?"

"Yes, I did."

"I never knew you had that in you."

"Well, unfortunately I did."

Colonel Fitzwilliam turned to Kitty.

"Amazing how when my aunt said that you Bennets would be a bad influence on us, it proved to be the other way around. For we keep placing you in the worst possible situations, do we not?"

"Yes, it is ironic." Kitty groaned, "And do not ever get angry at me without finding out the situation first again, mark my words, Richard."

"Yes, dear. I was hoping you were not going to get mad at me for that."

"Well, I am."

"Yes...I am in trouble, aren't I?"

"Possibly."

The carriage drove on as they bickered, yet Georgiana took no heed to them.

All she could think of was Jason and how he had lied to her. Yet the lie was not a harmful one, it appeared. If anything, it was counter-nefarious. If all proved true, then he would be a man who lied about being worse off than he was, rather than better.

Yet why so? What man lies about being of low birth when it proves to not be so? However, the answer could very well have been in what he confessed. He had said that women never looked at him for what he was, therefore, he pretended to be of lower birth to avoid that. Yet that excuse seemed to be such a flimsy one that she felt there had to be more intentions behind his deception.

Also, there was the fact that he was deceptive. He had, in all essentials, lied to her about who he really was, which meant that he could not be trusted fully. Could he be another Wickham in the end? The idea of it frightened her immensely. And the sudden change of her attitude toward him were not the only factors that allowed her to determine that when all that is right turns into all that is wrong, it can happen suddenly and at the blink of an eye.

Now she did not know what to believe.

Or who to trust.

29

MANY PERSPECTIVES UNFOLDING
IN THE END

Upon returning to Arruin, Georgiana saw why no women accompanied the men in retrieving her. They were all on an outing in the dress shops in the heart of the city. They were escorted by Mr. Bingley, who had the most patience with that sort of thing.

"How long will it be till they return?" Kitty asked Richard when they stepped down from the carriages.

"They are due back in an hour. Yet knowing Darcy, he shall have Jason remain here in order to meet him."

"He would do that, do you think?" Georgiana asked, apprehensive.

"Oh yes, he would have them all know what he looks like, so that they can be wary of him."

"He is not dangerous," Georgiana argued, "Just a liar."

Richard eyed Georgiana with caution.

"Your faith in him is shaken?"

"Of course it is. He lied to me."

Jason gave a fleeting look at her before he followed Mr. Darcy and Henry Darcy into the house, with Mr. Eastbourne following behind him.

"Georgiana," Richard said softly, "while it is strange that I am defending him, his deception seems to have more intent behind it than him just being false. Hear his explanation first before you forsake him."

"Oh, I did not mean to imply that I was going to forsake him. I unfortunately am just shaken by it all."

Richard eyed her once more.

"One thing I can see for sure...he is not Wickham. Therefore, do not fear it."

"Oh, now you get warm-hearted!" Kitty groaned quietly, still bitter with him.

"You are going to be angry with me for some time, aren't you?" Richard asked uneasily.

"Oh, Colonel Fitzwilliam, I have not even begun." With that, Kitty walked ahead and entered the house, leaving her husband behind to walk beside his cousin.

"I have caused a rift between you both." Georgiana sighed. "I did not mean to. I just needed an accomplice, so I used all the times she sacrificed her good name and ours to be with you."

"You...you did?"

"Yes, and now she has just seen how quickly you will wield on her, even though she risked much for you. And how you let my brother insult her unjustly."

Richard looked down, feeling heartily ashamed of himself.

"If you tell me not to forsake Jason, Richard, then do not ever forsake Kitty so quickly as to lash out at her without asking her to explain first. And remember all that she was willing to give up to marry you, and all the comforts that she also sacrificed to do so."

Georgiana walked forward as well and entered Arruin alone. Seeing her cousin wield on Kitty so quickly as he did filled her spirit with guilt. For she did not wish to be the source of discomfort and disquiet between two who were so akin in nature—yet now she could not help but find it essential that their love had been tested.

She feared that Kitty would not see it that way and might look coldly on her. So, she immediately went to find her. However, now that Richard knew he had it in his nature to verbally begin to berate his wife in so public an area without knowing the reason behind her actions, he could begin to rectify it.

Before Georgiana could make her apology to Kitty, she was ushered into the main study, where her brother stood with Henry Darcy and Mr. Eastbourne. Georgiana immediately saw how Jason was greatly outnumbered with three men who were much taller than himself looking down upon him, and therefore, it must feel daunting to him.

With a desire to not have him feel alone, or forsaken as Richard had informed her, she walked up to Jason and stood beside him.

"Brother," she began, "I know you're angry with me, yet please hear us out before you pass judgment."

"I have no choice, apparently," he hissed.

"And also mind your temper."

"Georgiana..."

"Fitz, who is perfect in this world? Tell me truly, whoever is? Not me, not Henry Darcy here, and perhaps not even you, Mr. Eastbourne. Then do not place an immediate judgment upon us before all the facts are revealed."

"Wisely spoken, Georgiana," Jason smiled.

"And you sir," Georgiana said firmly, "also owe me a truth, do you not?"

Jason blushed, guilty. "Yes, I do."

"Very well." Georgiana turned to her brother. "Please let him begin, for I wish to hear and understand it all."

Darcy nodded curtly so Georgiana sat down, and Jason Whitfield began his tale.

"The Whitfield family have been attorneys and judges for the last five generations," Jason began. "I was born into my lineage and position. Yet I am a younger son of a family of three sons. I am the youngest, but one. My father left me an inheritance, yes, but because I was not the heir to the family estate, I was allowed the freedom to travel to America, which I had done four years ago. I became one of the main attorneys here in New York. I steadily grew a disgust for how politics was run in both countries, between voting not being granted to all, yet also anger that the Trade had not been abolished in both Britain and the United States. I had joined some local abolitionist groups, yet it was not a very well-looked on interest and I knew that I would receive much defamation of character if I took a stand—call it a cowardly thing to do, yet it was so. Out of a desire to fight against an injustice still, I decided to gather a new identity: Jason Friend. Under that name, I would come across as an obscure street speaker without a penny to his name, but with a passion for preaching."

Jason turned to Georgiana, bashful.

"That is why you first saw me on the streets. I was wishing to make people question all that they do—and make them awaken to the fact that they let too much injustice against different cultures and women remain—when it should not be so."

Georgiana looked at her brother, who looked down at these words.

"And since you had seen me in my other identity, I did not know how to reconcile with you what I really was."

Jason turned back to the three men and continued.

"I wished to tell the truth, yet I never could think of the correct time. However, even if I did wish to confront it, there were other factors."

"Such as?" Darcy urged.

"I liked the way that Georgiana looked at me. She only saw me. She did not see my family, my profession, or my inheritance. She only saw me—and that was enough for the moment. And lastly, I wished to protect her."

"How is meeting my sister in secret protecting her?"

"Sir, those of us who wish for all to obtain liberty here, no matter their race or gender, are not looked on highly. I had to create a whole new identity to protect myself. What if I did not do so? And then afterwards, what if I began to court your sister publicly? People would shun her, simply for associating with me. They might even berate and attack her and your family. I changed my name to protect my life here, so why would I endanger your peace, names or even your very persons? Or worst of all, if Georgiana were to be shunned by any while she was here, all for associating with me, then I could not bear losing her all because of the pressures of the people. The world is rigid, you know this. And it bears down on those who attempt to change it. Well, I wish to change it, yet I do not wish to make social casualties along the way."

Every word he spoke, by way of an explanation, hurt Georgiana to the quick. While there was always the chance that Jason was not speaking the truth, it seemed too much to be otherwise, and she felt it all most keenly. Jason was correct—the world did bear down on those who dared to change it, even though it needed to alter terribly.

Darcy then turned to his sister, placing his elbows on the desk, and resting his chin on his fists.

"Well, Georgiana, since this affects you most, what do you have to say?"

"You are asking my opinion?"

"Yes, for this is your life," he said gently. Georgiana smiled slightly, found her voice again, and continued on.

"Brother, I know you must think me foolish and easily led by romantic notions, yet it is not so. It is true that I do feel for Jason very much, yet I was also drawn to him by his desire to open the eyes of those around him. And he reminds me that I have a voice. And I have the right to be heard."

Darcy looked down at the desk, wondering if he had always listened to Georgiana as he ought. He believed that he had in the past, yet now he was not so certain. Did he only listen when she said what aligned with his own sentiments—and did he ever encourage serious matters to be discussed if it caused him discomfort? Now he did not know. And it frightened him.

Looking between his sister and a man who had begun to find his way within her heart, Darcy thought of what to do before he continued onward.

"Very well. I cannot say that I approve of any of this. Yet I also know the repercussions of facing the world and being exposed to its bad opinion—and it is hard to face. Yet if you wish to court my sister in any way, Mr. Whitfield, then you had better come here tomorrow in more formal attire, like the gentleman that you claim to be, and be proper."

"I can do that, sir."

"And if you meet with her in secret one more time, then you shall be driven from this house and from her company permanently."

Jason nodded diplomatically.

"We shall let you both say farewell to one another," Darcy continued. "I shall see you to the gate, for you will not be alone together. And Mr. Whitfield?"

"Yes, Mr. Darcy?"

"Do not ever lie to my sister again. And never lie to me."

"Yes sir, though remember, I am still an attorney—and sometimes there is nothing for it."

"Oh, there is always something for it. Never lie to me—or her."

"Sir, I never shall lie again."

"Very good."

After Georgiana saw Jason to the gate, he promised her that he would return the next day and she knew him to speak true. Darcy observed them the whole while and his presence was enough of an intimidation to not allow Jason to take liberties.

Once Jason had left, Georgiana turned to her brother.

"Fitz?"

"Yes."

"I know that you are still angry with me, yet I must say something."

"What?"

"I am proud of you now."

Darcy blinked and then looked down at his feet. "Oh, I..."

She walked up to him, kissed his cheek, and walked into the house.

First, she went to Kitty and apologized to her for putting herself in that situation. Kitty was very forgiving, for she understood her sister-in-law's state of mind and emotions when she had done so. Richard still looked ashamed in the presence of his wife, yet that was how it should have been.

After she had made amends on that score, Georgiana had only one last thing.

She went to the servants' quarters in the house, and she was not surprised to find Jefferson, Mr. Darcy's valet, sharing some intimate words with a maid. Jefferson was not the most handsome of men, but he had a way about him that was alluring. And Georgiana had always known that if one needed him, she could always find him dwelling among the servants. Whether it was to woo one, or if it was to learn information about someone's whereabouts—it was Jefferson who could always be relied on for knowing everything that was going on.

"Miss Darcy," he said, when she found him sitting with the maid and kissing her hand. The servant woman left immediately, feeling embarrassed, and Jefferson stood up and bowed crisply.

"Forgive me, you caught me unprepared."

"Yes," Georgiana said, "I know the feeling."

She entered and sat down on a stool near the hearth.

"So," he began, "I did not ever think to find you in the servant's quarters. What would you need of me?"

"It bothered me," she began, "when I was returning with my brother to Arruin after we had been caught in the park. I wondered how we could have been discovered. For my brother did not just happen to be there, but was there with purpose and intent. In other words, he was told what I had committed myself to, but not by any who I confided in. No. He would only have been told by someone who knew that I had been meeting with Jason in secret before. By someone who makes it a habit to know everything that is of import to my family. Someone like you, Jefferson."

Jefferson looked down and then looked up again slowly.

"Well, Mrs. Darcy, you know my nature, and it is one that does not lie, unless I have something to protect."

"How long had you known that I was secretly meeting Jason Friend?"

"Since the first night that he came to see you."

"Truly?"

"Yes. Before I retire for the evening, I always take a turn around the grounds of wherever my employers dwell."

"You've always done that?"

"Yes."

"That sounds...lonely."

"Yes, Miss Darcy. It is the loneliest profession of all... my own. Yet it is necessary."

"Then, if you had always known, why did you not tell my brother earlier?"

"Because I could tell that he was not dangerous." He smiled gently. "And he made you happy."

"You cared about my happiness?"

"Miss Darcy, ever since Mr. Wickham pulled such a deception upon you, you have had very little opportunities of finding joy in being in the company of men. I know that you feel a distrust for us, or at least an apprehension, don't you?"

"Yes," she whispered, "I suppose that I do."

"I know. It is only natural. This Jason made you happy. And that meant much to you, I could see."

"That was very kind. Yet how did you know that he was not dangerous?"

"Oh, because I always knew who he was."

"You did?"

"Yes, I saw him at the court with the rest of the gentlemen and while he looks different without the attorney wig, I still was able to see the resemblance. A man who had that much to risk would not be romancing a woman of your birth and rank, only to abuse her. Therefore, I knew he was harmless."

"Jefferson, while your powers of being omniscient is frightening sometimes...thank you. For everything."

"You are welcome."

"I never fully understood you. Yet between all these new discoveries of everyone that I am learning this day and the many perspectives unfolding in the end, I am not afraid to know more."

"You have never cared to be ignorant of things, Miss Darcy. That is always a wonderful thing. Now enjoy his coming tomorrow and I hope it all goes well."

"You already know about Jason coming tomorrow?"

"Of course, I do."

"Thank you, Jefferson. Truly."

"And as I said, you are always welcome."

Georgiana smiled and left the room.

❧ 30 ❧

THE MAN BEHIND THE MYSTERY

"All this occurred while we were away?" I asked Darcy, incredulous. He had just informed me of all that had occurred while we were on our outing and I was still out of sorts, surprised by all the news.

"I can scarce believe it!" I gasped. "She had been seeing him all this while, the man from the street?"

"Yes."

"And it turns out that he not only was not a ragged beggar, but an attorney from a well-established family and was the same solicitor who represented the enslaved cargo on the Trekenna."

"Yes."

"Then you had seen him before?"

"I could not make the connection. Between those awful wigs that attorneys wear in the courtroom to the distance we were from the lower level—for our seat was in the balcony—he appears different close up."

"It is so unlike anything that one ever hears, is all. It feels more as if it were something that would occur in a Comedy of Errors on the stage."

"Indeed, we ought not to tell the Philadelphian Darcys about this, or they might tell their thespian friends, and they might transform this situation into a play."

"I would not put it past anyone to do so. Yet, Darcy," I said. "How did you respond when you heard all this? How did you treat the man?"

"I was angry to say the least."

"I am sure you were. Yet while Georgiana appears to be a delicate thing, we have to learn that she is not in full and is grown up. Finding her voice even. I daresay that it was her turn to want her own adventure. For she has seen all of us undergo ours."

"He shall come tomorrow, this Jason Whitfield."

"Would you like me to speak to Georgiana as well?"

"No, as you said, she is now grown. And for the moment, she will want to keep her own counsel. And it is high time that I let her."

"Yes, she is grown. It is just hard for you to naturally see her as so."

"It is. Yet if you would do me the favor of speaking with her after you have met this man, then that would be a great comfort."

"Well then," I replied, "I best prepare myself for this strange hero who walked right off the stage and into reality."

❧

The next day came and Georgiana waited in anticipation while we all sat with her. We all spoke of simple matters, however, she was clearly distracted until we heard a carriage arrive. Georgiana was the first to stand upon hearing it. We exited the house and stood there as the footman opened the carriage and the man I remembered from the street, stepped down—only he was greatly altered. Yes, he was short and slight in build, but he was a very confident man. His face was clean, his clothes fit him well, and he looked distinguished.

"Clothing may not make the man," I whispered to Jane, "yet it can help."

"Jason!" Georgiana cried, moving forward, and standing next to Jason who, when he dismounted, he immediately made a movement to embrace her. But he was able to stop himself in time as the eyes of all were upon him.

"Unbelievable!" Caroline Bingley hissed to Miriam, yet I was close enough to hear. "Georgiana is forgetting herself completely and acting like a wild animal. She calls him by his first name."

"Hush, Caroline," Miriam reprimanded.

Have I not said that I detested Caroline Bingley? I believe that I have. Yet I shall say it once more—I detest her.

Accosting us while encouraged by Georgiana, Mr. Jason Whitfield took off his hat and bowed.

"Mr. Whitfield," Darcy said, "welcome back to Arruin, and introductions must be made. You have met the men in company, yet here is my wife, Mrs. Elizabeth Darcy, her sister Mrs. Fitzwilliam you have met as well, yet these are her other sisters Miss Jane Bennet, and Mrs. Lydia Darcy. Also, this is Mr. Charles Bingley with his wife Mrs. Miriam Bingley and his sister, Miss Caroline Bingley."

We all bowed or curtsied while Jason bowed his head.

"I am humbled," Jason Whitfield said with ease, "And am very pleased to make your acquaintances."

"You are most welcome," I said, "And I must say, with your gift for articulation and speech, I find myself to be a simpleton for not suspecting you to be given the gift of the greatest educations before."

"Oh, my ragged appearance was a very good distraction from my formal tongue," he said, chuckling. We all laughed with him.

"Well then," Mr. Darcy said, "let us all go inside where there are refreshments, and we can get better acquainted with our guest."

"Excellent notion, my dear," I confirmed. We all entered the sitting room and Mrs. Hale served us all tea. When we sat in a standard formation, I looked between Georgiana and Mr. Whitfield, and I felt as if we all were intruding. They shared a great connection when they looked on one another and it could not be denied to any who looked upon them.

"Well," Jane said first, "Mr. Whitfield, I have been told that you were the attorney for the Trekenna Trial."

"You do me a great honor in taking a note on my history," he began, "yet as the main counselor of the trial, I not only was Miss Bennet, yet *am*."

"Yet we were told that the trial had ended, and the defense had won," Miriam commented.

"They did. Yet the abolition movement here and in Philadelphia have received news of the trial's outcome and they have sent petitions to the judiciaries, who have allowed us to make a re-appeal and have the case re-opened. I have a little over a month's time to form another solid case, for that will be the date of the trial."

"So near to Christmas?"

"That is all that can be done for it. Yet if I do not find victory this time, then all will be lost."

"And the cargo will be forced into the Trade," Lydia said, "that is awful."

"And it must not happen. We lose too many battles in the liberation for all people in this world. And we cannot afford to lose another one."

"And that is precisely why this country is so forlorn!" Caroline scoffed. "To descend to such a terrible act as the trade is monstrous."

"You forget that we did it as well in our country for a long time," Jason said.

"And we have abolished it."

"No, we haven't fully. Every country is flawed. In truth, Miss Bingley, it is our nation's political intent on the Impressment, that has led to it being so hard for the jury to take our evidence as valid. All of our witness accounts were European ones, yet it is hard for them to care for it when those accounts are committing atrocities as well."

"You berate you own country, sir?"

"No, I merely tell the truth. We all have our certain prides and prejudices that make us different but equal in both countries."

"Then pray tell me," I said, wishing to change the subject—not because I was not fascinated, for I was and I truly did wish to know the particulars of the trial—yet because I feared that Caroline would do or say something to offend Jason Whitfield, and I did not wish for him to leave feeling slighted by us. And I did not wish for Georgiana to be so embarrassed. "Where did you receive your education, and do you find pleasure in being an attorney?"

"My enjoyment varies from case to case, and those who I defend. Yet it never ceases to be interesting, whether we attorneys are on the right or wrong side."

"Do you fear ever being on the wrong side?"

"Yes, I do."

"That must be frightening."

"It is quite daunting, yet I still have hope."

"Then that is very well."

"Thank you, Mrs. Darcy. Yet I have received my education at Oxford."

"Oh, Mr. Darcy received his education there as well," I said, turning to my husband.

"Oh, did you, Mr. Darcy?" Mr. Whitfield said. "What were your studies mostly in."

"I preferred history," Darcy said, "be it general or topical. Yet I also specified in other languages, consisting of Latin, Italian, Spanish and French."

"You focused on much."

"Yes, I wished to focus on learning German as well, however I had no talent for speaking it, for some reason."

"No one can obtain all, sir, and four languages is a large accomplishment enough. I only learned Spanish and Latin myself."

"Thank you, sir."

Mr. Whitfield proceeded to speak to all of us in turn and he had much to say yet understood moderation of conversation. Never speaking too much or too little. It was a hard skill to learn or naturally possess, yet he did obtain it. He also proved to be charming and knew how to engage us all, while also confronting his double life that was developed out of survival. By the end of his visit, it was impossible to not warm to him. For he was a good sort of man, clearly—and he never wished to be far from Georgiana as well.

Eventually, his visit drew to an end, and we all saw him to his carriage. He gave us all a hearty farewell, while also requesting to visit on the morrow, to spend some time with Georgiana. His request was accepted, and Georgiana watched as his carriage rolled away.

We all entered, sat down to dinner and we spoke of other matters, such as taking a night at the theatre. Yet when all was ended and we readied to bed, I took that as the opportunity to visit Georgiana, so that we at last could have our sisterly communion and discuss all that she was feeling.

I knocked on her door and told her that it was I who had come.

"Come in, Elizabeth," she said. "I am fully dressed."

I entered and Georgiana was sitting on her bed, writing in a journal.

"Hello, Georgiana."

"Hello, I know why you have come," she said, still looking down at her journal.

"I did not come to lecture you," I began. Hearing my declaration, she looked up and closed her journal.

"You do not?"

"Know I do not. While I would recommend caution in the future, and to never entertain meeting men in the garden at night again, I still will not lecture you."

"I was protected by a gate."

"Even gates cannot keep out all dangers. Georgiana, all I ask you is to promise me that you shall be more careful in the future."

"Lizzy, I promise I will never put myself in danger."

"Thank you. Yet as for this man, this Jason Whitfield... you seem to adore him."

"Lizzy, I do."

"And he does with you, that much is apparent."

"You believe so. Then I am not seeing what is not there?"

"No, you are not. This is very much there, and it is plain. How do you feel when you are with him?"

"Like I am walking on air, or clouds. It all sounds foolish, yet it is so."

"Love can have that effect."

"You will not tell me that I am being foolish for falling in love so quickly, then?"

"I fell in love with your brother even faster, therefore I understand how you might feel so. Yet I want you to promise me or promise yourself, that you shall give this love of yours time. You shall see if it is genuine if you court him for months and if it is as powerful as you wish it to be. If the two of you are meant for one another, then you will then know that it is meant to be so. For it is very easy to mistake infatuation for love. In short, I do not want you to commit yourself and then be in a loveless marriage because you leapt into a romance rather than looked at it first."

"How many months should I wait?"

"Two months at the least."

"I see your reasoning. Yet if he makes me an offer sooner, I cannot guarantee that I shall remain obstinate."

"I know, yet I still must caution you. However, with all my warnings, Georgiana, he seems like a good man, and I am happy for you. As well as proud at how your mind has grown."

Georgiana then stood up, walked over to me, and embraced me.

"Thank you, Lizzy. Thank you."

"You are welcome," I replied, embracing her as well.

After I had spent time with her, I retired to my bedroom, where Darcy was waiting for me, wearing only his breeches and shirt.

"How did your conversation with Georgiana proceed?"

"To my satisfaction. Though I am not certain for yours."

"How so?"

"Fitzwilliam, she loves him, and this is a most complex sort. She will not recover so easily if it does not end in the way she desires it to. Yet she is strong and will recover from it in whichever way."

"I do not know what to feel."

"I know you do not. And there is no proper answer of how you should."

"Yet now that you have met him, what do you think of Mr. Whitfield?"

"Well, now that I know the man behind the mystery, I am not frightened at all. For his person is of a familiar kind. He is the sort that younger sisters of older brothers fall in love with."

"Do not joke now, Lizzy."

"Oh, but I must. I must."

31

A SCHEME MEANT TO SAVE MANY

The next day, Mr. Darcy sat in the study in Arruin, seeing to a set of letters that Jefferson organized for him, when there was a knock on the door.

"Come in," he said, then the door opened, and Georgiana entered.

"Georgiana..."

"Fitz, forgive me for intruding."

"Not at all, not at all. I suppose that we needed to speak soon anyhow."

"Yes," she said, closing the door behind her. "I wished to know how you feel about Jason now, for you must clearly see that he is worthy—at the very least."

"Georgiana," Darcy said, rubbing his eyes, "I still do not know what to think. His newly understood position in our society does put me at ease, yet I still am apprehensive. His conduct in the past does not warrant trust on my end."

"I know, brother, and I understand your hesitancy, yet I feel that all you need is more time to become better acquainted with him."

"Perhaps yet know that we leave for England in a matter of days so that we shall be back in London by Christmas."

"And that is the other reason for why I came to speak with you. I need your help, Fitzwilliam. Or rather, I believe that Jason does, even if he does not see it himself."

"How could I be of assistance?" her brother asked, dubiously, "For you can see my reluctance."

"And I am not frightened by it, though I do love you."

"Georgiana..." he sighed, softening to her proclamation.

"Brother, we cannot leave America now."

"I beg your pardon?"

"We cannot leave America, and I need you to write to your reluctant friend, the Prince Regent."

"What are you talking of?" Darcy gasped. "And why do you speak of the Prince Regent?"

"Because he is the only one who can send us information, facts, and hard evidence that the Trekenna ship made berth at a Spanish Colony that had abolished the trade and that it also passed along Scottish territory, where slavery is a felony. It is now punishable by transportation for British citizens, but also for foreigners. The minute that crew stepped into British territory, and Spanish as well, it had committed a crime. It does not matter that the Trekenna made it home, because some of its crew were English citizens, and they can still be tried along with the rest of the crew."

"Georgiana, how could you ask this?"

"How? How could I not?" Georgiana faltered. "Fitzwilliam, do you truly not see the importance of all this? You of all people?"

"I do," he muttered, and then he balled his hand into a fist, afraid of sounding spineless and like that of a hypocrite. "It is just out of our hands."

"What do you mean, out of our hands? It is *not* out of our hands. As it was not out of your hands to save that freed woman not so long ago. We are the sort of people who it should be in the hands of."

"No, you do not understand. Even if I were to gather royal decree that the Trekenna Crew are punishable and that the cargo should be freed, the courts in New York will not listen."

"Why not if we have the prince's word?"

"Because he is the prince of the country that has oppressed their sailors and maybe for the sole purpose of wishing to regain America as our colonies."

"What?" Georgiana asked, confused.

"I have been speaking with some political officials here in the city, Georgiana, and they hint at the fact that there is more to this impending war. There is a great likelihood that Britain wants to regain America as their colonies, and this war is the perfect way to do so."

Georgiana faltered, then sat down and took in what she was told.

"Britain might want America back?"

"Yes, it is not certain, yet it is very likely. And they feel that this might be the perfect time to regain it."

"Then Richard was right," she whispered, "We did grow to miss our colonies."

"If that is true, then yes, we did. However, it is not fact, mere speculation—though even I admit it probably is truth. My point, Georgiana, is that how can we get a people to listen to the words of what they would view as a tyrant who is trying to recapture their country?"

"Oh."

"And what is more, how am I to know that the prince will even listen to me?"

Georgiana thought on the matter and then, coming to a decision, she took her brother's hand in her own.

"Because he respects you, Fitzwilliam. The Prince Regent

always has and always might—though you both pretend to detest each other. And if you phrase it so, as if you are wishing to gather this information to defeat a New York Court, then that means that he has made a victory across an ocean. A victory that he will no doubt flaunt about—for he will be the one to come across as a hero, and that is something he will need to rally our countrymen to his side for these next few years. Make it appear as his benefit, and he will respond to you."

"Yet there is still the likelihood that the court will not listen to the message, and I could not blame them."

"Whether they will listen or not is not within our power, Fitz. What is in our power is if we decided to stand up and offer these innocent people our help. Sometimes it does not matter if you obtain victory. All that matters is if you decided to fight."

Fitzwilliam leaned back in his chair.

"Your words are immaculate, yet nothing is certain."

"Some things are certain, if we leave now and do nothing, we are as nefarious as the people who thought they could enslave another people—for we turned a blind eye. Brother, prejudice breeds blindness. Let your pride be of the right sort that will not care to remain in the dark. If we leave now, we will regret it forever."

For a while, Fitzwilliam was silent, and he looked out of the window, not knowing how to face her.

"You must understand, if we stay, then we stay in a land where we are the enemy. And we also stay in a land far from my sons, and I will have missed their first Christmas. Did you forget that I am a father?"

"I did not."

"I do not wish to miss anything. I do not wish to any way, shape or form be a bad father."

"Brother, please..."

"I shall think on it. And I am not the only one that this affects. I shall ask Elizabeth."

"Please do quickly," Georgiana requested eagerly, "And remember to tell her, this is a scheme that is meant to save many."

Georgiana kissed her brother on the forehead and then left.

※ 32 ※

WHAT IS RIGHT CAN NEVER BE
DONE TOO SOON

I sat in a chair in the library, listening to Darcy finish his narration of all that had occurred between him and his sister, and his final offer to me of us remaining in America to help save the Trekenna cargo.

"Georgiana said all of that?" I asked.

"Yes, she did," he confirmed.

"My lord, she has grown tremendously into a remarkable woman and practically shines as a speaker of social issues."

"Yes, she has. I must remember to compliment her on her accomplishments."

"Yes, do so when you see her next. She would excel as a stateswoman, it appears." I stood up, beginning to pace as I considered the dilemma we now faced.

"If we remain here in America," I began, "Then we shall miss our children's first Christmas and are away from Pemberley longer than you would like. Yet if we leave, then as Georgiana said, we are turning a blind eye."

"Yes, I am quite torn."

"I would be as well, if it were not for one view."

"What view is that, my dear?"

"The view that I love my sons, yet what memory are they more deserving of? Knowing that their parents came home to see their first Christmas, or that their parents missed their first Christmas because they were fighting for something? Because we stayed and risked much, in hopes of making the world better? Fitzwilliam, which memory do you think is more worthy of them?"

Fitzwilliam looked up at me and his eyes grew dark.

"Then... you are determined?"

"Are you not?"

"Yes, I am."

I took his face in my hands and looked into his eyes.

"Then it is settled. We remain... and we fight."

"Have you always been so perfect?"

"No, it is a side you bring out of me."

Darcy leaned in and kissed me passionately.

"Yes, my dear," he smiled. "Then we fight."

⚜

Darcy sent a letter express to England, which we knew that we would have to wait for almost a month to receive. The days passed slowly but pleasantly.

Jason Whitfield was told of the scheme, and he thanked us, even if the plan would lead to no fruition towards his side's success. In the meantime, Jason came every other day to court Georgiana, only ever spending days away to prepare for his case, phrase his arguments, and wait for evidence to come from England, which did sooner than expected.

Weeks later we received not only a letter, but also a parcel that was addressed to my husband from 'his Royal Highness, the Prince Regent'.

Darcy excused himself from the company that day and took me

to the library for us to read the letter in each other's confidence. At first, he read the letter to himself, his face growing softer as he did so, which gave me hope, for the news must have been profitable. When he finished, he lowered the letter, looked on me and smiled.

"What does it say?" I asked eagerly. Fitzwilliam handed me the letter, and I took it, then began to read to myself.

Dear you taciturn grouch!

Seldom do we write each other where both parties have a common goal that springs from different intentions, yet now we have found one. You seek to liberate a people who were forced into torture and bondage, and I need a victory and another reason for why our one-time colonies need our guiding hand once more, and this will be the perfect example. Therefore, not only do I send a decree attached to this letter that I verify that the Trekenna Ship passed through our territory, yet I also have a naval Captain by the name of Frederick Wentworth, who oversaw one of our patrol vessels that is a part of our West Africa Squadron. You know, we organized that unit to patrol the African Coast to arrest slaving vessels. Captain Wentworth specifically chronicled his captaincy and wrote down when his vessel spotted and chased the Trekenna, yet the Trekenna was a faster vessel. However, you are right, there is a chance that the court will not listen, therefore, I have given you a gift. Not only does the decree have my seal, yet in the parcel I sent is a journal of a harbor clerk in a Spanish colony who wrote down every ship that made berth there. The Trekenna not only made berth yet violated the colonies' strict prohibitions against slavery and—as it would have it, the crew are not just a mixture of American and English sailors, yet some of them were Spanish!

Therefore, Spain has the right to send emissaries to come and arrest the Trekenna crew, even if we cannot arrest our own. And lastly, the Trekenna's Captain, a certain Daniel Morgan, not only was foolish enough to make berth there, but the clerk required his signature and brand from his ring, which he gave in the records. That is proof enough that the Trekenna passed through that territory. That is the journal that is in the parcel. I trust you shall make certain that it does not fall into the hands of interested parties who would destroy it before it has served its purpose.

Now you shall win, Darcy, and with you, hopefully so shall I. Which means, luckily for you, I shall not count this as another favor that you owe me, for if so, then the debt would grow more sizeable.

You have your sword—do your best not to die by it. Either way, I can revel in saying you are welcome—and that I am brilliant beyond words. The man who you have no choice but to regard as your savior,

Your Royal Highness, the Prince of England

I closed the letter and smiled at Darcy.

"Well, Mr. Darcy, you do have your sword."

"Yes, I do," he smiled, "And I have no intentions of doing anything else but wield it."

⚜

Later that day, when all were assembled, including Jason Whitfield, Darcy gave Georgiana the letter for her to read aloud to everyone. At the conclusion of it, there were many sighs of relief and Jason Whitfield stood up amazed.

"Then there is more than hope," he began, "there is a chance now that we could find victory."

"Yes," Georgiana said, "there is."

In a burst of emotion, he rushed up to her and spun her around happily.

"I cannot believe you did this!" he cried. "You are a marvel!"

"Mr. Whitfield!" Darcy bellowed, "put my sister down."

"Right, forgive me," Jason said, lowering Georgiana gently to the floor. "I let my emotions run wild for the moment. I did not have hope before, and I was foolish to doubt you in any way. If I do win, and these people go free, then I will not pretend that it was not because of all that you have done, Mr. Darcy, Mrs. Darcy, and Miss Darcy. Thank you."

"You are welcome," Darcy replied. "Yet do not waste my time in stroking my vanity. Just win."

"Very well. I shall do my part."

❦

After a couple days, the Trekenna Trial resumed and each day, Mr. Whitfield returned, telling us of the success or failure of each day. Each day we had hope, yet each day we had to tell ourselves that justice might not prevail. While we waited, one day I was sitting with Georgiana, Kitty, Lydia, and Jane while Miriam, Samantha, and Caroline were on an outing. All the men were at the trial.

"This is the final day of the trial," I began. "I confess myself frightened."

"As do I," Georgiana said.

"I hope all goes well," Kitty confirmed, "Yet I do find it very hard in some ways."

"What do you mean?" Jane asked.

"I mean that all of this work that has been done, and the sacrifices that were made to free these people, yet will anyone ever see it? All they will see is Mr. Whitfield's closing arguments. If he is victorious, then the victory will be his alone. Yet you, Georgiana, and Elizabeth, you did much, but history will not remember it. History will not understand what you attempted to do and succeeded at doing it."

"I know," Georgiana whispered, "and at first my pride was hurt from it. Then I realized something."

"What?"

"That history does not always remember heroes. Or it does not remember us for what we ought to be remembered for. You are right, Kitty. If Jason wins and liberty and triumph follow, my name will be nowhere, but it does not cease that it was any less courageous an act. For some of us, there will always be a time for acts of valor and honor that gains no renown. Yet that does not matter, for I have found my resolve. I have changed, I think. And I cannot turn back now. What is right can never be done too soon. Yet it must be done either way."

We were all distracted when we heard a carriage arrive. Jane stood up and walked to the window, then turned to us.

"It is them. The men have arrived!"

We all rushed out to receive them.

"How did it end?" Kitty said first to Richard.

"What was the verdict?" I asked Darcy.

"Are the people free?" Lydia exclaimed to Henry.

"Jason please!" Georgiana cried. Everyone became silent, and we all turned to her as Jason and she beheld each other. "Please, did you win? Did justice win?"

❦ 33 ❧

A QUESTION

The moment between them both felt eternal and then Jason walked up to her and took her hands in his own.

"We..." he sighed, seeming out of breath. "Our side proved victorious. We won."

"You...you won?"

"Yes. And the slaves are now free. Because of you, Miss Darcy, those people are now free."

Georgiana burst into tears and then embraced him tightly.

"I am so proud of you, Jason," she exclaimed. "I am ever so proud."

"And I am beholden to you, Georgiana, my dear Georgiana! I am beholden to you. And I love you!"

"And I love you."

"Then I am not afraid anymore."

"What do you mean?"

Jason released her and then looked around at the rest of us.

"Forgive me for doing this so publicly, yet I have always been the rash sort, and I must do so now." He then turned back to Georgiana. "Miss Darcy, loveliest Georgiana. So early into our acquaintance, I saw a light within you that I have never seen before. A greatness of spirit, and shortly into my growing affection for you, a question had been growing from within me that echoed within my soul. A question that I feared I would never get an assured answer for. Yet now that I see your affection rivals my own, I am not afraid. Georgiana, I love you! Most ardently! And therefore, I ask you now, if you are willing, would you please do me the honor of accepting my hand, and making me the happiest of men?" With all the strength of feeling, of believing that he had achieved the ultimate reward, Jason got down on one knee. "Would you, my love, consent to marry me and be my wife?"

Georgiana began to weep silently, yet a smile never left her face as she breathed in and out, amazed and overwhelmed by the moment—then, slowly, she recalled that she must speak, so she opened her mouth and began to give her answer...

The End

Don't miss out on your next favorite book!

Join the Satin Romance mailing list
www.satinromance.com/mail.html